MURDER AT SPOLETO

Best Wishes

W Fgh Rnyn MD

Maurine Krimmy

Spoleto, 2003

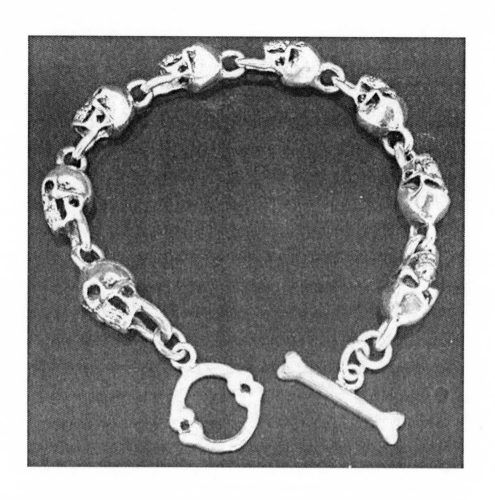

MURDER AT SPOLETO

A SPOLETO MYSTERY

MAURICE AND LEIGH THOMPSON

Elderberry Press

OAKLAND

Elderberry Press, LLC

1393 Old Homestead Drive, Second floor
Oakland, Oregon 97462—9506.
E-MAIL: editor@elderberrypress.com
www.elderberrypress.com
TEL/FAX: 541.459.6043

All Elderberry books are available from your favorite bookstore, amazon.com, or from our 24 hour order line: (800)431-1579

Library of Congress Control Number: 2002116079
Publisher's Catalog-in-Publication Data
Murder At Spoleto/Maurice and Leigh Thompson
ISBN 1-930859-54-6
1. Murder——Fiction.
2. Spoleto——Fiction.
3. Mystery——Fiction.
4. Forensic Pathology——Fiction.
5. Opera——Fiction.
I. Title

This book was written, printed, and bound in the United States of America.

Honoring 333 years of effervescence, insouciance and devotion to appreciation of the finer things in life of our Holy City

Acknowledgements

The authors thank their many relatives and friends for suggestions, encouragement, and corrections in hopes they will overlook the errors. Shelley Singer was a helpful editor. George and Linda Saint provided some of the gothic illustrations. Joseph Sliker, owner of the 82 Queen Restaurant, gave permission for use of his seat map of Gaillard Auditorium.

Contents

GAILLARD MUNICIPAL AUDITORIUM
MAIN FLOOR

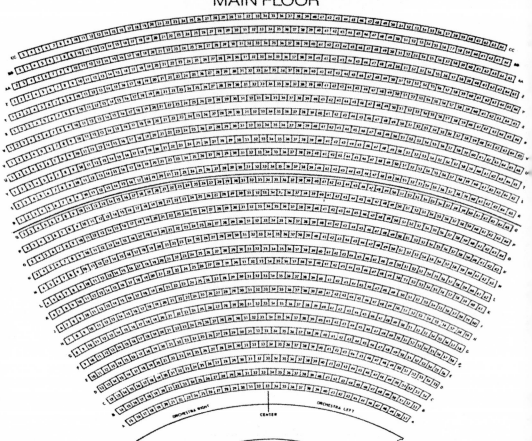

ORCHESTRA RIGHT   CENTER   ORCHESTRA LEFT

Dramatis Personae

Kasandrá	soprano playing Charlotte Russe Middleton
Esau Versey	bass playing Adam, the butler
Antoine Mazyck Middleton	Charlotte's husband
Evelyn	Adam's sister, the maid
Henri Vlad	bassoonist
Jean-Louis Guérard	maestro
John Bennett Gibbes IV	insuror
Hayden and Whilden	Charleston silversmiths
Henry Porcher Bissell Woodward MD	Professor and Chairman of Pathology
Palmer Bull Maybank	Mayor of Charleston
Augustus Ashley Cooper Hanahan III	Chair, Spoleto Board of Directors
Dan Ravenel	Chief, Charleston Police
Miss Tenney	schoolteacher
Mary Elizabeth Jervey Simons, MD PhD	Professor of Pathology and Medical Examiner
Bernard William "Bubba" Rhett, JD	Lieutenant of Charleston Police
Samantha Theodora (Teddy) Bonnet	producer, Gaillard Spoleto productions
Areana Oschkanova	choreographer
Alain Caponne	costumer
Bernardo Buontalenti Vernel	set designer, crime scene technician
Bill McCord, MD	fourth year Forensic Pathology Resident
Boone Hall	autopsy technician
Sinkler, Gibbes & Simmons	attorneys

Tom Waring	newspaper editor
Howard McIver	Charlestonian and drink inventor
Steve Bonnet	Teddy's husband and yachtsman
Yoki Ginsu	histology technician
Dirk Gadsden, PhD MD	Professor of Pathology, Head Analytical Laboratory
Shrimp City Slim	Blues artist and radio personality
Robert Mills	first US-trained architect
Ben Silver	London & Charleston fine men's wear
John	assistant to Mayor
Debby Kale	anchor, Live 5 News
Hiro	sushi chef and owner
Charlton deSaussure	famous Charleston internist
Dick Reeves	Charleston Gullah lecturer
Esmeralda	housekeeper of Mr. Reeves
Thomas Elfe	Charleston cabinetmaker
Milby Burton	Charleston Museum Director & author
Lee family	owners of Jones Hotel
Moreau Sarrazin	Charleston silversmith
Enos Reeves	Charleston silversmith
Louis Boudo	Charleston silversmith
Nicholas Trott	judge
DuBose & Dorothy Heyward	Charleston authors & playwrights
Peter Gazes, MD	famous Charleston cardiologist
Rutledge Moore	sergeant of police
Erik Ochsner	assistant conductor
Drayton Hastie Geer, MD	physician
Chenille "Shotzie" Geer	his third wife
Mary Ann Drayton	reporter
N. Ecru Filio	Charleston County Coroner
Buck Cathcart, MD	orthopedist
Harvey Est, MD	organ procurer
Kirk McLeod, MD	sports medicine specialist
Jack Gatgounis, MD PhD	anesthesiologist
Charlie Strange, MD	Director, Medical ICU
Joe Kurent, MD PhD	neurologist

Betsy Gilbreth, MSN	nurse
Giovanni "Digits" Personnoni	banker
William Deas	chef, inventor she-crab soup
Dr. Nemo	chief, Marine Biology, College of Charleston
Solomon Legare	detective 2nd grade
Sylvia Dennis	detective 1st grade
Edward Good	detective 3rd grade
Marian Read	audiovisual police expert
Beulah Manigault	police corporal
Shauntay Brown	detective sergeant
Faramarz Beigi	stagehand
Ismail Beigi	stagehand
Jim Riley	engineer and hair stylist
Will Evans	architect
Todd Palmer	clarinetist
JayJay Brown	police artist
James Corde	manager Gaillard Auditorium
Sarah Townsend	manager Gaillard maintenance and cleaning
Edgar Coulomb	manager Gaillard electricity and HVAC
Peter Bounetheau	postal clerk
KK Chen, MD PhD	pharmacologist and toxicologist
I. N. Hale	HazMat technician
Dr. Virginia Mixson Geraty	Charleston Gullah expert & author

World Premier

Jean–Louis Guérard

presents

The Charleston Nobility

Grand Opera in Three Acts

starring

Kasandrá

Esau Versey

Gaillard Auditorium
eight o' clock pm
formal attire
gala festival to follow

one

Diva's Dénoument

*F*riday, 10:52 pm

Kasandrá beamed. Triumph! The opening night audience, overflowing Gaillard Auditorium, was riveted to its seats, every eye on her. The maestro, who had written this vocal challenge just for her, beamed from the podium as the end neared. What a climax! Everyone else dies leaving her alone on stage to close with that final aria *di agilità*, sure to write new opera lore, rising in her best *Koloratur Sopran* to an unbelievable F two octaves above middle C.

She had struggled for three months to master that final scale, had emerged from her brief retirement just for it, and maestro Jean-Louis would hire her only when she proved up to this challenging vocal tour de force. She was the only star since Henriette Méric-Lalande who could sing this note cleanly and with the drama that would add this performance to all those adulations for her stirring performances of the Brünnhilde Immolation.

As the music swelled and she entwined herself on the divan with her young lover, her maid Evelyn, she knew the nudity and lascivious behavior could not eclipse her vocal glory. She could see the headlines now:

Diva Delights Spoleto Opening in Brilliant Comeback. She begins their final love duet: "All women's' lips are sweeter yet" which is interrupted by violent pounding on the door which gives way to the butler, Adam. His huge black chest, glistening with sweat, swells and his eyes are enraged as he confronts the pair. Kasandrá's voice rises as she torments him with memories of their own passionate lovemaking even as she caresses the compliant Evelyn.

Adam reaches the resonant low notes of his *basso profundo* as he decries a God that would punish him by perverting the desires of his true love, his sister Evelyn, now carrying their child. Kasandrá recoils in horror—Adam's jealousy is not for her but for Evelyn. As Adam jerks Evelyn from the divan and strangles her, Kasandrá opens the secret compartment in the wall and removes the jeweled Spanish pirates' chalice, stolen from the altar of St. Philip's. She fills it with champagne and raises it to Adam's lips singing: "This sacred draught erases sins."

Adam snatches the cup from her and drinks deeply even as his fiery eyes burn into her. He recalls her seduction, months before, first with drugged champagne and then with her voluptuous body, forcing him to cheat on his sister.

Kasandrá laughs: "My charms are more intoxicating than this fine champagne, and now the seed you planted grows lively in my womb."

He cries out in torment as he learns that she too carries his child. He rises up to strike her but staggers as she reveals: "This chalice cup, from God's own house, now kills instead of cures." Poisoned, he falls, calling on God for forgiveness for his lust. Her magic voice rising, Kasandrá begins the climactic aria *di sortita*.

In the majestic first part she reviews her life: falling from the pinnacle of high society to rejection by her family and friends, cheated on by her husband who killed himself. The middle part of the aria slows in a minor key as she describes how she forsook the values of her patrician family, consorted with her maid, and seduced Adam, her maid's brother. As this part closes, she drinks deeply of the poisoned chalice, and then tells the dying Adam that his lovemaking never could equal that of her own dear father. Adam dies.

The third part of the aria returns to a con brio F major, to usher in her triumphant last note. She mocks the dead Evelyn for getting pregnant. She chastises the dead Adam for not being faithful to her and her unborn child. Her voice rising she advances to the stage left apron. She draws a deep breath to begin that climb to the final F'" when she will collapse as the orchestra swells to a close and the hall fills with tumultuous applause, her applause. Her heart throbs in anticipation of her glory, threatening to leap from her chest with its thumping. She focuses on each note, to round it clearly, as she sings: "My loves, we've made our lives, it was not luck; and now, in death, through all of Hell we'll f•••."

This final note sounds clear as a bell, the stunned audience gasps, and she holds it two full seconds before beginning her climactic collapse. But, as the orchestra begins its swell, she staggers forward. The maestro looks up in horror as his golden diva, at the moment of their triumph, lurches away from her well-rehearsed moves. She stumbles over the floor microphone, and twisting in midair, falls backwards into the woodwinds. She crashes upon Henri Vlad, the bassoonist who had switched to contrabassoon for the climax. Henri collapses softly but not so his highly-polished antique Buffet-Crampon maple bassoon, with the unusual 20-key French configuration, resting upright in its stand. Kasandrá's ample torso fractures the topmost of the four wood sections. The sharpened wood fragment, still in its brass connection, is driven by her weight through her pink silk peignoir, through the fine wires of her concealed microphone (which she would have denied), through the back of her specially-made underwire uplift brassiere, through the rhomboid muscle between her left shoulder blade and spine, through her aorta and left ventricle, and through the intercostal muscles between her fourth and fifth ribs just left of her sternum to emerge beside her widely-displayed 38DD bosom in a spray of crimson that increases as her body slips lugubriously down the stops on the instrument to its butt.

The orchestral climactic swell sags to a cacophonous croak like an arthritic bagpiper. Jean-Louis Guérard, transfixed, baton aloft, stares unbelievingly at the scene as fine red dots pepper his ruffled shirt and pale face. Tall, Patrician, with flowing white hair caught in a ponytail and a huge diamond stud in his left ear, the maestro cannot believe his triumph has been so tainted as he thinks to himself: "Fat clumsy bitch. Ruining my triumph. I should have had her take grace lessons at Pigs R Us."

The horrorstruck patrons, glued to their seats, watched Jean-Louis to see if this was the planned ending to his horrible diatribe of debauchery, deceit, and death. A shocking tale of misbehavior, disgracing Charleston's elite, with a story that, even if not inaccurate, would never have been mentioned in polite society.

The ushers stood frozen by their doors. They had been waiting for completion of the curtain calls before guiding the 2734 patrons down the staircases to the elegant Gala below, for which the audience had been forced to pay an extra $250 each to get opening night seats.

Henri Vlad, stunned, with terrible pain in his neck, lay on the floor half under Kasandrá, hoping the Spoleto insurance would cover both his broken bassoon and his broken neck.

The first person to move was John Bennett Gibbes, IV, whose firm had insured Kasandrá's jewelry for the first act, rented from Hayden & Whilden Jewelers, oldest in the South. Leaping up from seat C18, he trod on 34 shoes in his clamor to the stage-right aisle, peering into the pit, and, bending far forward, splitting his old, too-tight formal pants.

A call for "any physicians …" was unnecessary as the house included half the faculty of the Medical University of South Carolina, also the oldest in the South, as well as more than half of their competitors, the private lowcountry physicians many from the best old Charleston families. Like a murder of crows they rose, tailcoats flapping, as they raced for the orchestra pit and slithered, climbed, and vaulted over the wall, landing on hapless musicians, chairs, instruments, and music stands. Some limped away on sprained ankles or wrenched knees and one had a broken fibula. Most rushed for the skewered soprano and the downed bassoonist whom they surrounded looking like the "Charleston eagles," i.e. buzzards, cleaning up the Market.

A Professor of Psychiatry argued with two private pediatricians over who was best at resuscitation. Three Cardiac Surgeons compared the lengths of their pocketknives to see who would violate the diva thoracically. Four plastic surgeons, impressed with her ample exposed bosoms, wondered who had siliconized them. Five members of Lowcountry Health Care Inc. wondered if her insurance extended to South Carolina.

Henry Porcher Bissell Woodward, MD, as a member of the Spoleto Board, sat with his children and guests in the center of the front row. Calmly stepping over the wall onto the conductor's dais he gently nudged Jean-Louis to one side, stepped down to the orchestra floor, and was first to reach Kasandrá. Forsaking any thought of gloves, Dr. Woodward felt the absence of pulse, attempted two breaths of mouth-to-mouth, and compressed her chest, spreading his hands around the protuberant bassoon. He was unable to move air into her lungs and his massage revealed a rigid chest which when compressed generated no pulse but only a squirt of blood to add to the crimson tide circling the body. He gently moved her to allow Mr. Vlad to wriggle free.

Dr. Woodard rose and said gently: "she's gone." The physicians, surgeons, chiropractors, podiatrists, and attorneys surrounding him began to dispute his credentials and lay hands on the devastated diva. Dr. Woodward arose to his full 6 foot 4 inch height and in a resonant voice bellowed: "She's dead, DEAD. Do you think she was born with a handle sticking out of her chest? Gentlemen desist." A Georgetown emergency physician insisted on attempting a few more breaths, a young ICU fellow tried more heart massage, and a Broad Street lawyer tucked his card in her panties, but they fell back as they realized they had been touched by her blood and she, of the artiste class, might be HIV positive!

The electronic and print journalists reacted almost as swiftly as the physicians. The TV reporters, distinguished by their careful coifs and upper-body elegance, barked orders to their technicians: "do we have a live link" or "get a wide shot" or "cone in on those tits." The cameramen, each with an eye glued to the viewfinder of their camcorders perched on one shoulder, hobbled around like half-blind pirates with overgrown parrots. They jostled each other for the best camera angles and soon flooded the scene with brilliant lights.

The musicians, veterans of many stage disasters, though none quite so lethal, began to safeguard their instruments, hunching over them as they quickly exited the mêlée by the tunnel to their dressing rooms. Henri Vlad, though, remained covered in blood, slowly turning the broken-off top of his precious antique bassoon in his hands as the physicians trampled his modern contrabassoon into splinters.

Esau Versey, the bass who had played Adam, was the only performer to rush to Kasandrá's side. Kneeling with one huge jet black hand on her golden tresses, his tears perfectly captured the moment, and the young AP photographer who captured the scene with his Nikon F5 with 300/ 5.4 lens won the cover of Time and later a Pulitzer as the news media savored the salacious nature of this scandalous opera of "old Charleston." The politically-correct Yankee press would love to sell papers with this shocking tale of Southern depravity. Only Esau knew that his tears were real—real disappointment at missing another night with Kasandrá when she had promised to make him leave his wife and give up black girls forever.

Friday, 11:09 pm

Everyone vied for power. Mayor Palmer Bull Maybank raced up, saw the cameras, smoothed his gray hair, and puffed up his political posture as he thought of something mayoral to pronounce. The portly Chairman of the Spoleto Board, Augustus Ashley Cooper Hanahan III, barked some orders but was stilled by the quiet voice of Dan Ravenel, the venerable Police Chief, who nearly whispered in his ear: "Gus" (a name Hanahan hated and few dared to utter), "let's get this mob into order before we have more casualties. Why don't you tell the audience that the Gala is beginning in the exhibition hall below and they should go down there immediately."

Hanahan, initially angry at this usurpation of his authority over Spoleto, seized upon this perfect out. If he canceled the Gala he might have to refund all those proceeds. But if the Chief ordered it to proceed, no one could accuse Spoleto of this crass disregard of the downed diva. So, as loudly as he could over the din in the Gaillard Auditorium, he screamed out: "The Gala is beginning — lead them downstairs immediately."

One and then another of the ushers heard his plea and seized on it as something to do. They directed the stunned and incredulous patrons to the doors. Soon the patrons start thinking of the $250 worth of bourbon and beer, peel-and-eat shrimp, crab cakes, hominy, collard greens, and big-band dancing they had been forced to buy. As they compared notes with their neighbors, not believing what they had seen and heard in this debauch, the plot seemed ever more dreadful in the retelling and that climax resonated as a fitting climax to Jean-Louis' dastardly portrayal of their beloved city and its vaunted inhabitants.

As more officials pressed into camera range, Chief Ravenel called for three of his officers to clear the orchestra pit and prevent further disturbance of any evidence.

"Evidence," boomed the bombastic Hanahan, his face as red as a baboon's behind. "What do you mean evidence. Don't you have eyes, man. She was tired and I could see her sweating like a horse. You should have smelled her after rehearsals—huh, diva indeed. She just got a little dizzy from the excitement and strain, staggered too close to the pit, and fell in. Happens all the time. I remember at my graduation Miss Tenney fell off the Memminger stage and broke her hip. Do you think Kasandrá was a unicorn with a slipped horn? She looks like an hors d'oeuvre down there—like one of Shuck's stuffed shrimp already dipped in hot sauce. What do you mean evidence?"

Chief Ravenel, in his quiet manner, leaned close to Hanahan and almost whispered: "don't you think this is a police matter now. If Dr. Woodward says it's over, I think you should leave this to police professionals. Why don't you go see to the press, and get them out of here." Only then did Hanahan notice that Jean-Louis and his flock of PR spinners had cornered the media and were giving out his story—his rescue of Spoleto, his magnanimity in accepting the leadership "for life" of this festival, the hardship of unapplauded genius, his mastery of the modern operatic art form, and the dangers to artistes not unlike, as he said, "grand prix auto racers or fighter pilots." Jean-Louis assured the cameras that: "This tragedy will not compromise the planned New York opening of this opera this Fall. No, not in the Met—on Broadway."

Charles Towne Reporter

February 13, 1736
The first performance of The Recruiting Officer was held last night in the new theater at Church and Dock Streets. This is said to be the first theater built as such in the colonies and the Lords Proprietors directed that said be built on Lot #113 of the Grand Modelle. The Recruiting Officer was well received by a crowd who for the most part behaved. During the more ribald moments there were scurrilous comments hurled at the actors who responded with their own lewd gestures and speeches, as is the wont of theatrical persons. There was only one injury. An actor, said to have imbibed two bottles of Madeira, became exuberant in delivering an obscene gesture to the crowd and slipped, falling on the bayonet of one of the militia who had been assigned to keep order. Fortunately his costume was mostly crimson and with a little bandaging he was able to continue.

two

Riotous Reaction

*F*riday 11:52 pm

The Chief approached the swallow-tailed physicians surrounding the bassoon protruding from its soprano butt-rest. Their balding heads bobbed up and down making them look like a bracelet of buzzards devouring a speared gazelle. As he shooed them toward the exit, he spied Dr. Woodward, whom he knew to be Professor and Chairman of Pathology at the local Medical School whose department included the Medical Examiner of Charleston, Mary Elizabeth Jervey Simons, MD PhD. He told Dr. Woodward that he had summoned Dr. Simons, who usually inspected the scene of unusual deaths. The Chief wanted Dr. Simons involved in this high-profile demise. He admired the young pathologist, whom he knew to have been promoted to professor in just seven years, authored several scholarly studies in the New England Journal of Medicine, and won two large NIH grants.

Friday, 11:58 pm

M.E., as her friends called her, was in her laboratory on this Friday night, as usual, working out the final details of a novel genetic test for cancer. She grabbed a white laboratory coat to cover her denim skirt and pink cotton blouse as she hustled out the door to her parking space. Roaring down Calhoun Street she was caught up in a sea of vehicles.

The evening news had been interrupted with a flash of the tragedy at the Gaillard. All three local TV stations had live shots of the melée on the Gaillard stage, replacing the expected routine opening of the Spoleto festival. Radio stations had interrupted their beach music, shag contests, or gospel with the news—what a way to launch this Memorial Day Weekend.

Everyone had jumped in their cars and headed to the Gaillard to gawk, be seen, or to break into the free-booze gala in the confusion. M.E. was trapped on Calhoun Street four blocks away. She pulled her British racing green Jaguar XKS up on the sidewalk before the Emanuel AME Church and hoped it would be safe. She sprinted down Calhoun with her evidence bag to the Gaillard Auditorium.

What a mess. Police were trying to establish corridors. Penguins with their ladies in ball gowns, pearls, and freshly coifed blue hair, were strutting on the sidewalk demanding their limousines. Chauffeurs, expecting a call at 1 am after the Gala, had been hastily summoned early. Teen drunks, alerted by the news, had cruised in, radios blaring, and now were bent on crashing the free-food-and-booze Gala.

M.E. ran across the lawn south of Calhoun Street to the Gaillard, dodging drunks. The main door was blocked with the surging crowd, but just then a side door popped open as some patrons burst through and she ducked inside and made her way upstairs toward the stage. She paused and showed her credentials to the young policeman guarding the stage left aisle. Each time she met new police they seemed incredulous that a young beautiful woman could be The Medical Examiner. She wondered if they expected a ghoul with a horrid nose in black habit. She laughed inwardly as he looked up from her ID like a high school stud meeting his rock star idol. "Right this way, ma'am."

"Is there a problem?" she drawled while strolling up to Chief Ravenel, Dr. Woodward, and the nearly-nude soprano with a bloody pole sticking out of her chest. "I forgot you were doing Moby Dick tonight." She wondered if one of the spear carriers had grown tired of his role as an extra and sought immortality with a final thrust.

Dr. Woodward quickly summarized the events. After a scathing review of the maestro's new opera he said: "She stumbled off the stage and fell onto this bassoon. Her weight seems to have shattered it and the sharp end perforated her. I tried resuscitation but her chest was filled with blood, I couldn't ventilate her, I couldn't generate a pulse, and from the trajectory I think this horrid thing has ripped open her heart."

M.E. pulled latex gloves from her lab coat pocket and quietly asked the police photographer to record each movement as she began to gently examine the chest wound. No mistakes, she thought, in a high profile case like this. Pressing the chest confirmed that it was rigid and blood squirted from the wound. Moving to the head M.E. found no evidence of head trauma, the pupils were fixed and dilated, and there was no blood in the external ear canals. The nose and throat were remarkably clear of blood. The projectile must have missed the lungs and esophagus.

She turned the body gently to the right and inspected the entry wound in the left back. She had the police photographers take several close-ups of the wound and then rolled the corpse back flat and palpated the abdomen which was obese but not rigid. As she probed the belly the corpse expelled flatus and feces which mingled with the blood and urine in the usual violent death gore. M.E. wondered if opera stars, like surgeons, had an obligatory visit to the restroom before starting a long performance.

She examined the extremities, noted the lacy panties and silk stockings with garter belt, and gently removed the elegant shoes. Three inch spike heels—how could a 180-pound older woman, with a large overhanging bosom, balance on those? Is this death by vanity? Why couldn't she wear solid Mephistos? Her feet were big enough to handle water skis.

Did she have a muscle or nerve disease to cause her to stumble? She found no difference in the muscle mass in either leg. The feet, ankles, legs and knees all seemed of normal configuration and mobility with just a trace of edema. Retrieving her evidence kit she carefully bagged the hands, shoes, and head. Then she asked the police for help in covering the body in two bags to preserve the position of the protruding bassoon.

Chief Ravenel offered that it would be hard to move the body with that pole sticking out like an obscene handle, but M.E. repeated: "Don't touch it. Be sure it isn't moved one millimeter. It will be important to see exactly where it is located."

Chief Ravenel thought: Located—hell lady. It's stuck right through her chest. Youall think it twists and turns in there and comes out her arse.

But he just said: "Yes ma'am." His mother had always taught him to be polite to white folks and never sass them. Earlier in his career he might have been tough on white perps, but now when those prissy-assed aristocrats killed someone drunk driving or rAAped a lAAte dAAte at AAte on the bAAttry, he just smiled, showed all his pearly white teeth, swallowed his pride in his Ph.D. in criminology, and said: "Yes suh," or "Yes ma'am." He knew that would fool them into thinking he was just a shuffling servant and their whiteness would be in charge. Then they made their fatal mistakes and he nailed their asses good.

Just then a tall handsome man strode toward the crowd. Chief Ravenel greeted the head of his forensics unit, Lt. Bernard William Rhett. Since his days as the star quarterback on the South Carolina Gamecock football team, everyone called the young lawyer, Bubba.

"Bubba," Ravenel said almost into the curly blonde hair, "we need an A-1 job on this one. It looks like she just tripped and fell, but every newsperson will want interviews and we better have all the answers. You know how important Spoleto is to Charleston, and there never is much other news over Memorial Day."

Bubba nodded in agreement with his boss and brightened as he saw M.E., glad to be working with her again: "Looks like a long night. What do you think so far."

"Looks like she tripped on that stage mike." She pointed out the flat gray microphone that was turned to face stage left, out of line with the others that were neatly aligned with the edge of the stage. "Then she fell on the orchestra and impaled herself. The musician was injured and his bassoon penetrated her."

"Where is the musician? Did he have anything to offer?"

"He was conscious but confused. Complained of neck pain. The paramedics stuck him in a Thomas Collar and hauled him off to the Medical University Hospital. I've bagged the corpse and all the pieces of that bassoon I could find. I've got all the photos I need."

"How did she end up in the orchestra pit?"

"I don't know why she fell. She seems to have sung a brilliant performance all the way to the last note. There's no evidence she was sick or weak or had a stroke, but you should see the tiny high heels she was perched on—like balancing a candy apple on a stick. She is soaked with sweat and it was a long act—perhaps she got dehydrated, overexerted, and had syncope, a fainting spell, or perhaps a brief cardiac arrhythmia. I'll check for drugs and it could be she had something like mild Parkinsonism that would make her unsteady. I wonder if all that singing, especially a long high note, could give her dizziness or a stroke? Maybe she got weak from food poisoning. What do these divas eat anyway—caviar and champagne? And you always hear about performers taking drugs of abuse."

"I remember the forensics lecture about Elvis. They loaded him up with speed and uppers on the way to the stage and knocked him out with Valium and Demerol when he got through. He died on the toilet of a drug overdose and probably could have lived another forty years with decent care."

"I'd appreciate your checking around here for any powders or liquids or drug bottles and any remnants of what she was eating. We'll do all our usual chemical tests, but it helps to have a clue for what to look for. Otherwise its just a needle in a haystack."

"Hell, ma'am," said Bubba with a fake drawl and a big smile. "Looks like that needle's done sticking out the middle of that there haystack."

M.E. chortled and followed the gurney carrying the corpse. The singer now looked like a boy scout tent.

Bubba supervised the crime scene technicians in collecting all the evidence. The dislodged stage microphone seemed similar to the others except that it had only a short piece of double-adhesive tape to secure it and that didn't seem very sticky. The others were much more difficult to tear loose from the stage. Finally when everything seemed secure, he allowed the waiting stagehands to begin to pick up the chairs. "Who's in charge here?" he asked.

"We're all just part-time help, mostly from the College of Charleston and the Dock Street Theatre. Teddy Bonnet is the only professional—the producer."

"OK," Bubba asks, "where can I find this Teddy guy."

"Ha," laughs the stagehand, "this Teddy barks orders like a stevedore, but she's all woman. I saw her a minute ago. Look for a knock-out with short black hair, thin, about five feet and a couple of inches tall, in jeans with a T-shirt that has the Spoleto logo on it. You won't miss that T-shirt for sure," he says giving Bubba a knowing wink.

Bubba walked through one of the set doors to backstage. He had helped out at the Dock Street Theater while in the twelfth grade at Porter-Gaud Academy. The huge Gaillard stage area dwarfed any he had been on before. Dozens of people milled about. He stopped several guys in white-tie who seemed still dazed. A couple were musicians worrying about the other scheduled performances of this opera. Two were Spoleto board members worried about the publicity. None knew where Teddy Bonnet might be.

A stagehand told him to try the "property room" and directed him to stage right where he found the room to be just a wire cage along the back wall and, in it, a strikingly attractive lady with her hands full of props, searching for the right place to store them. "Teddy Bonnet?" he called out.

Her dark piercing eyes swiveled to stare at him as she announced firmly: "I don't think you belong here."

"Well, ma'am, you would be correct, but I'm with the police, Lieutenant Rhett, and I'd appreciate your help."

Looking frustrated and impatient, Teddy snapped: "As if we don't have enough trouble tonight. Now the police! What do you want? Why don't you go fingerprint the corpse and let me get my work done?"

"Sorry to bother you, but I need your insight into this evening. I wasn't here," pointing out his suit coat, "and we didn't expect a death except in the script. I'm told you are the boss around here."

"Ha," she snorted. "Only the maestro is in charge, and he'll make sure you know that. I just do the scut work. But, you're right, the maestro killed off almost everyone onstage tonight in his big premier. I'll bet even he was shocked when one died in the pit and he didn't order it. He doesn't like anything to happen that he doesn't command. He wasn't eager for me to produce here and, after tonight, he'll probably blame me and I'll be lucky to get a job painting scenery. Oh well, what do you want to know?"

"I was told the star seemed perfectly normal up to her last moments."

"Well, perfectly normal isn't a good description of any diva. Like the others she was egotistical, demanding, and rude to everyone, especially me. Nothing could be right for her highness. The clothes were too heavy, the props too cheap, the champagne not cold enough or flat. She was getting old and her voice was past its prime, so she made up for it by blaming everything on me. And we had to put up with her for weeks while the maestro fiddled with the score and the designer, Alain, screwed with the costumes, constantly complaining about how hard it was to get the materials he needed in Charleston."

"Sounds like you haven't had a lot of fun with this show. Who were other important players."

"The choreographer, Areana, showed up a week ago to rehearse the ballet, but behaved in a dreadful manner—screaming in some Slavic tongue at the poor local dancers. After all the hard work I had done trying to assemble a chorus that looked good in formal attire, she only complained about their talents and posture and movements. Called me a fat pig! That bulimic bitch had some nerve. Her ballet looked like herding cats, right up to this afternoon. And Bernardo couldn't get his sets to work right. They are too elaborate and the maestro insisted he make everything for Broadway, not for this hick town. The first act set is especially luxurious with real crystal chandeliers and sconces everywhere. We spent all month trying to get his fancy stuff to work."

"Sounds like a disaster. Did the performance have problems, in addition to the star doing a swan dive into the sharp instruments?"

"The dress rehearsal this afternoon was a disaster, but most things finally worked tonight, not that it matters."

Looking around the cage that served as a property room, Bubba asked: "What is all this stuff?"

"Just props. We keep them in the property room all arranged by act and scene. Each scene has to be dressed with ashtrays and books and glasses. Everything goes in its place, outlined with tape, and labeled with a card color coded to the scene with a Polaroid picture of where it is to go. The stage hands still get things mixed up and put chairs in the wrong place. Then some dizzy actor falls over them or doesn't look where he's sitting. One time in a Hamlet I was producing a stagehand forgot the sword and the star reached for it, realized it was missing, and plucked a candle from the table for that final scene. Boy did the critics have fun with that one. I can't imagine what they'll say about tonight."

"Could you show me the system you use for props? It sounds neat. Did you invent it?"

"Goodness no. It's just routine. This may be a provincial festival with local help, but I designed it to be ready for New York next year," Teddy says proudly. "Now, I don't know."

"You mean this accident might screw up your plans?" Bubba asks.

"Who knows," sighed Teddy. "We'll never find a soprano who can sing that last aria. We probably can't find a good one who will take off her clothes. I don't even know how we'll do the next four performances this month."

"What were your plans after Spoleto? I heard the maestro was taking this opera to New York?"

"Not my plans. They're supposed to do Houston, Chicago, San Francisco, and Boston in the Fall and then open in New York around Christmas. But, will they find backers after this notoriety? Who knows?"

Teddy arranged the candlesticks, books, glasses, and other props. Soon all the taped sections were filled, except for two.

"What goes here?" Bubba asked as he inspected an empty spot and read the blue card stuck in the middle of it: "Champagne. Moët and Chandon Brut. Carefully open foil and the wire bail, screw out the cork slowly, and replace the cork half into the neck. Put in ice in the silver ice bucket on the table stage left beside the divan." The Polaroid shot showed the precise location on stage.

Puzzled, Bubba asks: "I thought you used tea or soft drinks on stage instead of real booze."

"Usually," answers Teddy, "but in this case the maestro demanded realism and that soprano could swallow a pint at a time. She said she needed to lubricate her pipes for that final aria and that only the finest champagne would do. She wanted vintage Dom Perignon but the best I could find in this town was the Moët. The bass said he'd be happy with ginger ale as he didn't like champagne, but not Kasandrá, only the best for her highness."

"I'd heard opera stars were a little tough to work with," suggests Bubba.

"Tough!" laughs Teddy. "Impossible! They are the most egotistical, picky, nasty, uncooperative beasts in the theater. And Kasandrá takes the cake. Areana called her the hippo. Instead of leading the dances, Areana just had her walk in the middle while the dancers twirled and leaped around her. The aging cow wanted Alain to make her look like a slim teenager. Tucks here, elastic there. We should have gotten a plastic surgeon to cut half of her off—and then take a vote on which half to keep."

"What goes here?" Bubba asks about the other blank spot.

"Oh, that damn cup. It's for the champagne. The star was too vain to realize you shouldn't drink champagne out of a silver cup. That way you can't see the bubbles and the clarity and color. But, oh no, she had to have champagne and the maestro said it had to be a church chalice, jeweled and all, to fit the plot. See, her character is supposed to be the epitomé of Charleston gentry—for three hundred years. Down here they think that is old and ritzy. In Europe, anything less than five centuries is just nouveau riche. Anyway, her fancy family has stolen this Spanish pirate's chalice from the big local church. The maestro said he needed this scandal to 'seal the plot.' Well, it got sealed good tonight I guess."

"So, where's this special cup? I'd like to see that for myself."

"I don't know," answers Teddy. "Kasandrá threw it across the stage like she was supposed to. That's why we had to get several made out of heavy pewter so they wouldn't get too dented."

"Do you have a spare?"

"Actually, we had three made. Each with fancy do-dads and four big fake jewels. The spares are all locked up in the cabinet back there," pointing to the back of the wire cage property room.

Bubba showed his interest and Teddy pulled a long keychain from her pocket and unlocked a grey metal cabinet. Inside were the small but valuable props, arranged neatly. She pointed out the silver bowls and candlesticks for the lavish first act on the top shelf. On the third shelf were two chalices with broad square bases that looked just like silver. Finely ornamented, each had four large jewels—one emerald, one ruby, one pearl, and a sapphire. Picking one up, Bubba realized just how heavy they were. "These would make quite a weapon."

"That would have worked better," suggests Teddy. "Kassandrá could have clobbered Adam with the chalice instead of poisoning him. Better yet we could have given her a cane to thrash him with. With a cane to steady her she might be back here now berating me for not having the champagne cold enough or the right brand or her jewelry polished just right."

"She wore real jewelry?" asks Bubba. "Was it valuable?"

"I guess. She and the maestro insisted on it. It came from a local shop, Hayden & Whilden, and I had the dickens of a time getting stuff to suit. They don't keep a lot of diamond tiaras in this town. But the shop arranged to borrow some stuff. The insurance was frightfully expensive."

"Did you keep that jewelry here?"

"Goodness no. Every stagehand in the place would have pocketed it. No, the insurance agent had a special guard at the dress rehearsal who brought the tiara, necklace, bracelet, and rings in a big Halliburton case. He got them out at the last minute and then collected them right after the rehearsal. The really good stuff is only worn in the first act and the guard collects that as soon as the curtain calls are over."

"Do you know what happened to the jewels tonight?" asks Bubba.

"No. The guard was backstage. I guess he got the tiara and necklace and stuff after the first act. I never saw Kasandrá in the pit, but she should have had a bracelet on her right wrist and big diamond earrings. I guess someone got those things off her. I presume blood washes off diamonds and gold."

"Do you have everything except the champagne and the chalice?"

"The used champagne bottle is just thrown out. This is for the new bottle for the next performance. I've got half a case of the Moët down in the bottom of this cabinet locked up to keep it safe from the stagehands. The chalice must still be on stage. Kasandrá threw it every which way in rehearsal and you never knew where to look."

"Can I help you find it?"

"Never mind," replies Teddy. "I'll find it eventually. It isn't worth that much; just pewter and fake jewels."

"Actually, it might be important to the investigation. The Chief is uptight about this accident and wants everything buttoned up. We'd better find it and tonight's champagne bottle too."

"OK," sighed Teddy, "let's look on stage. You look stage right and I'll try over here."

After searching the stage and the pit, no luck.

"Don't forget that niche," reminds Teddy.

"What niche?"

"Where the cup is concealed. Kasandrá goes over to it and gets the cup out of its hiding place. See, here it is." But it's empty.

"Where else could it be?" asks Bubba.

"We can look backstage and in the dressing rooms, I guess. Why don't we start over by the carpenter's shop." They look through pieces of set, wood, plumbing parts, and tools of all kinds, but no luck. Nothing behind center stage. Finally, in a large black trash can near the loading dock on stage right, Bubba finds two champagne bottles and one cork, but not the foil and wires that sealed the bottles. Carefully picking up each bottle with a gloved index finger in the throat he slips them into a plastic evidence bag he pulls from his coat. Then he adds the cork, wondering how to tell if it is from rehearsal or the performance.

"Let's look in the dressing rooms," suggests Bubba. "I need to check that the team has collected everything important from the star's room anyway. Do you know if she used any drugs, like before a performance? Or did she abuse anything—coke, grass, alcohol, speed?"

"I don't know that much about her habits," replies Teddy. "She drank a lot of wine and champagne, but I didn't see much liquor or hard drugs. She was always popping vitamins and herbal remedies and squirting nebulizers in her throat or nose."

"Was she an expert on herbs and drugs?" asks Bubba.

"Heavens no. All divas are hypochondriacs and demand attention. But she didn't know much about what she was taking—she couldn't tell Korean ginseng from gymkhana. And, as usual, she wouldn't listen to me."

"Did she have a stash in her dressing room?" asked Bubba.

"I haven't really been in her dressing room that much, but that's it over there."

Bubba left Teddy and found the tiny dressing room with the big star on the door. A uniformed officer was bagging evidence. The right wall was covered with mirrors behind a long plain table filled with makeup, brushes, combs, undergarments, telegrams, cards, and flower arrangements that spilled over to the floor. A day bed was pushed against the left wall. A closet filled the back wall— two rods from wall to wall filled with hangers, dresses, plastic covers, and two hanging cupboards of clear plastic filled with shoes on little shelves.

In drawers under the makeup table Bubba found eleven pill bottles: only one a prescription drug but five vitamin bottles, three antihistamines, and two decongestants. He picked them up with gloved fingers and dropped them in evidence bags. He found five spray devices with long shiny metal snouts and big squeeze bulbs, all of them filled with clear liquids. There were also seven bottles of liquid near the nebulizers, each with a neat label, some with droppers in the top. He confiscated everything: all the nebulizers, bottles of pills, jars containing powders and liquids and even some creams and tubes of stuff. There were many cards and telegrams, a few bunches of flowers, but few other personal items. He couldn't find anything that looked like illegal drugs—no crack pipes or needles. Not even marijuana.

In the lower drawer Bubba found an unopened bottle of Sauternes, Chateau d'Yquem 1987 and two pairs of bifocal eyeglasses. Between the makeup table and the makeshift closet was a basin, which contained a toothbrush in a glass and some Mentadent toothpaste, which he bagged. Nestled in the bowl lay a blue face towel and, in it, a chalice, just like the ones he'd seen locked up. He picked up the chalice with his gloves, touching only the edges of the foot, and dropped it into an evidence bag.

Just then Teddy returned to the dressing room and said her search for the chalice hadn't turned up anything. Seeing the chalice she asked where he had found it.

"In the sink, wrapped in a towel," replied Bubba. "Why would it be there?"

"I have no idea. Maybe a stagehand brought it here after the finale and just left it in the sink. They're supposed to clean it properly and then put it on that table in the property room, in the taped-off area marked 'chalice'. But I don't know where they wash the things. I can ask around for you."

"Not just now." He called for a crime scene technician on his radio, and asked for an evidence bag.

In a minute the technician, with the name Vernel on his ID badge, appeared with a cardboard box of plastic bags. Bubba took a large one, put all of his small evidence bags inside, wrote some notes on a card which he threw in, and used a special crimping tool to fasten a lead seal to close the bag. He then placed that evidence bag inside of a second plastic bag, sealed this with a regular twist tie, and asked Vernel to safeguard this with the other evidence. "Did you find a champagne cork or the foil and wire bail from champagne anywhere?"

"I don't think so," Vernel replied, "but there are three of us gathering up pieces all over the stage and down in that well where the orchestra was sitting when she fell on them."

"Where else did the star hang out around here?" Bubba asked Teddy, wondering about the habits of divas. It must be a tough life moving from city to city and performance to performance. He hadn't found that the soprano had any family or friends with her.

"She did spend a lot of time with Esau Versey who played Adam," she replied, "and his dressing room is right next door. Other than that, she wandered all over barking orders or complaining."

"Where was she staying in town?" asked Bubba.

"I don't really know. Most of us are given rooms in some of the big mansions belonging to local people who support Spoleto. Some groups stay in the dormitories at the College of Charleston or the Citadel, but they aren't available until a week or two before the festival opens."

Bubba knocked on the adjacent dressing room door. It was opened by a huge black man, muscular and very tall, wearing slippers and a black bath sheet around his waist. Bubba introduced himself, showed his badge, and asked to talk.

Esau invited him in, slipped into a black terrycloth robe, and sat in an easy chair while Bubba sat in the straight chair before the makeup table. This room was identical with that next door, but without the mess.

"I'm trying to find any clues as to what could have happened to your costar," said Bubba. "Do you have any ideas?"

"Ideas?" intoned Esau, in the deepest, most resonant velvet voice Bubba had ever heard. "Hell, man, she was skewered like a wild boar. We all joke about falling off the stage, and it does happen, but the worst I've heard of was a broken bone or two. This is awful. She was brilliant. I was lying on stage watching her last aria. She was really worried about that last scale. During the rehearsals she usually held that F''' very well, but I knew she was worried about opening night with the rehearsals all day, even though she just talked through her role and didn't sing at volume. You know, it's tough to use your instrument well under the strain of the performance and the dehydration."

"Dehydration?" asked Bubba.

"Yeah. It's terrible. We have all those hot lights on stage. The costumes weigh a ton and it's tiring to get through a long act with all those layers and layers. I don't know how some of the little ladies do it. Sometimes I have to wear armor, and even aluminum plates get heavy. In the first two acts Kasandrá had to wear three heavy ball gowns with all the hoop skirts and stuff. You don't know how much we sweat out there. Every performance the costumes are soaked and should be cleaned, except wardrobe usually doesn't trust the local cleaners. By the final curtain we are soaked. So, we drink a lot between acts to keep our voices lubricated."

"I understand that Kasandrá demanded real champagne on the set," stated Bubba.

"Yeah. I was happier with water or gingerale—I never drink until the final curtain. I'm told alcohol just makes you more dehydrated. But Kasandrá, she was so uptight about her final aria after that long act. She wanted something wet on stage and the score gave her a perfect opportunity to chug-a-lug bubbly just before her finale. I didn't need much for my voice, as I was about to die, and Kasandrá always insisted I not drink so she'd have plenty left for her."

"Was there anything different about the champagne or the cup tonight?"

"Nope. Looked just like in rehearsal."

"Do you think she drank enough to get tipsy and unsteady?"

"I'm not sure what she did between acts, but there wasn't that much on stage."

"What happened to that chalice after tonight's performance?"

"I don't know. I was so upset I didn't see much of anything," Esau said sonorously. "She was so beautiful and had the greatest soprano voice I've ever heard. She looked so pitiful in the pit with that gruesome thing sticking out of her. Horrible. I just sat beside her and cried. I couldn't help it. We had worked so hard on this challenging score. And we were headed to New York. To finally master it and have a wonderful premier, and then die for real just before the curtain. Too tragic. I bet someone writes an opera about tonight's tragedy."

"But what about that champagne cup today. What did you see?"

"I just don't know about tonight. After dress rehearsal today she took the chalice back to her dressing room. She didn't throw it in that rehearsal. She said it was too good to waste and she'd finish off the champagne later."

"Where was Kasandrá living in Charleston?"

Esau looked up slowly and in measured tones said: "She and I shared two sides of a little house on the East side of Meeting Street below Tradd. It is a guest home, called a kitchen house, for some rich women's doctor who donates it for Spoleto. We never got to see him much, except for a couple of fine dinners he threw for us. We got to meet some of the local gentry and he included a clarinet player, two ballerinas, and several string players. It's a nice place to stay, but has no parking places for the cars Spoleto lends us. The closest parking is up the street behind that building with the big columns, but I told Kasandrá just to park anywhere—they aren't our cars anyway. They wouldn't make the star of Spoleto pay a parking ticket do you think?"

"I don't know," mused Bubba. "Traffic isn't my department. But the Chief is mighty sticky about fixing tickets. I have to pay any I get. If he caught me weaseling out, I'd never forget it."

"If you'll write down that address," asked Bubba, "I'd like to go visit Kasandrá's apartment when we finish here. Maybe you'd be willing to show me around and show me your place too?"

"Sure," replied Esau. "But isn't this just an accident?"

"Looks that way," mused Bubba. "But we don't know if she fell because she was sleepy or tired from taking drugs, even an antihistamine, or how much alcohol she might have drunk today, or if she had any illnesses. Do you know if she was sick or taking anything?"

"Well, I do know she had a bunch of pill bottles, and was always gobbling down a handful of something or spraying her throat. But I never paid any attention. I didn't see any hard drugs; she didn't even smoke grass as far as I know, at least I never smelled it. She complained so much about hay fever and asthma and other allergies that I doubt she would smoke anything. She called her problem 'perennial allergic rhinitis.' Sopranos are like that. They all take a bunch of vitamins and herbs and all kinds of stuff and they are always spraying weird stuff down their throats and complaining about air quality. Me, I'm healthy as a horse. The only thing I take are two blood pressure pills. But I do get a flu shot each year, traveling to all those places. I wouldn't want to lose a week or two's performances by getting flu."

"Did Kasandrá get sick or see a doctor here?"

"I don't think so. It was pretty wet when we first got here and she complained about allergies. She also worried about pains in her joints and asked me about singers we both know who got arthritis of their vocal apparatus. She always complained about her instrument just like all singers, but I don't think she had any real problems and the humidity helps. And she didn't say anything about doctors."

"I'll wait while you get dressed. Then if you don't mind we could go to your place and we could see what Kasandrá might have in her rooms."

three

Slicing And Dicing

*S*aturday, 12:25 am

Dr. Simons followed the gurney bearing the corpse, draped in the body bags, with a prominent erection provided by the musical harpoon. On the way through the Gaillard foyer she peeked into the gaité in the Spoleto Gala. The formal attire and jewels flashed on the dance floor. The buffet tables were filled with shrimp and crab cakes with a big sign saying they were from Hanks and Mr. B's had provided roast suckling barbecued pigs, skewered just like the diva. M.E. thought: Maybe she should have worn an apple in her mouth. The food was being washed down with bourbon and Palmetto Amber Beer aplenty. Just like Charleston she thought. Nothing stops a party.

She remembered the history of the night Charles Towne surrendered to the British. They were having a big formal party that night too. To avoid any disruption, the host just locked the doors, trapping inside Frances Marion, the great patriot general called the Swamp Fox. He almost missed the war when he broke his ankle leaping out of a second story window to escape. Oh, Charleston, she thought. At least it's home.

She had the ambulance stop on Calhoun Street, retrieved her car, and followed the ambulance to her morgue in the basement of the Medical University of South Carolina Hospital. The morgue entrance was tucked away between the power plant and the receiving docks. As the Medical Examiner she had her own parking space next to the meat wagons, much coveted by the surgeons and ICU docs.

The gurney, bearing its shrouded body, with its tumescent wood-wind, was rolled up to the door of the refrigerated holding chambers. No way. It wouldn't fit. Not even diagonally.

M.E. asked the attendants to try the extra sized chamber, but it was still much too small. Now what? Despite being tired, she realized she would need to do the autopsy right away. So she asked the attendants to move the body to the number one stainless steel autopsy table. She looked up the on call list and telephoned Bill McCord, her most eager and talented fourth year pathology resident. Then she asked Boone Hall, the morgue technician, to prepare the tools.

M.E. retreated to the dressing room and changed into scrubs, plastic boots, double gloves, and her communication device—an earpiece she screwed into her right ear that had a projection for a microphone. It plugged into a footswitch that connected her to the videorecorders or to the telephone if it rang. Over this she fitted a helmet with a clear plastic face shield. Even guarded as she was against infection, she knew that other pathologists had gotten tuberculosis, AIDS, and Creutzfeld-Jakob "mad cow" disease in their work.

Like some astronaut bound for Mars she clumped into the autopsy room, turned down the thermostat, and greeted Bill, who had just arrived, and Boone, who was contemplating the fenestrated corpse. "What the Hell is that, Doctor Simons" Bill asked "did one of our bow hunters bag a 'dear' out of season?"

"Actually," M.E. replied, "that is an antique French bassoon made by the famous firm of Buffet-Crampon. Surely you know they have twenty stops as opposed to the modern German ones. I'm told they are more difficult to play, but that experts think the resonances are closer to the human tenor voice."

Bill, rarely at a loss for a comeback, stared at his gorgeous professor and admitted that: "My studies at Haaarvard College and The Johns Hopkins School of Medicine neglected the construction and sonorities of hollow tubes from Western European countries. The Abos in Australia did teach me a little didgeridoo, that looks sort of like that thing, but they hunt with boomerangs. I may not know how to make one of your fancy bassoons," he added sarcastically, "but that seems like a really hard way to blow one, or whatever you call it."

"I didn't know that much about them, but I got a quick lesson at the site. Apparently it is not that much different from your didgeridoo, being a hollow tube. What do they make the didgeridoo out of and how long is it?"

"They're made by termites hollowing out eucalyptus branches, but they can be any length. I've seen some that must be six or seven feet long."

"I hope they don't sharpen them. The bassoon is supposed to have a tube of eight feet to get the tonal range, but it is folded up into a four foot space in sections that fit together. That probably killed our singer as the top section split and formed a beveled sharp end right at a brass connector. By the way, one tidbit I learned was that because it comes in sections the Italians call it the fagotto—but no jokes please. It's going to be bad enough already."

"Thanks for the music lesson, but how did your bassoon or fagotto or whatever end up in the middle of a naked blonde stripper? I didn't know their customers included mad classical musicians."

"Obviously you haven't heard the news," M.E. chided. "Go get dressed and I'll tell you the saga of tonight's Spoleto opening, as best I've been told." She watched the tall handsome resident as he strode out, a little regretful he had never pursued her, even with all those silly harassment rules. Why was it only the unattractive men violated the rules? Turning to the corpse, she grimaced at the thought of all the dirty jokes she would hear from her colleagues about this impaling. "Raped by a wooden elephant? Are those splinters or wooden sperm? Bassoonocerus wound? Did she sound the note on key or was she flat? Did she climax or was she fagotted?"

M.E. pressed the footswitch and began recording her identity and that of Bill and Boone and the circumstances surrounding this corpse. The date and time were automatically inserted in each frame and the computer assigned a unique accession number, 04-188, to this postmortem examination. Instead of the old dictating machine and Polaroid camera, she now used two digital videorecorders. One covered the whole autopsy table throughout and recorded the audio notes without pause. The other had a pivot and a zoom lens she could control remotely while watching a large TV screen. Later she would use a third digital camera on her microscope to record the images of the tissue sections she would take. Her assistant would edit into a report all the key images, and then store on a

DVD the raw records as well as the tissue samples and slides.

She began by undressing the corpse, but found no identification cards or other personal items except for the business card of the Broad Street lawyers, Sinkler, Gibbes and Simmons, tucked in the elastic of her panties. The card advertised: 'Call if you've been injured,' but she didn't think the soprano would be making that call. She carefully cut away each article of clothing from the front. She was amazed at the underwire bra, especially as she rarely wore a bra herself and had never seen such heavyweight construction. She found a small transmitter pinned to the brassiere. The wire to the transmitter was flat and flesh colored. It was glued to her skin right up her back, up her neck, and then it was woven into her hair until it connected to a tiny microphone resting just above her right ear. M.E. documented all this on tape as she removed the device.

Then she measured the body and the protruding bassoon from all angles as she announced the measurements to the videotape. After capturing pictures of the front, she gently rolled the body to the right and captured pictures of the entry wound in the back with a short segment of bassoon still protruding. She was just getting close-ups of the wound when Bill, dressed like another astronaut, entered the room and clumped to the left side of the table.

"Did this French Tickler go in from the front or the back?" asked Bill irreverently.

"The bassoon, or more properly the brass connector between the third and fourth parts of the instrument" pointing to the offending perforator, "penetrated her from back to front. It looks pretty sharp, and there is a wedge of broken-off wood in the connector sticking out like a knife blade. The stage was about 63 centimeters above where this connector would have been located, judging from the bassoon cradle this was in and what is left of the instrument." She is 159.6 cm long and the wound is 33 cm below her scalp. So she could have fallen almost seven feet before her back reached the top of the instrument, broke it off, and then was penetrated by the sharp fragment."

"Glad she didn't fall on a sax," added McCord.

"Why?"

"We'd have to check for condoms to see if she had safe sax."

M.E. groaned and added: "We'll have plenty of jokes in the future, let's get to work."

Picking up the transmitter and microphone she showed them to Bill and told him: "I found these flesh-colored wires taped up her back between the microphone in her hair and the transmitter in her bra."

Rolling the corpse to the right she showed Bill the back. "The entry wound is jagged and, as you can see, begins just left of the vertebrae. If this instrument didn't rotate, the wedge-like broken wood entered her horizontally, probably parting the sixth and seventh ribs. How would you suggest we enter her to preserve the position of this thing?"

"Why don't we use the standard Y incision so we can remove the breastplate and have clear access to the chest. We can start the left arm of the Y as usual under the clavicle, but curve it to run just lateral to the exit wound."

"Well, that would work. But I'd rather cut medial to the wound and leave the wound itself and the track intact. I know we won't get enough exposure, but after we document the track we can go back and remove part of the chest with the wound for better exposure. Why don't you try it that way?"

Bill picked up the large autopsy scalpel and made the right side of the Y, running from the collar bone down to the xiphoid process at the bottom of the sternum, and then extended the left arm of the Y from the distal end of the clavicle, just cutting through the medial part of the breast, and medial to the wound. After inspecting the wound, they used the oscillating saw to cut through the ribs and remove the triangular shield exposing the chest cavity, which was filled with blood. They carefully sucked out the blood, avoiding the tissues. After documenting the exit wound they traced the track back into the chest. They observed that her breasts were all natural—no silicone or other implants.

"Darn thing goes right through the left atrium, down through the mitral valve, and splits her left ventricle," Bill observed. Gently lifting the impaled heart and sucking away more of the clotted blood, M.E. found the impalement to have also cut through the aorta, tucked away behind the heart, but to have passed under the left mainstem bronchus, missing the lungs, the main pulmonary arteries, and the vena cava. Documenting all with the zoom lens, and describing each millimeter of the path, they then cut away the part of the chest wall containing the wound and finally pulled from the body the killing stick.

The rest of the autopsy takes two hours and forty minutes as they proceed methodically through the chest and the abdomen. Each organ is inspected, carefully dissected out, washed, photographed, weighed, sliced, and then several sections are cut out for microscopic examination. They carefully preserve samples of the stomach contents and the heart blood and urine from the bladder to check for toxicology. Knowing that the concentration of some drugs and chemicals will change in heart blood, they also sample the more stable vitreous humor, using a needle and syringe to extract it from the left eye.

"I want to take some samples of the spinal cord," added M.E., "just in case she had multiple sclerosis or some neurological weakness to explain her stumbling." She had had a tubal ligation and scarring from prior pelvic inflammatory disease.

Then Boone gently flexes the neck and supports the head on a rubber block to expose the scalp. He cuts through the scalp in the back and reflects it up over her forehead. The oscillating saw cuts cleanly through the skull, and soon Boone pries loose the skull cap with its distinctive "pop", exposing the brain. They search carefully, but find no surface sign of pathology. So they put the whole brain in the pickle jar. After several weeks it will be firm enough to section with a long thin single-bevel Japanese sushi knife to search for any small lesions.

"Let's check the specimens," notes M.E. "Count the tissue bottles and make sure we have a sample of all the organs. Here are the six tubes of blood: the first sterile one for culture, one for chemistry, one hematology, one toxicology, one for DNA analysis if we need it, and one just to save. And here are the urine, stomach contents, and vitreous humor samples for the lab. Do you think we need any other samples?"

"That seems like more than enough for a simple accidental death," drawls Bill. M.E. thought he looked tired. Even though younger he seemed less resilient on these all night soirées.

"We haven't found anything surprising. Even high profile, I can't think of anything else to save except the cause of death, of course. We can impound the body for several days until we see some of the lab results if you like."

"Yes. Put a hold on the body. I don't know if she has any family to claim it quickly anyway."

"About that bassoon thing," asks Bill. "What should we do with that. It won't fit in our usual test tubes and jars and things."

"Well, for now rinse it off good, wrap it up, and store it in the fridge with the body. I'd like to add it to our museum, if Chief Ravenel or someone else doesn't steal it from us. Eventually we might want to handle it without gloves so we'll need to sterilize it first. Steam autoclaving might not work with that wood. Perhaps we can use the ethylene oxide sterilizer. Then we can hang it in a place of honor among all the knives, swords, axes, and other weapons in our display case. It will make quite a story."

"Can we call it a Soprano Skewer or Harlot Hâtelet or Diva Dildo?" asks the amused Bill. "Or maybe a Pig Sticker or even Fagotto de Sopranno?"

"Bill!" says M.E. sharply. "Respect the deceased. Soprano is OK, Harlot may be in context, but Pig I have a problem with. Remember the high profile here. One slip from us will be front page news and then I'll have another lecture from Mayor Rhett."

Bill helped Boone take the many samples to the robot processor. Each tissue block would go through a dozen solutions to dehydrate it in alcohols, replace those with a xylene mixture, and then replace that with paraffin. The dried tissues inside paraffin blocks would harden and then a histology technician would clamp each in the jaws of a microtome and slice it into amazingly thin sections for the microscope.

four

Morning Becomes Electronic Journalism

*S*aturday, dawn

Chief Ravenel had spent the night restoring order, directing journalists to the exits, and trying to shield from TV cameras and their lights the Charleston gentry who staggered, elegantly dressed but definitely inebriated, from the Gala. Too many of the Gala guests had also forgotten the Charleston tradition of personal anonymity and were all too eager to give on camera their versions of the evening's fiasco and the whole Spoleto story. The Chief knew that Mayor Rhett would be unhappy if the city didn't have an attractive image before the world. After all, without tourists, Charleston would be a container port with an old Fort half blocking the shipping channel. The Mayor had insisted on making the 333rd year, the Charles Town "Termillenium", coincide with Spoleto's 30th year to attract more and more tourists. Downtown residents felt the tourists already were like lemmings and hoped for them a similar end. At least during the night there were no other deaths and not even major accidents— just a few fender benders and the bruised physicians who, dreaming of James Bond, had leaped in their finery over the orchestra pit wall like penguins off an ice floe. Only one broken bone there, he had been told.

The news media had aroused itself until it climaxed in a feeding-frenzy on an otherwise slow news night. The breaking news interrupted all the local News at Eleven shows Friday night. Channel Five, that provided local feeds into the CNN Headline News, featured nothing else but Kasandrá, her career, Spoleto, Jean-Louis Guérard, the opera, and the "tragedy snatched from the jaws of triumph."

All four networks featured this story Saturday morning as Charlestonians awoke, some bright-eyed and many hungover. Those connected with Spoleto or the city's tourism industry wondered whether this tragedy would ultimately be good or bad.

For journalists, this story was too good to believe but never too good to report. Jean-Louis Guérard had been coaxed into highlighting this thirtieth festival, but only at an enormous price. Digging out the dirt they learned from some Spoleto contributors that he would now be called Director for Life. Spoleto would have to pay for two world premiers this year. First the maestro would write, produce, and direct a new opera, the equivalent of Porgy and Bess, but extolling the virtues of Charleston high society in its heyday "before the War of Northern Aggression." After Spoleto had paid for its creation and premier, he would have all rights to carry it to New York and the World. Second he would write, produce, and direct a new play with a classical historical focus, in concert with the Holy City nickname of Charleston. The Spoleto management had seemed wary but eager for special recognition of their thirtieth festival, and on the 333rd year of the city had acceded to the maestro's demands and prepared for what they hoped to be a glorious and lucrative opening.

Instead, the media spokespersons were told a tale of horror. Not of the soprano's impalement, but of the shocking theme of the "opera." The Spoleto management expressed as much shock as if their great grandfather had been proven a Yankee or perhaps just a private. The sacred Charleston heritage of chivalry had been besmirched by this this "opera" portraying Charleston gentry as incestuous pederasts, drunken charlatans, and miscegenators. The musically elite, however, spoke of the brilliance of the composition and drama, and complimented Kasandrá as the only living soprano who could do justice to the vocal range. They were equally kind to the muscular black *basso profundo*, Esau Versey, who matched her incredible F two octaves above middle C with equally spectacular fully resonant low notes rarely achieved in the modern repertory. The stars had complimented each other spectacularly.

The critics, official and self-proclaimed, were nearly unanimous in raving to the media about the flawless performance, the brilliant sets, graceful choreography, gorgeous costumes, and the spirited conducting of the aging maestro himself. All was reported as perfect up to the very last moment when the star, one wouldn't call her the heroine, was to collapse in death on stage. Instead she'd stumbled into the pit and impaled herself on a bassoon. The cameramen had gotten the most graphic pictures before the police shooed them away. Blood was everywhere and the soprano was largely exposed, very largely. The reporting became more and more lurid.

Only the distinguished arts editor of the New York Times, always on hand for Spoleto after the season had closed in The City, wrote a straight, conservative, unsensational review one might almost call "in the Charleston tradition of gentility and understatement." As arts patrons worldwide read in the Sunday Times:

Charleston opened this thirtieth Spoleto USA Festival to a packed house in the large municipal Gaillard Auditorium. Jean-Louis Guérard, perhaps the world's leading multimedia composer, beamed as brilliantly as the jewels adorning his audience, as he assumed the podium once again, acclaimed now as the Artistic Director for Life of this festival. The performance was nearly flawless, until the last note.

His new opera, in English, was sung exquisitely by Kasandrá who returned from her brief retirement just for this role. Esau Versey, the brilliant young bass, matched her musically but needed more experience to equal the theatricality of the electrifying Kasandrá who exposed more of her anatomy that was seen in her other vocal triumphs.

The theme of the opera is the decadence of Charleston aristocracy. Kasandrá plays the last heir of a thirteenth-generation family made rich as rice planters who excelled as politicians and Confederate generals but gradually dissipated to leave only Charlotte Russe Middleton as their scion. Raised in luxury, she attends Ashley Hall, learns dance at South Carolina Hall, and is prepared for her role in polite Charleston society. The opera opens with her debutante ball, in the family plantation house on the Ashley River, just after the tragic accidental deaths of her parents. The choreography, by the brilliant

*Areana Oschkanova is stunning—ready for the Met or Broad-
way, whichever Jean-Louis selects.*

*She meets the handsome Antoine Mazyck Middleton, is
wooed and wed as the act closes on another dazzling ball with
the stunning costumes of Alain Caponne. The sets of Bernado
Buontalenti resemble an English palace, with crystal chandeliers, sconces, and portraits of nobility.*

*The second act is tragic as the lighting gradually dims, the
music shifts to a minor key, and the glamorous portraits and
elegant furnishings seem to magically meld into the walls,
which turn from brilliant colors to beige under the artful
lighting, designed by the maestro himself, as the plot tells of her
husband's extravagant investments that are shown to be
fraudulent, ruining their friends. Her husband suicides and
most of her assets are repossessed, except for her family's plantation house. That is the setting for her husband's funeral that is
sparsely attended and garners little note. Rejected by "her"
society, Charlotte rebels.*

*The third act is stark tragedy. She seduces her black maid
as well as her maid's brother, Adam, who is her butler. Adam
discovers Charlotte and his sister in a passionate embrace,
nearly nude, and in a rage strangles his sister whom we learn he
had impregnated. Charlotte poisons Adam while revealing that
she too carries his child. Left alone on stage Kasandrá begins
her triumphant final aria, designed to show off her unique
vocal talents. She drinks of the poisoned cup and dies, prophesy-
ing that Adam, his sister, and their children will live a lascivious life with her in Hell. The last aria is an amazing vocal
achievement, ending in an F two octaves above middle C, and
in this performance she sustained it clearly and with great
power and drama.*

*The premier of a new opera is always an event, and the
excitement was heightened by the setting in Charleston, the
emergence from retirement of one of the most beautiful soprano
voices we can recall, the appointment of Jean-Louis to artistic
leadership of Spoleto, and by brilliant theater, music, and
visual spectacle. Surely as memorable as the earlier premier of
Gone with the Wind, this Charleston premier triumph was
tragically dimmed as Kasandrá, after her last glorious note,*

toppled into the orchestra pit and succumbed to her injuries.
We should only applaud her last performance as a vocal
triumph, capping her career, even if a more noble plot might
have made for a less fatal finale.

The Spoleto chairman, Augustus Ashley Cooper Hanahan III, searched the newspaper reports for his name. Only one of the CNN features had shown even a few seconds of him on camera and not even the local Post and Courier quoted him. He called up his cousin, Tom Waring, the editor, awakening him at home to complain about his omission from the news. The venerable Waring reminded him that proper Charlestonians used to appear only thrice in the paper—when they were born, when they married, and when they died, and they only got a fourth mention if they were resurrected. Hanahan harrumphed and hung up, still fuming.

The many Middletons in town were relieved that their family name, used by the maestro for his lead character, only appeared in passing in some reviews and not at all in others. Several Middleton attorneys framed in their minds the lawsuits they might bring against Jean-Louis or The F…ing Frog Bastard as they thought of him. Other Middletons, especially the hunters, wondered if the duelling code, which had been practiced in Charleston until 1880, could be revitalized. The family dueling pistols, in their lovely mahogany case, rested in the Charleston Museum along with much of their family silver and two beautiful Confederate swords, probably still stained with the DNA of former Yankee devils.

five

M.E. And Chemistry

*S*aturday 7:22 am

After two hours sleep Dr. Simons awoke, showered, and headed back to her lab. Dr. Woodward had called during the autopsy and said he would be in all day Saturday to help. He had suggested they needed to report as soon as possible. M.E. had called in Yoki Ginsu, an histology technician, to cut sections of the tissue samples and asked Dirk Gadsden, PhD, MD, her colleague who ran the analytical laboratory to process the chemical tests as soon as possible.

She slipped into the seat of her Jaguar and enjoyed the smell and feel of the leather and the beautiful cockpit. She ran her fingers over the burl walnut, which she polished when she had time. She switched on the Breeze, the radio station that blanketed the lowcountry with "Beach, Boogie, and Blues" just as they were doing an ad for Blue Monday with Shrimp City Slim. She smiled, shook off her tiredness, fired up the engine, admired its zoom zoom, and scratched off for the Medical University.

She went first to the women's dressing room and changed into the pink scrub suits they used in the autopsy room. Green was used in the main operating rooms and blue in the ancillary areas such as ICUs. Although she wasn't planning to perform any postmortem examinations today, she worked more freely in the baggy scrub suits and this was the only place she could enjoy slacks—Charleston ladies were never seen in anything but skirts, except on the beach.

Ginsu was busily processing the tissue samples to prepare them for microscopic examination. She removed the tissue sections from the processing robot and allowed the paraffin blocks to harden. Then she selected a block of left ventricle and clamped it into the chuck of the microtome. Sitting before the ultrasharp microtome knife she rotated the wheel with her left hand as the chuck rose and fell like a guillotine. With each passage the block moved a few microns closer to the blade and as it passed the blade, from top to bottom, that edge sliced off a thin section, thinner than a postage stamp. The paraffin made each section stick to the one just cut, so with each snicker-snack of the blade a ribbon of paraffin grew longer hanging down from the blade. Each white paraffin square had a grey patch of tissue in the center. It was like slicing bologna, but the ultrasharp blade was exposed with its edge upward so the operator could observe the action.

When Ginsu felt she had gotten appropriate sections, she gently lifted the ribbon with two large steel needles and placed a section on top of warm water in a bath. This made the paraffin ribbon flatten out. Then she slipped a clean glass microscope slide under the ribbon and picked up one section flat on the glass. She warmed it over a small flame and as soon as the albumin adhesive on the glass had bonded the ribbon, she marked the slide with the autopsy number and a code for the tissue.

At this stage the slides were just gray meat, but their beauty would be revealed with dyes that would highlight each feature. The great German pathologists a century ago had begun finding the right chemicals, but today this art was highly sophisticated. Ginsu would put the slides into staining robots that would expose each tissue to just the right dyes, for just the proper seconds. The resulting sections would be as lovely as a Seurat painting. For special structures antibodies were coupled to dyes, some of which fluoresced brilliantly in the proper light. Sometimes radioisotopes were used on slides coated with a silver emulsion, just like photographic film. As the radioactive materials decayed, they gave off rays that would darken the silver just like light would in a camera. Those dark dots indicated where the radioisotope had been attached in the cells and could identify the location of a cancer or a poison that shouldn't be there.

M.E. could have asked for frozen sections that could be stained and examined immediately. That was the procedure in surgical pathology, when a patient was waiting on the table and the microscopic views would determine if the patient had a benign lump or a cancer. Today, however, there was no urgency—no question of serious contagion or other emergency. So, M.E. and Bill would have to wait about a day until the dyes had time to color each section and they were ready for examination under the light microscopes, at magnifications of X10 to X2000. For even greater magnifications, to X100,000, they would use the electron microscopes.

Ginsu looked up as M.E. entered and said: "Dr. Simons, good morning. Sorry you had another long night. I should have the first slides ready for you within the hour and the last regular stains should be finished this afternoon before I leave. Just give me some warning about special stains."

"Well right now," replied M.E., "I know so little of her history that I can't anticipate anything special. It just looks like an accident, and we didn't find anything that unusual on the autopsy. The Provisional Anatomical Diagnosis will be probable accidental death from impalement, just like that drunk last month who fell off the John Rutledge House balcony onto that cast iron *fleur de lys*. This one was a little more musical, but the result was the same. Let's hope it is just the standard routine. I'm sorry to call you in on this holiday weekend, but this is a high profile case because of Spoleto and Dr. Woodward, who'll be looking in I'm sure, wants us to make a definitive statement as soon as possible—probably to make the Sunday papers."

Dr. Simons wondered what the analytical chemists were finding as she walked up to the floor above that held all the analytical equipment. Her research mass spectrometers and nuclear magnetic resonance analyzers were at the end of the hall to the right and the regular service laboratory on the left. She walked into the first lab on the left, put on her safety glasses, and greeted the lab chief, Dirk Gadsden. This tall, blonde marathon-runner was the fastest Charlestonian in the Cooper River Bridge Run, following the Kenyans, for the last two years in a row. He also was one of the sharpest analytical toxicologists in the country.

"Morning, youall," Dirk sang out with his usual pleasant deep voice, dipping his head to peek over his glasses. "We've finished the routine tox screen and found a handful of items, but we've also got a number of unknown peaks that I've sent to the more precise mass spectrometers. Look at this list. The low levels of ibuprofen, acetaminophen, and salicylate wouldn't hurt her, unless she were very allergic to them, but she must have had pain somewhere. She also must have had terrible allergies to something as she has a high concentration of terfenadine, ephedrine, and neosynephrine. In addition, I found relatively high levels of quinine—more than you'd expect from gin and tonic. I doubt she had malaria—more likely night cramps. We've got pretty high levels of a number of vitamins, especially vitamin E, but most of the other drugs are at levels lower than toxic. Then we've got at least one peak that we haven't identified before. What on earth was this woman taking?"

"I don't know. We don't have a medical history. Lieutenant Rhett was coordinating the collection of evidence and should have some answers. I'll call him and ask him to bring in all the drugs and whatever he has found out."

M.E. reached Rhett on his police cell phone. He had been up all night and was not through with his reports yet. "OK, M.E., I'll bring over the bottles, creams, tubes, and nebulizers as soon as fingerprinting finishes with them. It is a big pile. Looks like a drugstore. I didn't find anything that looked like a drug of abuse, but there are so many strange herbs and stuff she could have peyote or speed or whatever. Can you help us by analyzing some of these things?"

"Absolutely," replied M.E. "That's our job. Dr. Woodward is pushing me to have a final report soon and I know you're under pressure as well."

"You wouldn't believe how much. Reporters have been bugging the Chief all night. Everyone is trying to report a sinister side to this event and to blame someone. I can't see how it's anything other than an accident, especially if you didn't turn up anything suspicious at autopsy, well suspicious other than a bassoon through the heart that is. Are you comfortable with us beginning to paint that picture?"

"I'd hold off just a little," replied M.E. cautiously. "She was on lots of drugs and I just learned that she had high levels of a really dangerous antihistamine, Seldane, that might have caused heart irregularities. It is possible that arrhythmias caused her to stumble even if there were only a few abnormal beats. It doesn't sound criminal, but we also have a lot of unknown peaks we need to identify. But, at least I didn't find any pellets of ricin embedded in her skin, if the KGB is still using that."

"KGB? They used ricin? Isn't that the stuff in castor beans?"

"Yep, but ricin is deadly. One molecule kills a cell by stopping protein synthesis."

"What did the KGB do with it?"

"It may be before your time, but there is a famous case in toxicology of a Bulgarian dissident named Georgi Markov. He had fled to London and was broadcasting on the BBC."

"And the KGB didn't like that?"

"Actually they kept calling him up at home and threatening to poison him, but he paid no attention."

"Apparently that was a mistake?"

"To say the least. One lunchtime on the Waterloo Bridge Markov felt a blow to his thigh. It was a projectile fired from an umbrella. That night he got sick and was admitted to a Balham Hospital where he died three days later of what looked like septic shock."

"What did they do with the pellet?"

"They almost missed it. At autopsy the prosector saw it and thought it was a pin head. When he went to pull it out it rolled down the table and almost into the drain. Once they had it they knew it was special. It was made of platinum and titanium with two holes drilled in it with advanced laser spark erosion technology."

"Wow. So was it ricin in those holes?"

"They were empty, but they would have held about 350 mg or three or four lethal doses."

"OK, so how do we know about the ricin?"

"They also shot Markov's friend, Kostov. He was on the Paris Metro wearing a thick sweater and the pellet just lodged under the skin. The wax seals hadn't melted and they found the ricin inside. Kostov lived—all because of that sweater."

"So is the KGB still using ricin? I never thought of that when we had patients with sepsis."

"They may have moved on to bigger and worser stuff, but ricin is being used in medicine for cancer chemotherapy. They take the active half of the molecule and attach it to an antibody that seeks out cancer cells. If the antibody connects, the ricin kills the cell. I hear they are getting better and better at that."

Just then Dr. Woodward walked into the lab and greeted everyone with a big smile: "Well, what have you sleuths turned up?"

"We don't have anything unexpected except for two findings. First, she had high levels of both Seldane and quinine in her blood. Remember Seldane? It was pulled off the U.S. market a couple of years ago for causing heart arrhythmias. Quinine will do the same thing. Then we have a peak on the chromatogram that we haven't identified yet. Not sure what that is."

"I remember Seldane, sort of. How could she have gotten it?"

"Well, when they quit selling it there may be a lot left around and some other countries might still be selling it. Most people did well on the drug but a few died when they had irregular heart beats."

Lt. Rhett opened the door holding a huge garbage bag—well an evidence bag at least. "Hi, docs. I've got just the grabbag you've been looking for."

M.E. opened the bag and stared at the collection of bottles of all sizes and colors. Some labels were in Arabic and some in Chinese. One was labeled by Schwettmann's, a Charleston pharmacy. She had wanted some help with the search not a Niagara of help. Oh well.

Bubba observed her dismay and encouragingly said: "This is really all. I brought everything medical except an air purifier next to her bed. Even the cosmetics are in there. I hope that didn't overwhelm you."

"That's perfect," replied M.E. "It will just take us a little time to sort through it all. We have only found one unknown peak on her chromatograph. Maybe we can quickly find it in this gemisch."

M.E. asked Dirk to take charge of the medications, to maintain an evidence chain, but to get some help in calling all the pharmacies listed.

"See if you can find anything else about her from the pharmacists and call the physicians they knew about, not just the ones writing for these prescriptions. Maybe she had some occult disease that would make her unsteady. And Dirk, check me out on the kinetics of Seldane and quinine. I remember that both are broken down by the same enzyme, CYP3A4, so one slows the metabolism of the other. If I'm right, that could be an interaction that could have led to a heart arrhythmia."

"What kind of rhythm problem is it?" asked Dr. Woodward.

"*Torsades de pointes*," Dr. Simons announced proudly to her boss. "Remember that the heart cells are charged, like little batteries, until a wave of depolarization neutralizes the electrical polarization and causes the heart to contract. Then the cells regain their former charge and are ready to beat again. On the electrocardiogram you can measure how long that takes by the time from the beginning of the depolarization, called the Q wave, to the end of repolarization, called the T wave. Both Seldane and quinine lengthen this QT interval and slow the time to repolarization. They also cause variation in the rates of repolarization and wavefront propagation through the heart. Unfortunately, in some patients, this causes a severe arrhythmia in which the wave of contraction goes around and around the heart and the electrocardiographic record looks like a picket fence, so it's called *torsades de pointes*."

M.E. smiled, happy she was up to speed on this rather arcane point. When her boss asked about other drugs that cause it, she could recall a few: "There was just a paper in the Annals of Internal Medicine recording 17 patients with *torsades* from methadone given in high doses to treat morphine addiction, so it is not that rare. Interestingly methadone is also metabolized by that same CYP3A4 enzyme, but I don't know of any other connection. There also are some famous poisons that do it, like the group from the monkshood mushroom. Not what you want to slice onto your steak at Outback."

"Do you think she died of a cardiac arrhythmia?" asked Woodward.

"Well, it looks like she was bassooned," said M.E. with a smile, "but an arrhythmia, even for a few beats, could have made her stumble and fall. I just want to sort out all these medicines and why she was taking them. It could be that all the physicians she was seeing around the world never took a thorough history of the other medicines she was taking. We might find the same drug under different names given to her by physicians in different countries. As I recall Demerol has 40 or 50 different names around the world. And it looks like she was taking many over-the-counter drugs too. Remember that warning from FDA about Tylenol causing liver damage—they said the active ingredient appears in more than 200 over the counter remedies so a patient could easily take two or three with the same ingredient and get too much."

M.E. beamed as Dr. Woodward complimented her thoroughness and said how glad he was that she was in charge. He wanted to be sure that she would stay on as medical examiner, knowing some of the famous northern schools were recruiting her and she could always do full-time research and teaching.

She reassured him: "I enjoy what I'm doing. I've got sufficient funding, fine colleagues, and good support from you and the Dean. We have excellent residents who help with the routine and, remember, this is one of only two counties in this state that have medical examiners. It is a responsibility to be sure we do a professional job. And reporting some of these cases is notable. Remember the infected alligator bite last year and the fatal cases of Vibrio vulnificans in raw oysters we had two years ago? Those were good papers. I'm not sure bassoonosis qualifies for the New England Journal of Medicine, but I'm sure the resident will write it up somewhere. Maybe there is a Journal of Musical Mayhem. It is nice to be wanted by other schools, but my family have been here since the first Huguenots arrived in 1686 and I don't feel like abandoning them quite yet."

Woodward smiled and leaned close and said softly: "Would you like some dinner tonight?" Maybe Sushi Hiro or My Tho," he said mentioning two of her favorites, close together on King Street.

"Henry, that would be a super supper. I'll get through here and change. Would eight o'clock be OK?" M.E. was pleased. She had been to various functions with her boss several times recently, but he was still recovering from the death of his wife from breast cancer and she didn't think he was seeking romance as much as an alternative to an evening with his kids, as attractive as they were.

"That would be lov-e-ly," beamed Woodward.

six

Ballet—Political & Otherwise

*S*aturday, 9:15 am

At the Gaillard Auditorium the rehearsal of the San Francisco Ballet was going well. Highly professional, the dancers knew just what to do despite the tragedy of the opera. The orchestra, however, largely drawn from the same musicians who had performed the night before, was a little ragged. They still grieved the impalement, irreverently talked about the soprano lollypop, and tried to console Mr. Vlad. Vlad had been treated at the Medical University Hospital and after X-rays had been declared unfractured but badly bruised and he was sent home with a Thomas collar that make him look like an unhappy Puritan. He sadly joined his colleagues but without instruments and openly wept over his antique bassoon, noting it to be a member of his family just like an old dog. His fellow bassonist's irreverent thought was: "it sure had sharp teeth."

Several musicians refused to play until they were assured that the blood with which they had been splattered was not HIV positive. But, they gradually came together, focused on the classic and relatively easy to play music, and the dancers responded with the expertise and poise expected of this superb company.

Teddy Bonnet was busy directing the assembly of sets and flies and coordinating the work of the lighting and stage directors. There were only a few props, and by late afternoon everything was coming together.

When Bubba arrived she was ready for a break and delighted to see him. "How's the investigation, chief?"

"More like an Indian. We're not learning much. She had a bunch of medicines but we haven't learned much about her medical history or why she was taking so much stuff. What do you know about her?"

Teddy stretched, attracting his look. "I didn't know her too well. She was a loner. I did see her huffing and puffing on lots of nebulizers, but that is common, in sopranos especially. I also know she complained of arthritis in her hands and was afraid of it spreading to her jaw so she took lots of pills as well as liniments for that. And she had hayfever and said she had 'a touch' of asthma and allergies, and complained about the dust and air conditioning, but all singers are afraid of colds and runny noses. She even asked me about some herbal medicines she was taking, but she didn't seem to know anything about herbs."

"Well it's obvious she, ah hum, fell on her sword, but we still need to see if anything made her unsteady or perhaps faint momentarily. How's the ballet? Is anyone planning to leap into the orchestra and perhaps suffocate in the tuba in their tutu?"

"Please have respect for the dead. No bassoonery, sir. Besides our dancers are so thin they would probably not get stuck in the tuba—perhaps in a French horn or trumpet."

Bubba thought of what he could say about "French" but decided to leave that alone. "What is that row of cell phones for?"

"Not cell phones but radio controls for the fireworks. Several of the productions need fireworks to be precisely timed. See this allows us to blow things up at just the right moment, so we don't assassinate any actors or explode spears into the audience. Don't worry."

"But aren't they radio signals? How can you prevent some cell phone from setting them off?"

"Good point, but these are special frequencies and all require at least two if not three coded signals to work. Don't worry. I've got an explosives expert in to make sure it's all safe and the Fire Marshall comes in to inspect us during rehearsals. Besides which, we only blow up little things."

Bubba, smiling, picked up a notepad from a nearby table and, toying with it, asked: "Teddy, after you get through blowing up the ballet, would you be free for dinner? Carolina's and McCrady's are open late and have great menus."

Teddy paused. He was very handsome and accomplished, but she had not had a successful liaison since her husband's violent death almost a decade before. Her few brief affairs had ended badly and she just hadn't been involved seriously in a long time. Two weeks ago Kasandrá had misinterpreted her lack of swains and had hit on her seriously. She had escaped her advances, but was still angry about that assault and maybe what she needed to restore her confidence was a nice romantic evening with a handsome football star, even if he was also a policeman. She'd always enjoyed the dangerous pursuit. "Bernard, I'll be exhausted tonight. The first night of a new performance is very challenging, even if everyone survives. I didn't sleep well last night. If you can stand me wound up and exhausted, I'd be delighted to have dinner with you tonight."

Bubba beamed: "You've made my day, Teddy. Is it OK if I meet you backstage after the performance?"

"Yes, but I'll need to run by my place to change if you can wait twenty minutes or so."

"I'd be honored to wait for you as long as you like." Bubba said bouncing on his toes and tingling all over. Teddy was a gorgeous creature and so cosmopolitan and her dark hair and calm professional demeanor contrasted so much with the disposable flighty blondes he usually took to bed.

Saturday, 10 am

Mayor Maybank was in his office at city hall. The building sat on the northeast corner of the Four Corners of Law opposite the original colonial government building and first statehouse, the federal courthouse, and St. Michael's Church. This building began life as a branch of Bank of U.S., perhaps designed by Gabriel Manigault, and it was the second oldest City Hall in continuous use the country.

Maybank was trying to regain control of the media. He had already launched a campaign, perhaps belatedly, to greet all the media types flocking to town and give them tours while extolling the virtues of this charming bastion of the Old South. Now, checking with his staff, he asked: "John, are you sure you have all the passenger lists from the airlines that show new reservations?"

"Yes, Delta and US Airways are cooperating, and I've checked all the hotels to alert us for any walk-ins. And I've got some helpers at the airport to spot anyone showing up with a big camcorder or more than the usual tourist cameras."

"How about private aircraft and Amtrak?"

"The airport is calling me directly for each new private flight from outside this region and Amtrak has been booked full with no new reservations. I don't know what we can do about the drive-ins though."

"OK, let's go over the verbatims," suggested the Mayor. "Everyone should know the history of Spoleto and have lots of copies of the booklet on its thirty years of glory. We are honored to have Maestro Jean-Louis as artistic director for this thirtieth anniversary, but emphasize the thirty successful years and all the thousands of superb performances. Give the press the whirlwind tour of the historic district and emphasize Charleston as a center of culture and recreational opportunities that is drawing large numbers of visitors and retirees."

"How do we explain all the For Sale signs on the houses?" asked an aide.

"Just tell the truth," replied the Mayor. "We have more authentic eighteenth century and Ante-bellum dwellings than any place in this country, and there aren't going to be any more of them. Everyone wants to be a part of our history. Don't bother telling them that all those new money-eyed folks from 'off' probably won't live long enough to succeed. One Society now has a 35 year waiting list and if your father isn't a member it might as well be 105 years."

Saturday, 11:10 am

In the Spoleto offices on George Street, not far from the Gaillard Auditorium, Augustus Ashley Cooper Hanahan, III, was trying to control a contentious meeting of the Spoleto management committee. He had invited Jean-Louis to attend. Actually, Jean-Louis had demanded the meeting.

"What are you going to do to save my festival?" Jean-Louis demanded. He looked half dead. Large dark circles under his eyes made him look like a coon and his eyes were as red as a Citadel sash. His white hair was in total disarray as though he had peed in a light socket. He still had on his dress pants and fancy shoes, but with a turtle-neck pearl grey sweater.

"Actually, Jean-Louis," replied Hanahan. "We've been talking about canceling the remaining four performances of your 'opera.' This is a great excuse. You told us this would be an opera to 'glorify Charleston's heritage of gentility' as I recall your words."

Mayor Maybank and the other four members nodded their assent.

"You kept things secret. You even excluded us from your rehearsals. Last week when we heard rumors we called you in and you said you were rewriting the libretto to make us happy. Well, I don't know what you changed, but I can tell you I'm not happy."

The board murmured its agreement with this assessment.

"Actually, at the Gala, we huddled and most of the Spoleto local contributors suggested lynching you. Even if you have some distant cousins in town, I can assure you that even your own family was ready to get the rope last night."

Jean-Louis stood, placed both hands on the table, and, staring each of them in the eye from left to right, announced gravely: "I think my opera epitomizes your history. Powers' <u>Black Charlestonians</u> documents all of your relatives who raped their house slaves, fathered numerous mulattos, and then freed their chillun, even against the state laws. It is well known that Charleston had more freedmen, actually more freedwomen, than any other part of the South. Many of your ancestors' wills provided homes, education, trusts, and whatnot to care for their 'beloved Esmeralda' or whomever. Gentlemen, each of you has blood kin that are as black as this mahogany table!"

In the ensuing mêlée angry voices and fists pounding the table framed the denials. "Suh, my family never ...." "You lying cock-a-roach.... I'll never speak to you...." "You'll never be welcome in a decent...."

Hanahan gaveled and gaveled them to silence, thinking of the three black families with his name that he knew were descendants from one Hanahan or another who had dallied in the kitchenhouse while their dainty if frigid wives served tea in the parlor. "Quiet! Stop it! We'll never get anywhere fighting like this. Jean-Louis, I think the point is not so much whether your scurrilous thing is historically accurate but that we don't talk in polite society about unpleasantness, and we don't have our ladies prancing around half naked with their servants, black or white." The mêlée resumed immediately with Jean-Louis pounding on the table, his face multicolored as a babboon's rear end.

When Hanahan had silenced them again, Jean-Louis almost screamed: "I have a contract. The opera is mine. You agreed to feature it for five performances this year. I'm going to hold you to that contract and not all the lawyers on Broad Street can break it. If you don't come through, this will be the last Spoleto and your grandchildren will be paying mine. Don't forget, you and the other board members guaranteed the finances of this festival! You insult my magnificent opera once more and that fat soprano won't be the only one with a handle sticking out of her."

"Stop!" Hanahan screamed. "All of you. Remember we are here to protect Spoleto and Charleston. The story of this Gawdawful opera is already out. We can't squeeze it back into the tube. We have to live with it. Now what can we do to minimize the damage. No more grousing. We're going to work together on this, even if we all hate each other."

The participants gradually sat down, even if Jean-Louis was the object of the nastiest sullen stares since the British soldiers stole the bells out of St. Michael's Church across the street.

"Well, 'maestro,'" Hanahan asked derisively, "what do you want us to do. How can we replace the opera performances? Is anything else available. You must have an understudy—can't you use her?

"Ha," snorted Jean-Louis. "No understudy will perform my opera."

"But I thought that was what they were for?" said Hanahan with a smirk.

"She doesn't have the range. She would be a dismal failure. Her range isn't as good as some tenors. In fact," he said still smirking, "maybe I could get a tenor and rewrite it as a drag role."

The table erupted again. Everyone jumped up and started screaming at Jean-Louis. He just smiled enjoying his triumph. He had them just where he wanted them. That would teach these provincial prigs to meddle with Jean-Louis.

Hanahan gaveled and gaveled them quiet once again. "Gentlemen we have a crisis. We aren't going to solve it with bickering. Can we please work together. Jean-Louis, if the understudy doesn't suit you, what can we do?"

"I have already identified a suitable replacement who has a great voice and a great figure. She is available for New York as well. I'll have to rewrite some of the high notes, but I've already started that. She'd have to rehearse. You know, opera is the most complex art form and she and the cast, plus lighting, costumes, even the set must all find their harmony before the curtain rises. We'll have to make new costumes for her as the old ones would just fall off."

"Seems to me that's just what you wanted in your damn abomination," screamed John Gibbes as he began to unsheath his swordcane. "I don't know how you could get any civilized person to be on the stage for that piece of Yannnkeee Traaaash."

"We'll see what's trash, you hillbilly," screamed Jean-Louis shaking his fist.

"I'll barbecue your frog legs and roast your guts with collard greens," screamed the normally sedate Mr. Gibbes, as he lunged for the maestro. It looked like a restart of the War of Northern Aggression. In this mêlée the language, frankly, was not suitable for Southern ladies and gentlemen. It was far worse than that shattering "damn" in Gone With the Wind.

Hanahan imposed his considerable girth between the combatants and demanded silence. Slowly he regained control and they sat. "Jean-Louis would you pulleeasse see about a replacement and see if you can perform either Wednesday or Sunday."

"There is no way we could be ready for Wednesday and I doubt Sunday. I'll do my best to have excellent performances for the last two dates. If possible would you like to add an extra performance, perhaps on the closing night?"

"An extra date would be helpful, Jean-Louis. Let's look at the logistics of adding that. We only use Gaillard if the closing concert at Middleton Place is rained out, and that is unlikely. But we'd have to advertise and print tickets. What about the two dark nights. Can you suggest a suitable replacement for those nights? asked Hanahan.

"My goodness," said the Mayor. "If we have to refund all those tickets, at $150 a seat plus the required $100 reception, we'll have to refuse to pay the opera folks for the dark nights."

"You lying cheating cochon," cried Jean-Louis, pointedly looking at Hanahan's expansive belly and grunting like a sow. "You know my contract calls for guaranteed payments whether or not the performance is given. It is guaranteed not just for hurricanes, earthquakes, fires, terrorism, and so forth but for any other contingency as well. You'll pay even if you never have another festival."

"Let's just string up this frog bastard," roared John Gibbes, "and be rid of him once and for all. It is hard to imagine he is related to the distinguished Charleston Guérards."

"Harumph" roared Jean-Louis. "Your Charleston Guérards were Protestant Huguenots who betrayed Louis XIV and fled to this Godforsaken Hellhole. They even named a Huguenot enclave Hell Hole Swamp. My family remained loyal to the crown and moved to Paris with the proper King and God. How dare you question my family, you cheating pack of half-breed pederasts!"

Hanahan again physically pushed Gibbes back into his chair, restrained the Mayor, and gently pushed Jean-Louis, with his belly, back to a seat. He implored them to try to work together to save Spoleto and the reputation of Charleston. Turning to Jean-Louis he begged him to consider a replacement show, even an inferior one, for his opera.

"Nothing can replace my opera, and you know it," replied the maestro haughtily and with an air of hurt.

"What about that Russian ballet company we tried to book that had a partial conflict. Do you know if they might have those two nights free?" asked a board member. "Jean-Louis, I thought you were using their star dancer as a coach for the dancers in your opera."

"Coach!" the maestro roared. "Areana Oschkanova is one of the most famous dancers alive. She agreed to choreograph my opera, but could only stay through the second performance as she is on tour and her company is booked into Atlanta at the end of May."

"Could they help out with just two performances on the nights your opera was scheduled? Atlanta isn't very far away." Everyone talked at once.

Hanahan gaveled them quiet yet again. "Jean-Louis, what do you think? Is that possible?"

"Well, Areana did complain to me about a break in their tour and it was hard to book everything they wanted this late in the season. Her troupe is in Atlanta and awaiting her return for their performances there."

"What is their name again?" asked Hanahan.

"Stars of the Bolshoi. But," added Jean-Louis haughtily, "except for Areana you might call them 'Sagging Stars of the Second String Bolshoi.' They would never command sell-out audiences in Russia, and that is why they are touring here. Americans know so little of true ballet. You could sell a ballet troupe of teenage cheerleaders juggling those stupid flaming batons as long as they wore short shorts and jiggled."

"I'll get my secretary to find Areana," observed Hanahan as he walked out the door to his office.

His secretary found that Areana had left the guest home to which she had been assigned and demanded a suite in the Charleston Place Hotel, now run by Orient Express: Suite 401, the Charles Cotesworth Pinckney Suite. Hanahan thought about calling but instead asked his secretary to make an appointment for him to see Areana at noon if possible. His secretary called, made contact, and found Areana willing to meet Hanahan in her suite at noon.

Hanahan beamed then told his secretary: "Go get me a bottle of the best champagne, two dozen roses, and stop by Godiva at the hotel and get three pounds of chocolate. Meet me by the elevators just before noon."

Returning to the meeting, Hanahan announced that he would meet with Areana to explore the ballet possibility. "Meanwhile," he asserted, "Jean-Louis please help by finding a replacement soprano to perform your wonderful opera as soon as possible. We must not leave any turn unstoned or whatever," Hanahan intoned.

seven

Pretty Please...
With Candy and Kisses

*S*aturday, 11:53 am

Augustus Hanahan parked in the garage adjacent to the Charleston Place Hotel, walked down the stairs, marveled at the out-of-place Quadriga in the drive, and marched into the cool lobby as the doorman held open the door and bowed discretely. Shops ran in both directions, right to King Street across from the old Riviera Theater, now an exhibition hall, and left to Meeting Street near the Market and the recently renovated headquarters-museum of the United Daughters of the Confederacy. The paired winding staircases rose from the lobby to the ballrooms, but Hanahan first crossed the lobby to the public gentlemen's room on the left and checked his tie and zipper, combed his hair, ate a breath mint, and made certain his appearance was perfect if rotund. As he exited he saw his secretary loaded down with the flowers and a shopping bag. "Did you get everything?" he asked.

"Yes. The champagne was very expensive but I got it and the chocolates in the bag. Can I do anything else?"

"Just pray," replied Hanahan as he relieved his secretary of the burdens and headed to the elevators. He found the door to Areana's suite, checked his watch to be sure he was exactly on time, and gently rapped with the pitcher-handle door knocker on the double doors. He quickly inverted the flowers so the buds hung down in the European manner.

"Good day, Mr. Hanahan," Areana beamed as she opened the door. "What gorgeous flowers. Are they for me?"

"Yes, my dear. The Spoleto board is very pleased that you were willing to brighten our little festival with your gorgeous choreography and last night it was the highlight. The board met this morning and insisted that I bring you these, and some chocolate and champagne, just to show our appreciation of your artistry." Hanahan attempted a bow as he handed over the bag of goodies, and made it at least half way.

"Why thank you. I'm so thrilled. Won't you come in."

Hanahan was a master of polite conversation and flattery, being a Charlestonian. He did his best to woo Areana into feeling warm and fuzzy about Spoleto and the board. As the conversation turned to the dilemma of replacing the skewered squeaker, Hanahan saw his moment: "The next two performances on Wednesday and Sunday are a problem. Jean-Louis thinks he can find a replacement soprano for the final two dates.

"I hope he finds one who is bassoon-proof."

"Well, we have a problem with the next two dates. We don't want dark nights, but we don't know what to do and thought you might help. You are such a world-famous artist you know everyone of value. Do you have any thoughts of what we could do? We would be eternally grateful," he beamed.

Areana paused, thoughtful. What an opportunity. Her company had tried to get into Spoleto as the headliner, but their Atlanta date was firm and they couldn't get out of it. Besides Atlanta would pay a higher fee and have bigger audiences. But the company was dark for this week, rehearsing a new ballet without her. That was how she got away to save Jean-Louis' pitiful attempt at opera. The local dancers Spoleto had assembled were just clods, more like warthogs than gazelles. Not one with real talent. And Spoleto favored the cheap ridiculous ballets to fill their small theaters. This year they had some Cambodian peasants recreating village life, as though anyone cared, and another dance group at the Garden Theater wore combat boots and looked just as ugly. Her troupe could show them what real ballet was like, beautiful, disciplined, perfect.

"Well," she crooned lugubriously with her broadest smile, "I suppose you want only the finest attraction in accord with those ticket prices. It would be impossible to find something that could be staged in just three days with no advance planning. Yet, I believe there might be a possibility. Very expensive. Very difficult. But, at least it might be possible. And, this possibility would make your festival truly world class. It would become your headliner. And all those customers with the expensive tickets for the opera would be more than satisfied to have an even greater event."

"Oh, Areana," oozed Hanahan in his most supplicant adoring voice. "Oh, you are such a dream. What could possibly be such an opportunity. We had just given up. But of course we don't know the arts as you do. World famous personalities like you don't come here very often," he gushed, while hoping she didn't know how disingenuous he really was. Charleston needed Spoleto for the tourist revenue and publicity. He would help Charleston and Spoleto. But the last thing this conservative inbred town needed was a bunch of off-the-wall weird 'artistes' with their drugs, lovers of all genders, and wild behavior. It's OK if <u>we</u> do wild and crazy stuff, he thought, but not <u>them</u>. He thought of the beautiful painter and actress Alicia Rhett, Bubba's aunt, who had starred as India Wilkes in Gone with the Wind. She was as beautiful today as in her youth. Despite that triumph she had retired quietly to Charleston, not wishing to lose her good reputation by mingling too much with the Hollywood actors and actresses. Charlestonians still thought of that profession as being little different from the world's oldest. You can't even invite a nice divorced guest to the Debutante Ball in Hibernian Hall, he thought. If I showed up with an actress, I'd be voted out forever.

Areana beamed. It had been a long time. When she was the young star of the Bolshoi and the toast of Moscow she had handsome young men showering her with attention day and night—all night. Swallowtail coats, uniform braid, champagne, and flowers were *de rigeur*. But not chocolate. Only a pig like this one would bring calories to a prima ballerina.

"There is just a possibility," she crooned, "just a possibility that my Bolshoi company might be available for those two dates. On this tour we have been performing two different programs of Stravinsky. The first night we do the more classical ballets from his early Russian period when he collaborated with Diaghilev of the Ballets Russes. We have abridged each so we can fit Petrushka, The Rite of Spring, and The Firebird into three acts. The second night we extend to his French and American periods with The Fairy's Kiss, Persephone, and Agon."

"Which program would you recommend for Spoleto," gushed Hanahan.

"I will recommend the first program for three reasons. First, your orchestra will know the classical works and I want the same large orchestra you use for the opera. Second, we have the sheet music for the first night as, you may recall, they are not copyrighted in their original versions because of the Czar's refusal to sign the Berne Convention. So you don't have delays in renting scores and they are fully orchestrated. Third, I'm not sure your audience will relate to the complexities of his latter works. In Agon particularly the middle part is largely serial rather than tonal and is not often heard. Experienced critics have lauded our presentation of these six works, but some yokels have not understood the later more complex pieces."

"I know how to reach all the principal dancers," added Areana thoughtfully. "Of course we are very busy. To interrupt our work would create an enormous workload. We'd have to work doubly hard. And some of the dancers, not as limber and resilient as I, might not want to take on the challenge. And of course, it would be very expensive."

Areana was pleased to see Hanahan beaming as he gushed: "You are the brightest and the most beautiful artist ever to grace Charleston. What a wonderful thought. You know we wanted your troupe to headline Spoleto this year, but you couldn't fill all five of the key dates."

She wondered if he was always such an idiot or perhaps was drunk. "Yes," she smiled. "I remember the negotiations. You suggested we take second billing to Jean-Louis' opera, use recorded music, and accept only a tiny fee. Then you wouldn't compromise on the dates."

Hanahan thought of her rudeness in refusing to adjust dates and her insistence on an enormous fee. Oh well, if he'd gotten her maybe he'd have done without that monstrous "opera." It would have been better to have Areana do a Black Mass on stage than that Guérard piece of liabelous trash.

"But, can you do it for us?"

"Well," Areana replied. "Perhaps if we were guaranteed the lead position for next year with funding for new productions and a large orchestra, then I might ask my colleagues to consider it."

Aghast, Hanahan reflected. It was a mess. If he had to refund more than a million dollars in sales for two nights, for they were all sold out, it would be a disaster. Even if he made Jean-Louis sue to get his fees, Hanahan knew that the contract was ironclad for Jean-Louis. He felt like the original Charleston submarine, the Hunley, sunk off Sullivan's Island. He was sunk, the Spoleto board was a crew all drowned, the Mayor was a leader undone, the city would be disgraced, and having dark nights on a major festival bill would taint it for years. Oh well.

"Areana," he smiled his most earnest smile, "I think we can work together on that if you can get the troupe to give outstanding performances on those two critical nights. We can use the whole orchestra we have for the opera if you think they can master your music in time. I'm sure we can arrange to use the opera set if you wish. Do you think your colleagues would come?"

"Well, I'm sure the fee would be no less than $200,000 per performance," she asserted haughtily, remembering the paltry $75,000 that had been suggested for each of five major performances.

Hanahan sputtered, turning even more red than usual. Areana thought his face was like a pimple. She mused: I wonder if he's going to have a stroke right here and add a second body to the festival lore.

"I'll do my best to get the board to agree, Areana dear, if you'll just contact your colleagues and see if they are available. When could you let me know?"

"When would your board know about the fee? And, the company will need excellent housing and chauffeured limousines. We want all our meals catered from McCrady's, Magnolia's or Anson's and a staff of people to see to every need."

"In this crisis I'm sure we can arrange luxurious accommodations," he replied. "How many people would be coming?"

"We should hope to get all 15 of the dancers to fill the stage. And we have 7, no 8 production assistants."

They agreed to talk again at 3 pm and Hanahan rushed out. As soon as he was in the elevator he called his secretary and had her reassemble the board for a meeting at the Palmetto Restaurant in the hotel for 2 pm. That way they could be available to meet with Areana themselves if need be. Seeing it was 1 pm, and he was famished, he decided to try out the restaurant himself and walked across the lobby to its entrance. The chalkboard announced the specials to be Rockville Blue Crab Cakes and shrimp and hominy, his favorites. Things were looking up.

Maybe one dead Soprano wouldn't sink the whole festival. After all they had booked two dozen major groups for 82 total major performances, and with the Piccolo Spoleto festival run by the city, all together there would be more than 300 total events and a budget of more than $12 million. And, he could get the credit. He might come out as the savior of the season, the savior of Spoleto, and the savior of Charleston. His chest puffed out as he sat down and fluffed his napkin which was soon lost in his vast lap. He savored his new position of eminence just as he savored the menu.

"I'll have your best white wine," he told the waitress imperiously, knowing he would have to go by the price as he didn't know that much about grape varieties and vintages and had grown up in Charleston on Mr. I. M. Pearlstein's Budweiser. "And let's start with the crab cakes and then have the shrimp and grits." He began to think of where he could house this horde of prima donnas. He knew that the local Carey Transportation owner was a Spoleto supporter and could probably spring for some extra limousines. And the restaurant owners were very helpful, especially if the board paid the bills. It might just work, he thought, as the waitress opened a bottle of Far Niente Dolce 1993. If not the best, it was certainly the most expensive white wine they served. For really fancy vintages you had to go next door to the Charleston Grill for dinner.

Saturday, 5:00 pm

By late afternoon Hanahan felt relieved for the first time in almost a day. The Board and Areana had signed the contract and her troupe would arrive Sunday to begin rehearsals with the orchestra. They would do the first night program as she had suggested. He had directed his staff to print the programs and put up posters at all the Spoleto sites. And he had reached many of the newspersons for a press conference at 5:30 pm to be followed by a live shot on the local evening news.

By 6:00 pm he was seated at the anchor's desk of Channel Five News with the lovely anchor Debby Kale who introduced him as having important news about Spoleto. It was such a slow news day that he had made top billing.

"Debby," Hanahan beamed, "we have wonderful news that in addition to our fine regular Spoleto lineup we are adding two exclusive performances of the Stars of the Bolshoi Ballet who are getting rave notices on their American tour. We tried to get them to headline a Spoleto program, but the dates wouldn't mesh, but now they have agreed to give two very special performances on Wednesday and Sunday next week in the Gaillard Auditorium."

"Mr. Hanahan," replied Ms Kale, "is the ballet to replace the opera you premiered last night?"

"Yes. The opera will be shown for its fourth and fifth scheduled performances and we are considering adding an extra performance, perhaps on the last night of the festival. Everyone with tickets for the Wednesday or Sunday opera can now use them for this superb ballet. If others also want tickets, we'll provide everyone with the best opportunity to participate. Debby, we've had a terrible accident. It's shocked everyone, and we are very fortunate that we will be able to perform the opera for two more dates. As always, Spoleto hopes to please all its customers. We're going to keep open our usual box office lines to allow those who wish to turn in their tickets for Wednesday or Sunday week to swap them for another performance. If seats become available, we'll offer those to other customers. Everyone has to be patient with us as this is obviously unexpected and may take some time to sort out."

"What will the ballet perform?"

"In the classical Russian ballet tradition, they will perform three wonderful works of Stravinsky all of which were produced with the famous impresario Diaghilev and the original Ballets Russes. We are very fortunate to bring such an impressive classical performance to Spoleto and I'm pleased to announce that they have agreed to highlight next year's Spoleto as well."

"Is there any further word about last night's tragedy?" asked Ms Kale.

"A terrible accident, terrible" replied Hanahan. "To lose a star of the magnitude of Kasandrá is unimagineable, but Jean-Louis is working on a suitable replacement and the opera will go on."

"Well, good luck with the rest of Spoleto," beamed Ms Kale.

As the stage director indicated he could slip out of his chair off camera, Hanahan wiped the sweat off his face with his ever-present white linen handkerchief. A union audio technician retrieved the two tiny microphones clipped to his tie and complimented him on its design. Hanahan was wearing one of his yellow ties with the Babar figures on it and replied: "This is one of Ben Silver's cute ties. In addition to all the stuffy clubs and regiments, they have some of the best whimsical ties I know of. And they support all of our local efforts. They even make a Spoleto tie and cuff links, with that round wrought iron window piece from City Hall."

eight

Peaking

*S*aturday 5:30 pm

During the day Dr. Simons reviewed all 83 tissue sections but found nothing of significance. Kassandrá had more atherosclerosis that would be expected in a woman her age with significant narrowing of all three major coronary arteries, but no sign of an acute myocardial infarction. Her bronchi suggested mild asthma with some chronic and acute inflammatory cells. Her larynx seemed thickened with some edema. She had a chronic urinary tract infection and her serological testing revealed that she had a positive test for syphilis, probably an old infection now cured. M.E. was pleased her HIV tests, including the P24 antigen that showed up early, were negative. It looked like the toxicology laboratory was the only loose end. So she went over to the analytical laboratory to help Dirk.

"Hi," called out Dirk on seeing M.E. at the door, "you are just in time. We've identified all but one peak on the chromatograms. Most are just harmless ingredients in standard herbs and drugs at fairly low concentrations. I don't know if any of these might change the metabolism of other drugs, such as Seldane, but I'll search the literature. Her blood ethanol concentration is only 0.06% which wouldn't by itself make her unsteady. Even the 0.08% threshold for conviction for drug driving in this state doesn't cause much unsteadiness by itself, but added to other drugs, even Seldane, it might be a factor. The quinine peak is quite high. We found sesamol, the active principle in sesame seeds. We see that fairly often as benne seed or sesame seed or sesame oil is used so much in cooking around here."

M.E. smiled: "I love benne. You've eaten some of those flat benne seed wafers I made and brought in last month. I just use the recipe from the Junior League Charleston Receipts cookbook. Charlestonians got addicted to benne when the slaves from Sierra Leone brought it as an aphrodisiac. I'm not sure if it has that activity, but we sure eat a lot of it down here. What does the unknown peak look like?"

"I can't find it yet in our standards. I'll run a high-precision mass spectrometer scan on it and get the exact molecular weight. This new time-of-flight mass spec can give precision down to 0.01 or 0.001 mass units. Then the computer can figure out the molecular composition and I'll use the Chem. Abstracts on-line database to identify it. It will take a little time, though."

"Well, I'll tell Chief Ravenel that all indications are an accidental death, but that we do have the complication of a large number of legal drugs used together and that possibly could have made her unsteady and contributed to her fall or possibly could have caused a cardiac arrhythmia. I'll say we are continuing to investigate. Would that suit you?"

"Sure," replies Dirk. "It doesn't sound like we need to worry about foul play, just the possibility of some unusual drug interactions. Maybe her pharmacists and physicians can help us out."

Mary Elizabeth left her laboratories at 7:10 pm and drove quickly to her home at the foot of Church Street, just behind the William Washington House. She loved the eighteenth-century homes in Charleston. Her home was a former kitchen and laundry, separated from the main house to avoid fire and heat. It was brick and had a small living room, dining room, compact kitchen, and two bedrooms and baths upstairs. One bedroom served as her office and library where she often worked all night at the computer. The other, with an authentic Charleston Rice Bed, had lovely antiques. She always wondered why George Washington had rented the Heywood-Washington House when he visited Charleston in 1791 rather than staying with his cousin down on the Battery. She parked her Jaguar at 7:25 pm, raced through the shower, and pulled on a lovely teal dress that complimented her eyes. A minimum of makeup, two classic gold earrings, a small steel and gold Rolex, and matching stockings and shoes completed her outfit just at 8:00 pm as Henry Woodard rapped on the pitcher-handle doorknocker. She greeted him with a light kiss and invited him in, but he said: "I think we are both tired enough we should head off to dinner. Tomorrow will probably be a busy workday."

Henry opened the door of his grey 1976 Mercedes 300D. M.E. asked: "Any trouble with this old tub yet?"

"Nope. It has only 235,000 miles on it, the original engine is going fine, and it just needs a little prophylactic medicine every few months."

"Well, the diesel still stinks. Don't you know that some people are allergic to chemicals in diesel fuel."

"Some people are allergic to anything. Those food-allergy specialists can make you eat nothing but purified corn syrup, but are you allergic?" he asked playfully.

"No."

"Well my kids aren't, the maid isn't, and that's all I chauffeur around usually. You are a special guest, young lady."

Henry found a parking place just across King Street from Sushi Hiro and when they entered Hiro greeted them warmly and beckoned to two seats near the end of the sushi bar, by the ceremonial basket of sake and the sheaf of rice. "Good evening Hiro," noted Henry. "M.E., would you like your usual chirashi sushi or something special?"

"Chirashi would be perfect, and I'd like some miso soup to start, one of the delicious house salads, and some green tea."

"Hiro," added Woodward, "I'll have the soup and salad, an Ichiban beer, and I'll order a la carte sushi. I see you have the crawfish roll and spider roll specials, and I will indulge in your amaebi with the shrimp heads, hamachi, ikura with the quail eggs, baby octopus, uni, and miragai. M.E., I hope you are not too tired."

"No, one night without sleep is OK. Life is too exciting to spend it unconscious. I still think a drug that shortens our need for sleep is possible, and would be a terrific advantage."

"And make you rich as well," added Woodward. "I didn't know you were working on neuropsychiatric drugs."

"Well, not yet," added M.E. thoughtfully. "But we are getting closer to defining the function of some of the genes that are only expressed in the hypothalamus, amygdala, and pineal, and I bet one or more is related to sleep patterns or possibly memory consolidation. Maybe we really could learn new things while asleep if we can turn on the right genes. Am I making you miss Spoleto tonight?"

"No, there are so many performances of each major event that I try to spread them out. My kids get tired and they went to both chamber music performances this afternoon. I'll get to see the San Francisco Ballet next week, I think. Would you like to go with me?"

"Well, let's see. That would be very nice, but I'm really getting some hot data on the stomach cancer project. Could I give you an answer in a day or two? I don't want you to have an empty seat."

"That would be great. I can wangle a seat out of the box-office. Frankly, I get all these seats just to help support Spoleto, and give my kids some culture."

"What did they think of Friday night?" asked M.E. "They must have had ringside seats."

"I worried about that," replied Henry. "They are so morbid. They hang on all the gory details of my work. They were first shocked but then they were beaming that they'd seen a real death. I hope they don't get the reputation at school of being ghouls, just because I'm one."

"You know," replied M.E., "I've always wondered about the inappropriate humor we all use when confronted with death whether resuscitating a patient or in the autopsy room. I know how we are confronted with our own mortality at those times, and humor is a release, but sometimes it is really off the wall. I hate to think of all the jokes at our medical school about the fenestrated soprano. Maybe it is good for the kids to have a little release and a dose of realism. At least it wasn't some horrible homicide or maniacal serial killer like you and I often see. Maybe they'll wear their bicycle helmets now."

"And not go near the edge of the stage if there are any sharp pointed musical instruments around."

Ninety minutes later they were back outside M.E.'s home. Walking her to the door, Henry said: "M.E., I'm growing very fond of you. Is that a problem? I know that romance between faculty isn't favored and I'll back off if you are concerned."

M.E. holds Henry close and gives him the most passionate kiss they have exchanged. "Henry, I am falling in love with you, and you know it. You've been so gentle and so chivalrous, I thought you didn't find me attractive."

Henry, squeezing her, says: "M.E., you are very special and I don't want to do anything that isn't exactly what you want as well. I'm 45 you know, 7 years older than you, and I've been out of the romance mode for the three years since Emily died. I'm not sure I know how to date any more. I'm sure you find me old and awkward and foolish."

M.E. rubs herself against his shirt, slips her tongue deeply between his lips, and runs one hand firmly down to his crotch. She breaks off the kiss at his sudden inhalation of surprise and says: "Doesn't feel broken to me. Why don't we see if it snaps to attention like a Citadel knob."

Henry, speechless, follows her into her living room with his heart racing with not a thought about Spoleto, sopranos, bassoons, or mass spectrometers.

nine

Private Policing

*S*aturday, 10:25 pm

The San Francisco Ballet was spectacular. After the dual tragedy, of the opera's theme and the star's death, a few patrons turned in their tickets but there was a line of hopefuls at the ticket office in the Gaillard Auditorium lobby. By curtain there were standing room patrons and the audience was expectant and responsive. Standing ovations were not that unusual at Spoleto, but this audience was especially rewarding, even delaying their rush to the goodies at the reception.

Teddy Bonnet had an evening with few problems. No one screamed at her. The sets and props all worked well. The ballet company took care of their own costumes and she only had to help them with local cleaning at the nearby Arrow Cleaners. No one died or fell off the stage. She had added a fluorescent 4" wide lime green tape two feet from the edge of the stage and warned all performers not to cross it. She finished earlier than expected and looked up to see the smiling Lieutenant Rhett in a handsome dark grey pinstripe three-piece suit, a gorgeous red Ben Silver tie with little pelicans on it, and a matching silk pouf in his pocket. He handed her a beautiful array of yellow roses from Charleston Florists, stems-up.

He also handed her a box of Godiva chocolates from the shop in Charleston Place.

"Thank you my good sir," she curtseyed deeply feeling somewhat out-of-place in her jeans and black turtleneck. "I am ready to leave, but remember I need to change if you don't mind."

"You certainly shouldn't change a thing, as you are just perfect," said the chivalrous Bubba with a big smile, "but I'd be honored to accompany you anywhere and wait while you make any adjustments you feel appropriate."

"Oh, you Southern charmers!" Teddy replied with a broad a smile as she took his strong arm and headed to the exit. As they walked out Teddy asked Bubba about his family and their roots in Charleston and kidded him about some of the ancestors he described more candidly than he often did. As soon as they exited by the side door, she was led to a gleaming Ford and asked: "Did you wash the chariot, sir?"

"Yes, just for you. Watch out for the radio and the gunmount."

"Wow," said Teddy. "I've never been in a gunship before."

"Well, I'm supposed to use police equipment so they can reach me and so I could respond to any emergency. I put the weapons in the trunk, but I can't move the radio or the gunmounts. I'm sorry."

"Oh, this is a unique experience. Do you have a siren too?"

"Of course, but the lights are concealed in the grill so we don't have the bubblegum-machine top of the black-and-whites at least. Where are we headed? I don't know where you are staying."

"Oh, I'm sorry," replied Teddy. "My father-in-law and I are staying in the Louis de Saussure House at the corner of East Bay and South Battery."

"Oh, that is one of my favorite homes in Charleston. Have you seen the wonderful painting that hangs in the Yale Library of the view from the Battery up East Bay that features that house before the piazzas were added?"

"Yes, we have a reproduction of it. The lovely Mrs. Appleton lets Spoleto house artists in her top-floor condo and this year they offered it to us. I think it has the best views of the harbor, James Island, and Fort Sumter."

"Jim Island," corrected Bubba, "in our local parlance. You know the Battery is the favorite place in town to park and smooch. Sometimes more than smooch."

"I thought you did that in those horse-drawn carriages under a parasol."

"Only during daylight. By the way, the current deSaussure is perhaps the most famous physician in Charleston, but lives on Meeting Street in the Daniel Elliott Huger house, built by his wife's family about a century before the one you occupy. When he was Chief Resident in Medicine at Washington University in Saint Louis he began the <u>Washington Manual</u> which is now carried by every intern and medical student in America."

They found a place to park and walked to the elevator on the west side of the house. On arriving at the third floor they knocked and called out for her father-in-law, but there was no answer and only a few lights were on.

"Be careful," Teddy noted, "there is still some repair work on the piazza here—don't stumble over anything." They paused on the piazza to take in the magnificent view over the Battery to where the Ashley and Cooper Rivers join to form the Atlantic Ocean with the low brooding Fort Sumter in the middle of the distant channel. It sits on one of the many sand bars that kept the British and the Yankees from bringing their big men of war into the harbor itself. In the brisk breeze Teddy wrapped her arms around herself until Bubba moved close and put a long strong arm around her shoulders.

"Would you like my coat?" he asked quietly.

"No, sir, your arm is much better. What are those lights to the left?"

"They are from Mount Pleasant and Sullivan's Island. Right at the tip you are looking at the famous Fort Moultrie, where the British first lost a major battle to the patriots."

"I thought most of that fighting was up north?"

"Actually, there were more injuries during the Revolution in South Carolina per capita than any other state. What happened at that fort is that Sir Peter Parker brought a fleet of more than a dozen large men-of-war to capture Charleston. The patriots were hurriedly building a fort out of palmetto logs and sand to guard the harbor, but they had only half finished it. The British cannonballs hit those soft logs and the sand and just sank in without doing much damage. Although the patriots only had a few small cannon, they wounded everyone on the flag ship and shot off Sir Peter's pants, better to expose his namesake."

"Bubba!"

"Well at least the British retreated and left us alone for a few years. Because of that victory our state flag is the palmetto with the half-moon crescent that the patriots had worn on their helmets."

"I better get showered and changed. Even if Carolina's would let me in dressed like this, I wouldn't want to embarrass you."

"Teddy," said Bubba softly, "you could never embarrass me. And, you look perfectly gorgeous and you know it."

Teddy led them to the living room and seated Bubba while she disappeared into her bedroom. Bubba was thirsty and wandered into the kitchen. Unlike most Charleston kitchens this was quite modern, and filled with gadgets. Bubba counted three blenders, a large food processor, and lots of pots all in stainless steel like a laboratory. And there was a large all-glass still hooked up to the cold water supply with the cooker sitting on a gas burner.

Bubba drank deeply of the cold Goose Creek water, and then returned to the living room to read one of the coffee-table books by Poston on Charleston Dwellings until the door opened, and his heart almost stopped. Teddy was wearing, or almost wearing, a gorgeous maroon silk sheath that looked like it was about to fall off. Her black hair was glistening and stunning and she had woven a brilliant Hermes scarf into it. Her tanned skin was a perfect backdrop for the dress and her dark eyes, with minimal makeup, just glowed. He noticed that she was not wearing a bra, but her magnificent breasts supported the dress, which ended high on her slim thighs. Her high spike heels made the top of her head reach just to midchest on Bubba, who arose and paid the appropriate polite compliments, while thinking some private ones.

Bubba almost whispered: "I can't image who gave you a boy's name like Ted? You are the most feminine person I know."

"Well, it is actually worse than that. My father was Samuel and my mother Theodora and so they named me Samantha Theodora. For awhile I was known as Sam but my husband always called me Teddy and I like that name."

They turned off the lights, exited, and he helped her into the car wondering what her skirt might expose.

Carolina's was packed, but for the police lieutenant and football hero a table was quickly available. The din was about average. Charleston had excellent restaurants but few quiet ones.

Bubba asked Teddy what she'd like to drink and relayed to the waiter her request for a dry white wine by the glass so she could sample several. Bubba ordered a "McIver."

"What's that?" asked the waiter.

Bubba explained: "Three-fourths Charleston iced tea, one-fourth ginger ale, a sprig of mint, and a twist of lime."

"I think we can make that," replied the waiter. "That's the first time

I've heard of it. Why is it called a McIver?"

"It was invented by Howard McIver, who is now in his nineties and going strong. He says it is the strongest thing he ever drinks and many attribute his longevity to that habit. Howard is the guru of the Charleston fertilizer business, from all the phosphate deposits here, and I just like his drink. It has just enough fizz and great flavor."

When the McIver arrived Teddy tried it: "That's neat. But tonight I need some wine if you don't mind."

Teddy decided on a Thai appetizer and sesame-encrusted local grouper while Bubba had the shrimp and hominy. After they had ordered, Teddy pointed out her father-in-law across the room at a corner table beside the bar and pulled Bubba with her to introduce him. Her father-in-law, the center of attention of four couples still in black tie and cocktail dresses, rose and kissed Teddy on the cheek. He introduced her to his companions as his daughter and she introduced Lieutenant Bernard Rhett to her father-in-law and his companions, but Bubba remarked that he had already had the honor of meeting the famous Jean-Louis Guérard.

Back at their table, Bubba held her chair, stealing a glance down her décolletage, and said: "I didn't know your father-in-law was the maestro."

"Well, things have quieted down over the last decade. This is the first time we've worked together, or really even seen each other, since just after my husband's funeral."

"I'm sorry, I don't think I know that history."

"Jean-Louis's wife died suspiciously of an insulin overdose about a dozen years ago and he became withdrawn and sour and unforgiving. He drove himself mercilessly—it was his most productive period. But he tortured his son, never letting him succeed on his own and dominating every moment. I think that is what lead Steve to take his mother's maiden name and to date me so aggressively when I was just finishing the Philadelphia College of Science. We had a whirlwind courtship that Jean-Louis never really accepted and he almost destroyed our wedding. He kept interfering with every success Steve accomplished, except sailing. I had been in student theater and turned from science to the stage, but Jean-Louis did everything he could to block my career."

"But I've read some of the reviews. You were doing very well on Broadway and then two movies and some TV. Rave notices!"

"Well, not raves, but I was working hard and trying to succeed. Recently I've done better behind the footlights in producing and directing. I suspect that is going to be my future."

"What happened with your husband. You mentioned a tragedy?"

"You don't know? I thought everyone in Charleston knew that story. The maestro had a huge fight with Steve who retreated to his sloop, Rhett's Revenge, where he could be alone with the wind and the waves. He sailed down the Intercoastal Waterway and reached your harbor on December 10 in a terrible storm. But, he was so proud and so angry that he wouldn't stop. That night, after midnight, they found him hanging in the shrouds of his boat, crashed into the Battery just above Water Street."

"Oh my goodness. I never connected that with you. It was the lead story in Charleston for a week. But they never figured out what happened, did they?"

"No. It could have been an accident, but Steve was a wonderful sailor. The storm was bad, but I am afraid it was suicide. Jean-Louis just tortured the poor man and never let him be himself."

"Well, why are you working together?"

"We aren't, really. I produced both operas for Spoleto last year and they asked me to produce all the Gaillard shows this year, long before they mentioned Jean-Louis. I almost quit when I heard, but I wanted the opportunity. But it isn't working."

"What's wrong?"

"You know how headstrong he is. His ego is boundless. Everything must be just his way. He has gone out of his way to belittle me. He curses me. Friday afternoon at rehearsal he told the pit orchestra that I was his son's whore. I've really had it."

"That's intolerable."

"In theater you have to put up with egos and dominating personalities, but this is personal."

"Personal?" asked Bubba, querulously.

"I shouldn't tell you this, especially not you, but I'm furious. Jean-Louis is a predator. He hits on all the beautiful young performers, male and female. He is notorious. Every night he brings someone else home to the apartment now that he threw out Alain Capone, with whom he had lived for several months. They had a terrible fight that woke me up as Capone kept threatening to kill the maestro and vice versa. I thought being his daughter-in-law would protect me, but no. Wednesday night he beat on my door in the middle of the night. I keep it locked, especially when he is around, but I opened it thinking he was having a health crisis or something. But no, he attacked me. Thank God I'm reasonably fit as he came roaring in like a bull, a drunken one at that. But I kneed him in the right spot and clobbered him with a brass table lamp. It dropped him splat. He lay there holding himself, rolling from side to side, and moaning while I grabbed a coat and ran out. Since then I've been careful to avoid him as much as possible and to keep my door locked. Spoleto thought they were doing us a favor to house us together, as we were family, but I told the staff they had to find me another place and soon. I told them to get me either a new apartment or a gun."

"Good for you. What can I do to help? I'll be glad to help you move. If you like I'll be happy to go over and cut pieces off the bastard right here. Or I'll cut out his heart and they can serve it up like Peruvian *anticuchos de corazon*."

"No. I appreciate your thoughts and support, but the maestro will get his comeuppance. For one thing he is trying to raise money for Broadway from some pretty rough Mafia types who don't mess around. I wouldn't be surprised if he, or pieces of him, don't turn up in some New Jersey Italian sausage."

"Speaking of sausage, how was your grouper?" asked Bubba.

"It was just light and very tasty. How about your grits?"

"That actually is grist—corn grist from the mill. Shrimp and hominy was the standard breakfast when I was a kid. The street vendors pushed their carts filled with shrimp right off the boats calling: Shrimp. Shrimp-e-raw-raw. and you would buy a pie plate full and then they'd give you an extra handful 'for broaddus.'"

"Who's broaddus?" asked Teddy.

"That is a Gullah expression for something extra, as for the boss, or buckra."

"Isn't Gullah a black dialect? Certainly the Gullah festival scheduled for Tuesday at the Gaillard has an all-black choir."

"Gullah is a beautiful language and spoken in its purest form on the sea islands by the descendents of the slaves from Sierra Leone and Barbados who brought the language here. It is close to the Creole of Africa or the Bajan of Barbados. But the culture overall, the spirituals, the wonderful ethics, and the language belong to all of us raised in the lowcountry. You know, despite the horrors of segregation, in Charleston we were fully integrated at home. I was raised by black nannies, I played with their children, and we all grew up loving each other and our distinctive way-of-life. We have many African influences. Our sweetgrass baskets are the same as they make in Sierra Leone. Gumbo is their word for okra. We are very much 'we' people."

"I'm amazed. You hear so much about slavery and racism."

"Certainly that was horrible, but don't forget that many slaves lived with their owner's families and cared for them. They grew very close. We were the only city in the South that educated slaves and allowed slaves to sell their services and earn their freedom, but many house slaves were also freed. There were more than 3000 freedmen in Charleston by 1865 and many of them owned the best businesses or were notable scientists and artists and many owned slaves themselves."

"Is Gullah the reason you speak so funny down here?"

"Thaaank youuuu, mammm," drawled Bubba. "Actually in Charleston we use a long 'A' a little different than in Boston. We say: 'aa laate daate aat aate on the baatry.' And we mispronounce 'c' and 'g': 'ciar', 'giarden' and bird is 'bud' and church is 'chuch' All of our words and inflections are heavily influenced by true Gullah. I hope you'll hear more of that Tuesday. They are supposed to do some Gullah tales as well as spirituals and a part of Porgy and Bess."

"Now the maestro has added a second opera about Charleston."

"But Porgy is real life. My parents knew Goat Sammy."

"I'm looking forward to Tuesday. At least they didn't make me find a goat for the performance. You know Charleston in many ways is quite modern, but in others retains a charm, perhaps even from colonial days."

"We certainly don't adapt rapidly to modern advances. I recall my cousin, Dick Reeves, talking about when telephones were first introduced. He heard his housekeeper, Esmeralda, answer the phone and say: 'Yessir.' Then 'Sho nuff is sir.' And she rang down the phone. The phone rang again, and the same exchange. Cousin Dick said he called her over and asked: 'Esmeralda, who be dat dere on de phone.' Dick was a gullah expert who often gave talks about the language and he often used it in his everyday conversations. He told me Esmeralda explained: 'They say is this be 2-3-9' and I answer 'Yessir.' Then they tell me: 'Long distance from Noo York,' and I agree, 'Sho nuff is.'"

"Sounds like your cousin should be part of the show."

"He's gone now, but he had a weekly radio program and told tales first in Gullah and then in English. Everybody listened and loved the funny little guy. He really had a twinkle in his eye."

Bubba paid the bill, held her chair, and they politely waved good-bye to her father-in-law and wandered to the exit, attracting attention all the way. In the car Bubba asked: "Would you like a motor tour of our town?"

"Someday soon, for sure," replied Teddy. "But I'm a little tired and have to be up early to work on the maestro's play. Another world premier and many props and complex sets. At least we'll open in the Gaillard rather than on that tiny stage of the Dock Street Theatre. They put so many things in that space for Spoleto the crews are falling over each other and have to store some sets outside in Queen Street."

"OK," said Bubba. "Home we go."

On the piazza, Bubba drew her close, enveloped her in his arms, and lightly kissed her eyes, nose, and lips. Teddy pressed closer to him and returned his kisses, but when his hands began to wander lower on her back she gently said: "Bubba, thank you. It has been a delightful night and I have enjoyed your company. But, I'm really tired and I have an early morning."

"I am honored you have shared your evening with me," intoned Bubba, trying not to show his disappointment. "I hope we can do this again?"

"Absolutely," said Teddy tenderly, reaching up to give him a deep kiss. "I'm not saying no—just not tonight."

Encouraged, Bubba headed down to his car, the old elevator clanking. He wondered if they ever fell free. Oh well, two floors wasn't that far to drop and the way he felt he might not even notice it.

ten

Sunday Sojourn

*S*unday, 11:00 pm

Hanahan beamed. The Sunday papers had focused on the San Francisco Ballet and several of the other Spoleto events very positively. The chamber music series at the Dock Street, under the venerable Charles Wadsworth, was spectacular and sold out as usual. They were thinking about adding a third performance each day and repeating the programs at least three times. The response to the announcement about the Bolshoi Stars Ballet had been frantic, but it looked like they would end up with a full house. The replacement soprano was en route and the maestro was rewriting the music to suit her. They had agreed to add an extra opera performance on the closing night of the festival, when Gaillard was scheduled to be dark. That would provide more ticket flexibility and less lost revenue. This evening's Westminster Choir had, as every year, been super. They usually performed in the local Episcopal Cathedral, but tonight in Gaillard with a large orchestra they had tackled some spectacular pieces and the electronic organ was acceptable, if perhaps not quite as resonant as the beautiful tracker organs at the Huguenot Church or in Grace Episcopal Church. He thought that problems were over, the solutions were at hand, and now let's have several weeks of fantastic festival.

Chief Ravenel was relieved. A perfect evening. No one died. Nothing exploded. No traffic tickets even. The audience was orderly and quiet. They had all filed out to the reception below and few had left yet. He guessed his staff would be there until 2:00 am. At least he was going to get a good night's sleep.

Teddy Bonnet had spent the day with the cast of the maestro's play as he reworked once again several scenes and she helped block some of the movements. They had closed the Gaillard to all visitors and had started at 8:00 am to be through in time to vacate before the orchestra and choir took over for the evening. She was worried that it was still rough in several scenes, and the stagehands were not smooth with the changes, but it was improving. When this opened it might create even more controversy than the maestro's new opera.

Jean-Louis was busy raising money. The publicity of the opening night tragedy had scared off some of his deep pockets and was in trouble. Doors were being closed and he was desperate. He had thought that publicity, even of this shocking kind, would bring the investors running, but not this time. At least he had had the foresight to sign up a replacement soprano in advance. He did have some contacts with the Jersey mob, but he was afraid of the price of using them.

M.E. was enjoying a quiet night at home. She had written the Provisional Anatomical Diagnoses and finished everything except the toxicology report on the soprano. Dirk and she had looked at some of the results. As the jars and creams and pills were identified, partly with Bubba's help and partly with the analytical laboratory, nothing very significant had turned up. The quinine was in an Italian preparation for nocturnal leg muscle cramps. Although it had once been sold in the U.S. for that indication, it had been withdrawn by the F.D.A. from over-the-counter use. The Seldane had been in an unlabeled jar, but it looked like some old pills, possibly from the U.S. before it had been withdrawn, or possibly similar pills from another country. It looked like they could finish this soon. She also had signed off on five other cases, cleaned up the experiments in her laboratory, and had things moderately buttoned up, for her.

M.E. leaned back in her chair, glanced away from the computer screen, and thought about Henry. She had been thinking a lot about him today. When they had finally arisen, just in time for church, she hadn't wanted to shower off his scent. Now, she wanted him again. He had lit a fire within her she had never experienced before. Despite the lack of sleep, she was tingling all over and very alert. Did she overdo it? He seemed very happy and loving this morning. Should she call him? Just then the doorbell rang. Snapping back to reality, M.E. arose and walked quickly to the intercom, but no one answered. Cautious now she detoured by the drawer with her stun gun. She didn't often get pranksters on lower Church Street and especially not at this time of night. She couldn't see anyone through the peep hole and was debating calling the police. Instead, she made sure the sturdy chain was on, primed her stun gun, and gently slipped the door open. There on her doorstep was a beautiful Baccarat crystal vase filled with gorgeous red and white roses. She quickly opened the door and grabbed the gift, thinking that it would be a neat way for a rapist to gain entry. With the door securely locked again, she held out the gift. Incredible. She looked all over for a card until she finally found the linen envelope taped to the bottom of the vase. The logo of the printing firm, Walker Evans and Cogswell, was discretely embossed in tiny letters on the envelope. Wow, she thought. They had printed Confederate Money but the building was turned into condos a decade or more ago. Must be a Charlestonian with a vintage card. Inside was the formal calling card: Henry Porcher Bissell Woodward. She smiled and turned over the card to find on the reverse, in a gentle script, the word: love. She ran to the phone and called him, but no answer. She thought, I guess he has said it all, and her thoughts wandered to the future.

Bubba struggled all day. He had the day off, but couldn't be with Teddy on the closed set. He waited, nervously, until the rehearsal broke at 5:35 pm and met Teddy, as she promised, at the stage entrance in back of the theater. She walked out between the moving vans holding the props and costumes and was stunning. After working all day she seemed as vibrant and alive as ever. He greeted her warmly, wanting to crush her in his arms, but opened the car door and asked what she would like to do. He had tickets to the Westminster Choir, but she said she was beat and would rather have a quiet and early night as this was the only show that didn't require her attendance as the producer.

"We could go out. If you're tired, would you like to come over to my place for a relaxing dinner et al." Bubba's mind raced. Was it a wreck? Had he left dirty clothes lying about? Were the towels clean?

"That would be just woonnderfull," she crooned.

It wasn't as bad as he feared. Most things were neat, the towels were fresh, the air conditioner made it comfortable, and he quickly offered a drink. She flopped in an old leather easy chair, propped her feet up on the ottoman, and suggested some iced tea.

"Iced tea?" he asked. "After your hard day I'd have thought you'd want a pitcher of martinis or a single-barrel bourbon straight up."

"Nope. I have mostly stopped drinking and besides, I'd be asleep in a few minutes. Then what would you do as I snored," she winked.

"Give me five minutes to make your vintage tea? Would you like sugar, lime, ginger, or fresh mint?"

"Mint would be nice, but you can be my sugar."

Bubba tingled as he boiled the water, added the Charleston tea from the Wadmalaw Island Tea Plantation, and filled two glasses with ice, a slice of lime, a small piece of crystallized ginger, a sprig of mint, and two squirts of ginger ale. "Here is the quintessential Charleston drink," as he handed her a frosted glass wrapped with a linen doily. "Is it too tart."

"No, gracious sir, the lime and mint make it perfect. It has a wonderful unique flavor. You are an accomplished bartender."

Bubba sat on the floor before her, gently unlaced her black Mephisto walking sneakers, and began to massage her feet. She leaned back and sighed, closing her eyes. He massaged her delicate ankles and up her muscular calves. She parted her legs and he continued to her knees, his fingers massaging the hollows behind each, and then up her thighs.

"You weren't a trainer in your former athletic life were you?" she breathed.

"Nope, just a dumb jock."

"Well, does this abode come with indoor plumbing?"

"Yes...."

"Then it's time for us to hit the showers."

"Us" he asked hopefully.

"Unless you have a robot to scrub my back."

Monday, 8:12 am

Bubba awoke to tiny kisses over his eyelids and cheeks. He sighed, wrapped his arms around her, and kissed her deeply. "Wow" he said.

"And double wow and triple wow and who knows how many wows," she replied. "My dashing knight, in no armor at all, you don't know how important that was."

"It was all your perfect lovemaking, and you know it."

"No! This is the first time I've climaxed in almost a decade."

"But you are so soft and loving and warm."

"Maybe I was. But after Steve died I had a horrible experience. I was beaten and...violated. I've avoided romance ever since—until you. You'll never know how scared I was last night. If you hadn't been so gentle and kind, I'd never have come home with you or come at all."

"My dear," he softly intoned, "forget the past. Let's focus on the future, our future. I'm here to protect and nurture and satisfy your every need" as he wrapped his strong arms about her and felt her shiver. He had learned from his police work that so many people had been wounded or tortured in the past—it amazed him they didn't turn out to be "perps" seeking revenge.

eleven

Pilot's Choice

Monday, 11:00 am

"Dan, thanks for coming to my office," Hanahan said, extending his hand in a vigorous handshake and beckoning the Chief into his office.

Hanahan enjoyed entertaining visitors in his colonial office with its lovely original mantel and woodwork and the many Charleston-made pieces of furniture. His desk was one of the few pieces accurately attributed to Thomas Elfe by the venerable Milby Burton. He smiled remembering that in the 1850s the home had been owned by the Lee family, freedmen who also owned the best hotel in Charlestown, the Jones Hotel adjacent to St. Michael's.

"Would you like some tea or coffee?"

"Well, I would never refuse a cup of your tea if that is handy."

"Actually," Hanahan said beaming, "I just got a box of the first-flush, hand-picked tea from the Charleston Tea Plantation out on Wadmalaw Island. Let's try it."

Hanahan called for his lovely secretary and told her to use the best setting. He watched as she placed the Moreau Sarrazin (1738) teapot on the salver and got the Charleston tea in the Enos Reeves tea caddy (1792).

She selected a Louis Boudo teaspoon (1809) to help it into the cups. He savored that first sip of good tea and thought of the special first-flush Darjeeling he had hidden away. He got it at Harrod's each year on his June visit to the London Olympia antiques show, and he rarely shared that tea with anyone, even his wife. He beamed, feeling the epitome of a Charleston gentleman, as he poured the perfectly-brewed tea into the Tobacco Leaf teacups, unfortunately not original but good reproductions. They settled into two matching armchairs, upholstered in the Charleston pineapple pattern.

Dan asked: "Is this about the horrible tragedy Friday? We've been investigating, but so far it looks like an accident possibly related to her taking alcohol along with some antihistamines and other sedatives that may have made her unsteady. Dr. Simons said she wouldn't have the final laboratory studies for several days and the Final Anatomical Diagnoses won't be available for weeks."

"No, Dan," frowns Hanahan, "I wanted to ask your advice about that threat we got. We get them every now and again, but this seemed odd. Should we take it seriously? Is there a real risk? Has there been anything else?"

"Nothing else. Just the telephone call your answering machine recorded at 4:30 am this morning. We've been analyzing it but the voice is disguised electronically and we can't even tell if it's a man or a woman. The words: 'God will suck the breath out of everyone at Gaillard and make 333 into 666' make no sense. Do you think 666 might refer to Satan?"

"Hell. I don't know. Should we restrict the alert to Gaillard or do we have to worry about all the other venues?"

"We are putting extra security at each site, but we will focus most of our attention at Gaillard. We haven't figured out the 'suck the breath out' reference. It might be one of those petroleum bombs that uses up all the oxygen, but the Air Force Base security folks told us those things are huge. But why 'God?' The only thing religious there is the Gospel and Gullah concerts and they aren't controversial."

"You obviously haven't heard about tonight's play."

"Only the title. But I thought it was about travel or airplanes. Isn't it called 'Pilot's Choice?'"

"Right title, wrong pilot. Guérard has screwed us again," sighed Hanahan.

"What do you mean?"

"That bastard has been so secretive, none of us knew much about the play. He has kept the actors and rehearsals out at Woodlands in Summerville. No one has been allowed to watch. He even kept the play-bills under wraps. We've just been advertising it as a Gala World Premier of a new Guérard play."

"So, does it have a helicopter fly down like in Miss Saigon? Or are the pilots dropping those petroleum bombs and killing innocent Vietnamese or Somalis or Serbs? Seems like everyone we bomb is an innocent some-body. Or maybe it is about an athletic team that crashes in the Andes and eats each other and the pilot gets first choice?"

"You know I've always hated that book, Alive. I see myself going down with a team of young thin athletes and they are all looking at me like a prize ham in the deli section of Harris Teeter."

"So, what's the story? Does anyone get killed with a musical instru-ment? Perhaps someone smuggles a flute on board and starts beating the flight attendants?"

"You'll understand when I tell you I finally got a staff member into a rehearsal and we found out the pilot is Pilate as in Pontius."

"Oops. So it is religious. That might be interesting. I don't recall much about Pontius Pilate. I seem to remember that the Copts are positive about him but the rest of Christianity wouldn't mind if he fell in a cesspool and drowned. I don't think we have any Copts in Charleston—just cops. So, what's it about?"

"Do you want the short version or the long one?"

"What's the short?"

"Its sacrilegious and our fundamentalist friends will probably want to hang Jean-Louis, then crucify him, then burn him at the stake."

"But what has that to do with God sucking out the breath?"

"I'm not sure. Maybe you can figure it out."

"OK, what's the long version."

"Sit back and have another cup of tea. What I found out is mostly boring. Apparently he wanted the play to begin with historical accuracy. I think he must have thought he was doing The Nine Commandments."

"Nine?"

"Well, Charleston has never recognized adultery. Remember, Charles II himself had 14 illegitimate children."

"OK, you got me there. Give me the long version."

Hanahan sighed, got out his notes, and began: "It's the Passion Play seen through the eyes of Pontius Pilate. The first act is set in the new

Roman villa Pilate has built on Mount Zion near David's Tomb outside the Zion Gate of the old Jerusalem city walls. Pilate is seen being browbeaten by his shrew wife who is demanding a team of four horses instead of two to draw her carriage. Pilate says he can't afford the extra hay, slaves, or expansion of their stable. The Board of Architectural Review will never approve expanding the historic stables. Besides, he'd have to pay the luxury tax for extra horses and hay consumption. Then his wife is fussing about her mother, who is dying in their villa of the febrile coughing disease. She demands Pilate employ Dr. Luke of Antioch, who is rumored to be visiting Jerusalem for the Passover, but Pilate hasn't been able to find him. We learn that Pilate is afraid his lovely daughter is having sex with a young gangster who is running the numbers racket outside the Temple of Athena. His son is a drunk and addicted to opium. Besides, Pilate's chief scribe, Miriam, is blackmailing him after he broke off their affair."

"So," shrugs the Chief, "Pilate is having a midlife crisis. Sounds like Guiding Light. That won't disturb the religious right."

"Just wait," retorted Hanahan. "It gets worse. Pilate has invited his mentor, Sejanus, to bring his family to Pilate's villa for a Passover feast, but Sejanus said they had to meet two days earlier for an urgent matter. Sejanus, a close friend of the Emperor Tiberius, got Pilate his job as procurator of Judaea, now a third rank Roman colony. Pilate is bitter that Sejanus had promised to expand his power to include more of Herod's kingdom of Palestine but Rome has resisted. Tax collections are down and Tiberius himself had sent his chief scribe, Petr Marwick, to examine the books."

"Still just Roman history," says Dan.

"In the second scene Sejanus arrives. He has been protecting Pilate but is very angry. He accuses Pilate of inflaming the Jews, who are the dominant force in Judea. Although Pilate professes Judaism, he acts more Roman and shows off his knighthood in the Samnite clan of the Pontii. Then he put up portraits of Tiberius all over Judea and that inflamed the Sadducees, the leaders of the Jewish community. Then he minted coins with Tiberius on one side and a lamb on the other. That infuriated the Pharisees who regarded themselves as the protectors of the Jewish faith, including the slaughter of lambs on Passover and they viewed the coins as graven images. Some of the senior scribes had complained directly to Tiberius that Pilate was cruel and had executed some suspected rebels without proper trials. Sejanus was angry and concerned. Pilate was defensive but frightened."

"We never thought of Pilate as a humanitarian," says Ravanel. "I'm going to sleep. Maybe it is just going to suck the intelligence out of the audience."

"Have patience. Sejanus tells Pilate that the Sadducees have insisted that Pilate help them get rid of a usurper who is challenging their authority and disrupting their prerogatives. Pilate knows that the supreme legal authority, the Sanhedrin, which is dominated by Sadducees, is unable to execute a criminal, but refers them to Roman law. Sejanus tells Pilate that in the traditional Roman trials before Passover the Sanhedrin will recommend death for this troublemaker and they insist that Pilate agree. Pilate asks who this person is and is told Jesus. Pilate asks if it is the Jesus of Damascus who was caught fornicating with a ewe. Sejanus says he doesn't think so and he recalls being told this guy is from Nazareth and belongs either to the Qumrān sect or is a Zealot."

"So far it sounds like Roman history," says Dan, clearly bored. "So what is the big deal. It sounds like a prose Titus Andronicus. The maestro doesn't write blank verse does he?"

"Just wait. I want to give you the whole picture as best I know it. Sejanus leaves and Pilate sends for his chief scribe. The scribe arrives and Pilate demands to know the agenda for Friday's court. The scribe says they have two prostitutes caught outside the Shrine of Vesta on March 1, the annual festival of the Goddess. Pilate recognizes the impertinence of this sacrilege and suggests that cutting off their noses as usual might not be sufficient and the clerk agrees that cutting off their ears as well seems appropriate to the crime. Then the clerk says they have caught three robbers, including the troublemaker Barabbas, trying to rob the tax collections. Pilate recognizes the opportunity of showing Rome just how careful he is with their taxes and announces that he will make an example of those three especially with Tiberius' agent in town. Pilate tells his chief scribe to be sure to accept anything from the Sanhedrin, even without the proper paperwork."

Dan insists: "Well, it still sounds like one of those historic PBS specials or maybe a Biography of Pilate. Big deal. I don't think there will be any audience left at this point. They will be seeking Oprah."

"Patience. Patience. Next Pilate calls in the Centurion whose troops guard the prison and handle executions. He goes over the upcoming court session. He asks the Centurion to get a good person with a sharp sword for the prostitutes. Then he explains that they need to make an example of the robbers. The Centurion notes that the robbers have been causing trouble in prison, complaining that they were raped by several of the huge

Nubians. He adds that it will be easy to cut off their heads. Pilate suggests they need a more horrible slow death to show Rome their resolve and strength. He reminds the Centurion that two years ago he had a rebel boiled in sheep manure and urine in the central square. The Centurion reminds him that the screams might have been notable, but the stench was horrible. Pilate agrees to find a less odorous horror. The Centurion says he'd read in <u>Valorius Maximus</u>, the army magazine, that a Roman general had rebellious townsfolk tied to trees until they slowly died. Pilate thinks that is a good idea, but says he wants everyone to see the agony of the robbers and wants them more on display. Pilate says let's string them up on that skull-shaped hill, Golgatha, beside the town. That way if they are up high enough everyone will see them and hear their screams but as they rot the stench won't reach town. The Centurion suggests they tie them between tall poles, but then thinks that their arms might pull off after a few days. Pilate, gazing thoughtfully into the courtyard, sees baskets of flowers hanging from a crosspiece fixed to an upright. 'There is the answer,' he says, pointing it out to the Centurion.

'Bury them like flowers in baskets?' the Centurion asks.

'No,' angrily, 'put up one of those crosspieces for their arms and hang them on it.'

'That's a great idea and we can find some tall trees for the pole so everyone will see them. But if we tie their arms to the pole won't they just pull loose, struggling and sweating and all and then slip down the pole?'

Pilate thinks for a minute and then says: 'I've got it. We could use spikes to attach their wrists and feet to the wood. Of course that might shorten things, and even if the heads of the spikes are big enough and you nail through the wrists they could pull out. I tell you what. Let's show Rome a controlled experiment. That will impress them. Pick half the prisoners, randomly by throwing dice, and use rope. For the other half use spikes. And we'll inform Rome of the result.'"

"That is a little strange," says the Chief, "it sounds like Guérard's warped mind, but I don't see anyone blowing up Gaillard because of that. What happens next."

"The second act is the trial. The prostitutes are sentenced to mutilation. The three robbers are sentenced to this new mode of slow execution and the crowd loves it, cheering on Pilate. Then the Sadducees bring forth Jesus and say they have examined him and found him guilty of sedition and recommend execution. Pilate is careful to have a real trial. For every accusation of the Sadducees, however, Jesus has an appropriate reasonable answer to refute the charge. Three times Pilate finds Jesus not to be guilty of a capital crime and says he is just a homeless crazy person like the others they have had trouble with since the Temple of Jupiter stopped providing a place for them. Pilate recommends exile, probation for two years, and 200 hours of community service. The Sadducees go nuts. They insist Pilate examine him in private."

"Obviously not in sync with our justice system. Here he'd plead guilty to jaywalking and get off with a reprimand."

"Pilate talks with Jesus a long time and gets to like him. In addition to the common Aramaic, Jesus speaks perfect Latin and Greek. Pilate sees Jesus as a strict traditionalist. He asks Jesus: 'What about the gamblers, loan sharks, insurance salesmen, and money-changers you threw out of the temple?'"

"Pilate is concerned because he gets a cut of that action. Jesus cites the history of the Temple of Solomon, whose rebuilding was started by Herod the Great, and points out that Jewish Law does not allow such activities in a holy place. Pilate asks: 'So you would have no trouble if these functions were in the Temple of Venus or the Temple of Vesta? 'Of course not,' replies Jesus, 'I have always said render unto Caesar....'"

"Pilate is relieved. If he could cut out the Jews from running their casino he could capture the highrollers and ply them with better drinks and free nights with the priestesses or even the Vestal Virgins. Besides, the food they were giving them in the Temple of Solomon was terrible— tough meats with all the juices drained out and flayed fish. He could give them some of the new lamb quarter pounders. No one had figured out that most of the livestock out back were pigs and they didn't sell wool. Wow, he could clean up."

"Pilate and Jesus are soon playing Pursuitus Insignificus and Jesus is terrific. He seems to know everything. Pilate is impressed until Jesus confides that he gets a lot of information from his father. He says his father has a world wide information network, like a web."

"Soon Pilate tells Jesus he is going to let him go, but Jesus reminds Pilate that the prophecies, tradition, Jesus' mission, and God's will all demand that he be executed before this Passover. Pilate is horrified and they talk further. Pilate, upset, says that he believes such action to be unfair but that he has a plan that would allow God to so direct the outcome if that is truly his choice. Jesus agrees, sure of the outcome."

"The scene moves back to the court. Pilate announces that his wish is freedom but that powerful forces suggest God's wish is execution. Pilate says that Jesus has stated that God is all powerful and can move mountains. 'So,' says Pilate, 'he certainly can determine which side of a coin comes up.'"

"Taking a local gold coin from his pocket he says: 'If the side bearing the image of Caesar Tiberius comes up, the choice is mine, and I will exile Jesus as I have proposed. If the side of the lamb comes up, it will be a sign of God's wish and, despite my reluctance, I will yield to God and offer Jesus up to the Sadducees for execution. Now let's do this right.'"

"He summons the two high priests, Annas and Caiaphas, to stand in a line on the right of his throne and he arranges the Centurion and his chief scribe to stand on the left facing them. 'Now everyone shake hands,' he orders. He summons a blind beggar from the crowd, instructs him, stands him between the two pairs, and has him flip the coin high into the air."

"The four observers bend over and gently blow dirt off the coin. Annas stands first and announces it is lamb. Pilate sighs but turns over Jesus to the Sadducees and soldiers for execution. Then they choose Barabbas to be set free as is the tradition on Passover."

"An amazing twist on an old tale," says Dan. "But it still doesn't seem too bad. What happens next."

"The rest of the second act is the familiar Passion Play. Jesus is led off, appears in the next scene on the cross, dies, the earth quakes and the sky darkens, and the Centurion looks up and says: 'Surely this was the Son of God.' Then there is a brief scene at the tomb of the resurrection and later the ascension with concealed wires flying Jesus to heaven just like Peter Pan."

"I thought you said there was a third act. Is that the apostles and the spread of the church?"

"Nope. The third act begins again at the trial with the coin flip. This time it comes up Caesar. Pilate exiles Jesus from Judaea and privately wishes him well and suggests that he pursue his carpentry and not anger the powerful Sadducees."

"Well, that is a twist," adds Dan. "What next."

"The final scene is a reunion in Jerusalem of Jesus' brothers and sisters and some of the disciples on Passover in 141 après JC, 'after the birth of Julius Caesar'. It is 11 years since the trial. Pontius Pilate has been fired after his cruelty to the Samaritans and two years before he has hanged himself on the orders of Caligula. Herod's Kingdom of Palestine has been mostly reconstituted for his grandson, Herod Agrippa I, who is completing the rebuilding of Solomon's Temple. Times are good in the land. They are meeting in the huge villa of Dr. Luke, now the most famous physician in Judea and a pupil of Aulus Cornelius Celsus. Luke runs a hospital, a pharmacy, a nursing home, a home health care company, and a spa of eternal beauty and runs his practice with many assistants and scribes to keep up with the paperwork. His villa is on the shores of the Jordan. Jesus' family is impressed even though James, Joseph, Judas, and Simon have formed a major construction company and his sisters have good marriages and lots of happy kids. The disciples James and John have formed the Brothers Zebedee Red Sea Fish Company and are doing a booming business. Peter is a well-known builder of minor temples and outhouses. Andrew ventured to Hadrian's Wall, went north to the Blue People, and hasn't been seen since. Asking around they hear that Paul is doing a terrific tent business in Syria but Matthew was killed in a terrorist attack in Baghdad. As they share stories of their various lives and families, they reminisce about their early lives. They admit to being wild and crazy in their youth. Philip of Bethsaida remembers that he was almost caught when they worked the loaves and fishes scam and the young kid found the hidden baskets of food. Thaddeus says that was just like the time the watchman caught them switching the jugs of water and wine. They all revile that blackmailer Lazarus."

"They ask Jesus' brothers and sister where he might be. The reply is that when he left Jerusalem eleven years before he had traveled to Greece and then Rome as a magician and had had some success. He had picked up a German animal trainer and they incorporated animals in his act, even making elephants and white tigers disappear. Peter asks Jesus' family how Jesus is doing, and brother Simon replies: 'He got bitten by a tiger five years ago and died in the Macedonia General Hospital.' They are saddened and all agree that he was the most charismatic con man they had ever met. 'He had a real flair for the big con,' adds Peter. 'Who else would have tried to pull off that Son of God caper.' John says: 'Well, we had some good times. Remember that great dinner we all had with Jesus just before his trial. It was upstairs in the Long Room at Miriam's and she had baked the best flat bread and even found some wonderful wine. We all got drunk and then Miriam brought in a dozen of her girls and everyone made out all night.'"

"The last line is from Jesus' brother Simon, raising his glass: 'To our brother, sister, and friend Jesus—may Jupiter find a special place for all his tricks in some bright corner of Mount Olympus.'"

Dan frowns: "I see. Yes, that will really upset our fundamentalists. I can see the pickets now: 'Guérard the Antichrist.' And it does connect somewhat to that threat. Is there any chance the maestro would stop after act two? That is sacrilegious enough isn't it?"

"No," Hanahan replies. "I thought of that. As soon as my staff leaked to me the rumors of the content I talked with Jean-Louis. Yesterday after the tragedy on Friday I talked with him again. But he is adamant. He says it is brilliant. He says the critics will applaud it and it will be famous on Broadway. But I think he's gone nuts or senile. He told me we wouldn't have any trouble with the Christian right because, quote: 'Roses are red, Violets are bluish, If it weren't for Jesus, We'd all be Jewish.'"

"But how many people know about this? If they only find out at the performance, there wouldn't be time to plant a bomb."

"I'm not sure. I've begun hearing rumors. Some of the Woodlands staff may be talking. It is only 20 miles up the road."

"Well, I guess that means we need to raise the level of security. We can put metal detectors at all your major sites, bring in lots of plainsclothes, and sweep with our dogs."

"How about Gaillard. That holds a lot of people and is a big arena."

"I think we should use metal detectors. We could set up ten or so in the foyer outside the auditorium entrance. If we allow one hour for every-one to be cleared, that would be about five per minute per detector. That's doable unless we catch a lot."

"Catch what? Nail clippers like those cretins at the airport?"

"No. You don't realize what your friends and neighbors are packing. I bet at least one in ten will be packing a gun. And if the threat is from the religious fundamentalists, they've got a lot of gun-toting, snake-handling, skinheads."

"Oh no. No strip searches. I'll get run out of town. What a preamble to Jean-Louis' idiotic play. I never thought about someone in the audi-ence getting mad and starting to shoot the actors. Even Jean-Louis hasn't thought of that."

"We can warn people at the front door and allow them to return to their cars and lock up their goodies. Then we can provide bags they can fill and seal and we'll safeguard them. But we'll have to see what they put in them so we won't be storing a bomb. Otherwise, no questions asked."

"I hope you won't arrest any of my relatives."

"I'll check with Judge Trott. My officers won't like it, but I believe we can agree not to officially notice whatever goes in the bags."

"Well, I'll leave security up to you. Just don't hassle our customers. We have enough trouble with them. I sure hope this doesn't turn out like that Chechen invasion of the Moscow theater. All we need is 100 or so hostages dead and we'll live in infamy forever."

"We'll just keep your audience alive and safe—would that be OK? You try to make them happy with this play. We can keep out a real bomb, but I bet Guérard's great premier is a bomb on its own."

"I'm afraid you're right, Chief. But we all greatly appreciate your help. Remember when our biggest problems were just the half-naked Brazilians with their fingers up their noses?"

Monday, 11:55 am

After the Chief left, Hanahan eased himself into his favorite chair and sipped a third cup of tea. What a Spoleto. Usually they just worried about selling tickets or artists getting sick. Terror. Amazing. Who would want to attack an artistic production? Hmmmm. Jean-Louis. He needs money for New York. Apparently he's having trouble getting it. Now we hear he is borrowing from the Mafia. Publicity brings fame…and customers. The target has got to be Jean-Louis' crazy stuff. No one would attack the other productions—too bland and nice and well-liked. Well, if they do attack this darn play, I hope it is when it opens in Gaillard Auditorium. That is a modern concrete building. After the opening it moves to our lovely Dock Street Theatre. That building has only a few exits and is built of black cypress—lovely but it would burn like a candle. Maybe we can get the play moved to Memminger Auditorium. It's abandoned and broken down. We've put other controversial stuff there and no one has blown it up at least. Maybe we could talk Jean-Louis into playing Christ himself, he thinks of himself as the messiah, then we could use real spikes…

twelve

Crucifiction

*M*onday, 9:51 pm

Chief Ravenel was pleased. No pickets had shown up. The dogs had swept the auditorium three times. The metal detectors had delayed entry with no end of grumbling, and the check room was filled with signed paper bags filled with weapons, each stapled shut by the owner and guarded by police. No weapons had been detected by the magnetometers at the entrance to the auditorium. His staff had been amazed at the array of guns, knives, phones, cameras, tape recorders, etc. they saw going into those bags. The first act had started only a little late and with polite applause. The first intermission was uneventful. The Spoleto Society members, who had each donated at least $1000, raved about the wine and food catered by Brett's. The rest of the audience bought Cokes, coffee, or champagne in safe plastic glasses. The second act was nearing a close with the scene opening at Golgotha with the three crosses, the soldiers, and the condemned.

The robbers were tied to their crosses and those crosses were erected on either side of the stage. Jesus's cross had the sign attached at the top proclaiming him King of the Jews and he was stretched out on it and hammering was seen. Actually his wrists and feet were attached with flesh-colored plastic with nailheads glued to the center over his carpal bones and tarsals. The soldiers erected the cross and Jesus hung there wearing brief breeches. The soldiers cast lots for Jesus' clothes, they offered him the sponge with vinegar, and they used a lance to pierce the flesh-colored bag on his lower abdomen that had two compartments filled with wine and water.

Later the Centurion looked up and observed that Jesus was hanging motionless, his chin on his chest, with urine wetting his briefs and running down his inner legs. He whispered to a soldier: "Look at Christ's legs. We didn't rehearse that. That's realism. I'd be too embarrassed to do that."

Another soldier, overhearing, turned to watch this spectacle when they all observed that the flow was turning brown. "Oh my God," exclaimed the Centurian. "He isn't breathing. Help me."

The Centurion jumped up from where he was sitting and summoned the soldiers who rushed to the cross, unseated it from its hole, and laid it on the stage. The Centurion frantically signaled the stage director and called for help. Then he rushed to the head of the actor and started furiously doing mouth-to-mouth resuscitation. They cut the actor free of the cross, laid him on the floor, and tried closed chest cardiac massage. The Centurion had taken the Red Cross course and correctly felt for a pulse. Feeling none he assessed the airway as being open and instructed the soldier in giving two quick breaths between each set of five chest compressions. He pumped vigorously, feeling a rib or two fracture. He called for help and told the stage director to summon an ambulance.

The audience was stunned. Was this part of the plot? Had resurrection been replaced with resuscitation? After Friday night, anything was possible, especially in a production by Maestro Guérard. Just then Teddy closed the curtain.

Several of the physicians remarked to their spouses that blowing into the mouth was biblical, but coordination of chest compression with ventilation was invented at Johns Hopkins about 1960 and was not appropriate in a presumably 2000-year-old scene. Others were just stunned by the sacrilege.

The stage manager, transfixed, looked back and forth between the script in her hands and the action on stage. Finally she called for an ambulance.

One Roman Soldier said: "That really screws up the scene at the tomb.

What do we do now, resurrect a robber? Maybe we could build a giant slingshot and catapult him into heaven? Or maybe next Wehrner von Braun enters stage right."

The audience slowly broke into polite applause, the auditorium lights gradually came up, and the audience stood and started to file out for some refreshments or to visit the facilities. Everyone wondered what was going on, what the next act would bring, and wondered if another tragedy had marked a Guérard premier.

Soon the stage was filled with police, stagehands, and Chief Ravenel trying to control the flow. The Chief finally had his men clear a circle around the actor. Henry Woodward, MD, again in the front row, sensed the problem and calmly mounted the stage. Approaching the actor, he took charge of the resuscitation. He moved to the head and listened to the chest and felt for the carotid pulse. He told the ventilator to be more vigorous and showed the chest compressor how to bear down hard and hold the downstroke. He quickly examined the rest of the actor and asked if anyone knew his medical history.

The actress playing Mary Magdalen and the actress playing Jesus' mother both spoke up. They glared at each other. The first said: "We were seeing each other and I'm pretty sure he's healthy and had no problems except diabetes and herpes."

"Herpes!" exploded the second. "The bastard told me he had no sexually transmitted diseases. Damn, now I'll have to tell my husband."

Dr. Woodward kept examining the actor's eyes and feeling for pulses in the neck and groin. The ambulance arrived and the paramedics, pushing everyone aside, took over. The paramedics attached the resuscitation vest around the chest, powered it from the oxygen supply, and intubated the trachea. Dr. Woodward asked them to draw a blood sample and give intravenous glucose to this known diabetic, but the chief Paramedic just injected the glucose solution. When they got the heart monitor hooked up Dr. Woodward saw ventricular tachycardia and asked if they had bretyllium. The chief paramedic retorted: "Them doctors won't let us have it. Now back off. Even if you're a doc, we're in charge until we get this GOMER to the emergency room." They rushed the gurney from the stage, into the ambulance, and went screaming into the night.

Monday, 11:35 pm

Augustus Hanahan had been sitting with his guests in the front stage-left section. He was stunned. His staff hadn't warned him about a resuscitation on stage. More blasphemy. He pulled himself upright and shooed his companions out into the aisle so he could find the maestro and complain. He tried to follow the stage left passage to backstage, but the police stopped him until he confirmed his identity. Backstage was bedlam. Another disaster. He accosted Chief Ravenel and loudly accused him of not having enough security.

The Chief, calmly, said: "Augustus, calm down. We've no idea what has gone on. The actor was thought to be young and healthy and no one was observed to do anything to him. Maybe he just got sick. He's off to the hospital and we'll just have to see. Dr. Woodward thinks he might have had a diabetic seizure or coma. Why don't you go take care of the audience."

Hanahan, cowed and still confused, wandered around the stage. He accosted Teddy. "What next? Why did you do that? What happens now?" Teddy, not sure herself, spotted the maestro with a crowd of actors on stage left and she and Hanahan approached just as Jean-Louis instructed the cast to forget the interruption and run the third act as rehearsed. Any standin can play Christ in that act as he has no lines and only a brief appearance.

Jean-Louis said, exuberantly, "This will work fine. Almost as though planned."

Teddy directed the stagehands to change the set back to the courtroom and told the actors to prepare for the third act which she will delay for fifteen minutes.

Hanahan asked Jean-Louis if he should make an announcement before the third act about what had happened.

Jean-Louis, horrified, insisted he be silent. "I may change the second act to incorporate this. The realism was terrific, wasn't it. It was brilliant. I just need to think it out. Resuscitation—wow. Suppose it had worked? Do you think? Say nothing!"

"But," Hanahan replied, "we can't keep it out of the papers. My goodness, the actor looked dead."

"Oh that hospital will fix him right up. Probably just food poisoning. You know the shellfish here can be deadly in a non-'R' month."

Hanahan watched as the maestro almost ran to the backstage exit, muttering to himself about rewriting the script and replacing the actor.

Tuesday, 3:15 am

Bill McCord was dreaming of a deer hunt and just when a huge buck appeared before his blind he heard bells. He startled. What idiot would make noise at a time like this. On and on they rang. No stopping them. He awoke with a start. The ring was on his bedside table, from the phone. Groggily he picked it up and rasped: "Yeah."

"Bill," said M.E., "I'm so sorry to disturb you but we need to do a careful postmortem examination now and you are the senior resident on call. We've got another Spoleto death."

Twenty-two minutes later Dr. McCord arrived with a slight beard but wide awake. He quickly changed into scrubs and joined M.E. beside the corpse. "Which musical instrument killed this one?" he said smiling, "did an ocarina get stuck in his carina or was he circumcised by a Jew's harp?"

"Now Bill," said M.E. smiling. "This is a 24-year-old actor who was playing Jesus Christ in the Spoleto play tonight at Gaillard. While he was on the cross, everything seemed to be normal and he made no unusual noises or gestures, but he suddenly slumped down and was incontinent of urine and stool. When this was observed they noticed he wasn't breathing, quickly attempted resuscitation, but were unable to establish an effective rhythm. The paramedics gave him 50 cc's of 50% glucose at the scene, but without drawing a blood sample. Dr. Woodward was there and is furious. Apparently the paramedics pushed him out of the way and wouldn't listen to him."

"But without that blood sample how will we know if he had low or high blood sugar? Did he have any ketoacidosis?

"No, and at the hospital his blood sugar was about normal. So, skipping a meal and having hypoglycemia is the best bet, even with the stress of performing."

"They should have been able to resuscitate him, though."

"Well, despite what I'm told was a full-court effort at the Trauma Center, they pronounced him dead at 1:48 am. Chief Ravenel is very upset. He told me that two actors dying dramatically on the Spoleto stage within three days cannot be a coincidence. With all the newspeople here, they would like as clear a statement as we can make when the sun comes up. So, I'm sorry we meet again in the middle of the night."

"I'm glad I'm not starring in any Spoleto productions," mused Dr. McCord. "That would really make you think, wouldn't it. Talk about Warhol's fifteen minutes of fame. Do any of the stars last that long? Are they giving them purple hearts yet?"

"Let's get to it," said M.E. soberly. "He arrived in a body bag with no clothes. I've already dictated the header for the videotapes. Let's examine him. I only know a little of his medical history. His parents were at the Trauma Center and said he had juvenile diabetes and had had several hospitalizations for diabetic coma or hypoglycemia, but not in the last three or four years. He had some kidney damage, had one photocoagulation of retinal vessels, and had bad neuropathy with almost totally numb feet and some trouble walking in the dark. They said he was taking good care of himself, measuring his blood sugar before each meal and using three or four insulin shots a day. They say he used the Lilly Humalog insulin together with Lilly Lente insulin in two pens. He takes no other drugs to their knowledge, does not drink or smoke, and does not take illicit drugs. They were already talking about the connection with the soprano and mentioning lawyers."

"We better double glove and treat him as HIV positive until we get the results," added Bill. "I don't see any lesions on his scalp or face."

The endotracheal tube is in place. There are catheters in the left subclavian vein, the right external jugular, the left antecubital, and the right femoral. There also is a chest tube between the left 2nd and 3rd ribs. The electrocardiogram electrodes are still pasted on his chest with the wires hanging off them, and there is a prominent burn about the one on his right upper chest.

"They must have put the defibrillation paddle right on it," mused Bill.

He had many old insulin injection sites on his shoulders, abdomen, and thighs and there was some diabetic lipodystrophy, especially on his thighs. His fingertips showed multiple old sticks. His lower legs had lost some hair, had trace edema, and had those slowly-resolving bruises and thin skin characteristic of diabetics.

Bill brightly asked: "But, what do you think of this?"

M.E. bent and took the magnifying glass to examine the left foot.

There appeared to be two puncture wounds, 12 mm apart, at the base of the first metatarsal at the great toe. M.E. said: "That's strange. Diabetics usually take careful care of their feet and never inject anything there. Why would he do that?"

"Perhaps it isn't an insulin injection?" suggested Bill. "It looks like a snake bite. Perhaps it is just an injury, like two splinters. Was he walking barefoot tonight on stage?"

"Good idea, Bill. But, to be thorough, let's take two tissue blocks through the skin of the foot and into the deep tissues. Besides histology we can assay for insulin. If those wounds are from splinters, there may be some microscopic evidence of wood or metal."

They did not find anything suggesting foul play. The eyes and kidneys showed some signs of diabetic damage. There were many tiny petechial hemorrhages characteristic of suffocation. The endotracheal tube was well placed. They considered severe asthma or laryngospasm obstructing his airways, but the larynx seemed normal and the lungs had no trapped air. The coronary arteries were of usual configuration and there was no gross evidence of myocardial infarction, fresh or remote. The stomach was empty and they felt that made it more likely to be a case of hypoglycemia. Certainly the lungs did not show aspiration.

At 7:40 am they had completed the gross examination, videotaped all the significant features, obtained all the tissue samples, and obtained fluid samples from the heart blood, stomach, vitreous humor, and urinary bladder. They labeled the specimens for proper handling, documented everything on the videotape, and turned over the materials to the technicians. M.E. carefully cut the two tissue blocks from the wounds in the feet so that they contained the entire needle track, or whatever it was. They wouldn't put these through the usual robots but flash freeze them. That way they could cut some sections for histology and use other slices for toxicology.

"Bill, we should send the blood and fluids off for insulin, glucose, C-peptide, and hemoglobin A1C. But after a full resuscitation I'm not sure what we will learn. Any other special tests you would like?"

"Nope, boss, that about does it except for the holes."

Glancing at her Rolex, M.E. said "I guess it's time to get up."

"Well, I'm going to get some breakfast in the hospital," yawned Bill. "Care to join me for some coffee and a bagel?"

"I'd love to, but I better prepare a short statement for Chief Ravenel and tell the coroner what we've found, or rather what we haven't found.

Unless toxicology turns up something in one of these cases, it looks a lot like two accidents. Would you be comfortable if I said that this is probably an accidental death and may be related to hypoglycemia that caused him to suffocate in the unusual crucifixion position."

"I think that is the best we can do right now," agreed Bill. "I sure wish they had gotten a blood sample before they gave that glucose. You know, there really is always time."

M.E. called Chief Ravenel's office and asked him to call her as soon as possible. She called the coroner and left the same message. Channel Five called her but she deferred to Chief Ravenel. Fearing she might have to be on camera, she showered and changed from her scrub suit into a business suit and then, clipping on her namebadge, she walked to the other end of the hospital to the cafeteria for several deep cups of very black coffee. This was the time she liked best. The nightshift was getting one last refreshment before signing off and going home and the newly arrived dayshift was getting perked up before morning report. Although the hospital was vitally alive 24x7, this seemed to be its most vibrant moment.

Apocrypha

II Aaron 3:1-5

It came to pass that a tribe of evildoers invaded the land of Canaan. They worshipped the camel, held loud races in the main streets, and constructed a large platform of cedar on which they exhibited a golden idol of a camel. At first the peaceful Canaanites tolerated the barbarians, but they became more bold in wearing offensive symbols, fornicating in public, and relieving themselves on the temple. And so the Canaanites prayed together in the temple and left the evildoers outside. God came to them in the form of a whirlwind and spake: 'Thou who hast turned from truth to a graven image will not regret the loss of that which thou cans't see or feel' and he enveloped them in the whirlwind which sucked from them all their breath. So ended the history of the Angels of Hell.

thirteen

Aftermath

*T*uesday, 8:15 am

When Chief Ravenel reached his office he had five messages. The most urgent calls were from Hanahan and Simons. He called Dr. Simons first and her phone rolled over to her cellular phone. He asked about the actor.

"So far it looks like an accident. Diabetic. Possibly hypoglycemia. Weakness. Suffocation from hanging on that cross. We did find two small wounds in one foot, but we aren't sure what that means. I know it sounds crazy to have two fatal accidents on one stage in three days, but that's all we have so far."

A little relieved, he called Hanahan.

"OK, so its just another accident. Makes us look like bumbling idiots—killing off two stars in as many days."

"Well three days, Augustus."

"We're slow down here. Do you think we can make this weekend without doing in someone else? I'm not sure I'm going to walk on that stage again. I'll sure be looking up for some poisonous cloud to be descending on me or a big pelican to snatch me up."

"I think that would be a record-sized pelican. Speaking of poisonous clouds, do you think your threat might have been related to the actor's death, if he suffocated on the cross?"

"Hey, Chief, that's your end of the business. You tell me. I was worried about the whole audience turning blue. Too bad it wasn't Jean-Louis. I'd suffocate that bastard anytime."

"Well, if you examine the threat it was during this sacrilegious play, the actor did quit breathing, and maybe the 333 thing is about this silly "Termillenium" and the 666 is Satan. What do you think?"

"You didn't see any skinheads or other crazies around, did you?"

"Well, no more than usual at least," added the Chief. "Let's keep the threat secret. I think it begins to focus us on the religious right fundamentalists and we have a whole notebook full of notes on those local troublemakers. They've killed abortion doctors before. We think some of them have been burning down black churches. If they had prior word of the play's plot maybe one got angry enough to even knock off the symbol of their so-called faith. What do you think?"

"I don't know anything about them. I just go to St. Philips every Sunday and sit in the balcony. I avoid any arguments about religion, creationism, or which rite to use."

"Have youall got a noncontroversial minister yet? That one who shacked up with the witch certainly made life interesting."

"Now, Chief. Don't get caught up in the rumors, although I'm afraid that one might be right" Hanahan replied. "By the way, Channel Five asked me to appear on the nine o'clock news. Do you want to be there?"

"No, Augustus," answered the Chief. "Just be sure to say we continue to investigate but that we have no evidence at this time of anything but an accident and that the actor had juvenile diabetes. I wouldn't say anything about the hypoglycemia yet."

Tuesday, 8:35 am

M.E. answered the ring in her office. Her phone had rung several times in the autopsy room, and the caller ID showed it to be Dr. Woodward, but she hadn't wanted to talk while cutting and gloved and when there were others listening. When she heard his voice her heart raced and she invited him to the library. She did a lot of lookup early in the morning, when the library was almost deserted, and she loved the old books and their wonderful musty smell. Most of her real work was now done on the computer, but she was still drawn to the worn leather bindings and the thoughts of all who had turned those pages before her.

As soon as she saw him she wished she had chosen an even more private place. If she did what she wanted and they were caught in the library…. She wrapped her arms around his neck, gave him a deep if quick kiss, and thanked him for the lovely flowers. "I called you right away but there was no answer. I guess you were out delivering flowers to all your other girls."

"You know better. Actually, Mary Elizabeth, I was afraid to talk to you last night. It is a little easier in daylight and workclothes I guess."

"Oh, is it bad news?"

"No, I am just mightily smitten, mightily, and my emotions are controlling my judgment. This is all too wonderful, too perfect, too desirable. Just don't let me run off the track and behave like an adolescent in public. I can just see the rumors—Department Chairman drools over subordinate. Sounds like sexual harassment to me."

"I thought I harassed you," said M.E. smiling. "At least I tried."

"Well, if I recover enough stability to trust myself in public with you, would you consider dinner tonight? I've got several guests to take to the Gullah and Gospel Gala tonight and can't get out of that easily. Would you like to go with me?"

"It sounds great, Henry, and I have my own ticket, but I'm not sure. I was up most of the night and if I can get away for a couple of hours this afternoon I'd like to go and join you afterwards. Let's not be too public quite yet. But if anything else from Spoleto blows up, or the lab hits something hot, I'm sure I will be working right through and sleeping this evening. Is that OK? If you want to get another date I'll understand."

Woodward drew her close, kissed her ear, and whispered: "Mary Elizabeth, I couldn't even think of anyone else but you. I don't know how I'm going to get through work today. I may not be able to think of anything. What will they think if during my lecture on lung cancer I start singing like Bing Crosby."

M.E. gave him a hug and thought singing would brighten up that depressing lecture. Pathology was intellectually exciting but not a lot of fun.

"By the way, what were your findings on the actor? You said on the phone that it looked accidental."

"I do think hypoglycemia-asphyxiation is our best bet. He seemed to be taking just insulin and caring for himself. The only thing that's odd is that he had the usual numb feet but we found two puncture wounds, maybe, in his right foot. I doubt he took insulin there, and Bill McCord suggests they are just from splinters from the stage. We'll do our best to check them out."

"If he had numb feet, could someone have injected him with a poison without his knowledge?" Woodward mused. "A morphine-like opioid, perhaps Fentanyl, would knock out his breathing and keep him from struggling or crying out. How about a muscle paralyzing agent such as tubocurarine? I doubt you could inject enough potassium and that would really hurt subcutaneously even if you were numb. Maybe the Romans were trying lethal injection and hit him with squill or some other ancient poison."

"Wow you're really full of ideas. Why not hypoglycemia and a simple asphyxiation from the crucifixion."

"Well, he was a young man. Kassandrá wasn't that old. Our festival has knocked off two stars in three days. I wonder if Spoleto has insurance against accidents like these? If I see Hanahan I think I'll kid him that I heard of a 100-million-dollar lawsuit. He'd croak. When was the last time Broadway killed a star on stage?"

"Now, Henry. Be nice. We have just two everyday accidents— bassoonation and crucifixion. You see that all the time. Maybe the star tonight will aspirate an okra and die of gumbo poisoning."

M.E. squeezed Henry's hand at the library door and walked back to her office in the hospital basement. She reached Bubba on his cellular phone and told him of the postmortem examination of the actor. "Could you examine the stage and his dressing room and I guess the cross for splinters and see if he was barefooted or wore slippers or shoes on stage. Diabetics should be taking care of their feet and keeping them covered. It's most likely these wounds are from splinters, but they might be the tracks of needles or tacks or small nails or staples. You might also see what can be found, tiny now, on the stage and wherever he went."

"Is there a possibility this was injection of a drug of abuse? Did you find any tracks or signs of skin-popping?" asked Bubba.

"No other marks except what is probably from insulin so I don't think so, but we'll check that out in toxicology. Actually, I think it's just a red herring but I don't want to leave any avenue unexplored with the high profile these two deaths have assumed. When did you ever think Spoleto would include bassoonation and crucifixion."

"Well I have heard some board members suggested crucifixion for the maestro and I know where they would like to put that bassoon," replied Bubba with a chuckle. "Do you think this has anything to do with the threat the Spoleto director received?"

"I'm not sure. The 'suck the air out' reference might sound like suffocation. Let's keep that quiet. The newspeople would go crazy speculating on that one."

"Well I bet the audience had a sharp intake of breath when they figured out the plot of Guérard's new play. Why doesn't that guy stick to wholesome classic opera themes like roasting young children in your oven or the fiery end of the world?"

M.E. chuckled. "I guess there's lots of violence on the classical stage after all. Oh well, spirituals and excerpts of Porgy and Bess will be redeeming. Now don't forget to get your team to look for something tiny and sharp that might have stuck in that actor's foot."

Tuesday 4:30 pm

M.E. was ready to collapse, but went to the analytical laboratories on her way out. "Anything new and exciting in the lab, Dirk?"

"Well, we've mostly finished identifying all the medicines the singer was taking. There is an amazing variety of legitimate medicines as well as herbal medicines of all kinds. She was spraying things down her throat that we've found in the various inhalers. She was using liniments on her skin. She was apparently brewing teas with mixtures of ingredients including chamomile, which isn't entirely harmless, despite Peter Rabbit. But all of these are at low levels in her blood and urine or undetectable. I've even done some hair analysis to look at long term exposures, but it comes down mostly to the Seldane and quinine if anything is causative, and I don't know how to prove that."

"Well is that the final report so we can wrap this one up and make Chief Ravenel and the others happy?" asked M.E.

"Not quite so fast, Dr. Simons," replied Dirk. "We've still got one peak on the blood analysis that I can't find in urine, in hair, in the vitreous humor, or in any of the pill bottles we have sampled. That suggests it was just being absorbed and was mostly in blood. We've never seen this peak before in this laboratory and it is not in the usual references about drugs."

"What did you find on the high-resolution mass spectrometer?"

"The molecular weight seems to be 645.76 and from the fragments it looks like 34 carbons, 47 hydrogens, one nitrogen, and 11 oxygen atoms. I've been running possible structures on the 3-D computational chemistry program, but I've gotten only one hit. I ordered a physical sample of the stuff from the National Toxicology Laboratory of FDA, but they said they had only a tiny amount. It should arrive tomorrow by priority FedEx."

"Does this thing have a name?" asked M.E.

"Well…" Dirk hesitated. "I'd feel better if you gave me a few hours to search our databases and also to test the mass spectrometer analysis of a physical sample. You know with minor peaks from the liquid chromatograph the MS can be unstable and often gives you a lot of fuzz. Can I have a few hours?"

"Sure" replied M.E. firmly. "The last thing we need is a red herring, especially when this woman obviously fell off the stage. I've tried to soft peddle the Seldane and quinine story as we don't have any electrocardiographic evidence of her QRS duration or QT interval, we can't prove she had an arrhythmia, and all we can say is it was an unfortunate example of a well-traveled lady who took multiple drugs from multiple doctors and multiple sources and these two, at least, might have been a bad combination for her. It still is an accident. Do you think you'll have this last peak buttoned up by tomorrow night?"

"I'll do my best," replied Dirk. "Go home and get some sleep."

"Actually, I want to hear the performance tonight."

"I know you love our local music, but aren't they doing this one several times? Go sleep and catch a later show."

"I might, but I love Porgy and Bess. I never hear it without a few tears. It's home."

"Wow. I can't imagine the tough professor with tears. See you tomorrow."

"Well, keep that to yourself. I don't want to appear too human. Spoils the ghoul image."

Tuesday, 5:45 pm

When Bubba returned to his office he found his team beaming. They had several large bags of sweepings, vacuum debris, ferrous items picked up with a magnet or discovered with the metal detectors, and X-ray of the trash. In an evidence bag was a tiny object. "So," Bubba said, "you found it. Fantastic. Did you use the magnet or the X-ray?"

Sergeant Rutledge Moore explained: "We were sweeping the stage when this actor who plays a Roman soldier, in a dress no less, came up and asked what we were doing. I told him we were looking for something small and sharp and he replied that the stage was dangerous and that he had almost been wounded. When I asked what he meant he said that a wire had stuck in his sandal. He had thrown it away, but we went through his trash and found that wire thing I put in the evidence bag."

Bubba complimented his staff: "That's really finding a needle in a haystack. Super work. I knew you guys could find anything."

He carefully removed the object with tweezers from the evidence bag. It was about a half inch in length, hollow, sharpened on one end in a long bevel, and crimped shut at the other. He carefully replaced it so the medical examiner could photograph it under the scanning 3-D microscope.

"Did you find any medicine droppers or syringes or any other works that might go with this?"

"No, boss. We searched everywhere. We asked all the stagehands and actors we found, but they seemed like a clean crowd. No tracks we could observe. My guess is they might do grass or crack or speed, but it didn't seem like a big smack crowd."

fourteen

Gullah And Romance

*T*uesday, 8:15 pm

M.E. was late. She had pushed snooze too many times. Finally she raced to dress. Ordinarily she would have worn a simple dress with no jewelry and little makeup, but she tingled all over at the thought of Henry and dressed carefully. The Stoll's Alley Shop's simple print dress of green Thai silk was exquisite. She chose the small James Allan pearl and gold earrings she had gotten from her parents for graduation from medical school as they were very special. She added a Gump's gold giraffe as a pin, a simple white leather bag from the Gucci's in Charleston Place and matching white shoes—it was after Memorial Day when ladies in Charleston switched to white.

Parking was terrible. She had to go to the highest level in the garage adjacent to Gaillard. Then she had to wait for the first break in the great gospel hymns that made up the first act. Finally, she was in her seat, W29, at the back of the main floor, under the balcony. She couldn't even see Henry Woodward, but knew he'd be down front. He contributed generously to Spoleto and always took guests to provide them with even more revenue. That was especially generous when, for this anniversary, they had almost doubled the price of the main events and, for the major performances, required that you buy tickets to the gala receptions that followed down below on the exhibition floor.

Henry had invited her to join him at the Spoleto Society room during the intermissions, but she didn't want to confront his children and guests just yet. She waited until the crowd had passed by the entrance at the end of her row and then, to stretch her legs, she walked down the ramp inside the auditorium rather than out in the hallway. She saw a few friends and relatives from the town and more from the medical university. She was a little thirsty, but drank very little as she never liked to use public toilets, knowing as she did all the things you can pick up there. You might not get knocked up, she said to herself, but I'd hate to get herpes or another sexually transmitted disease from a toilet seat all by myself. Besides the line was always long and filled with ladies squirming with the wait.

The second act was exquisite. A large gospel choir drawn from many of the churches in the Lowcountry, all the way from Beaufort to Georgetown, sang old favorites as well as some lesser-known and more authentically African tunes. The combination of piano, organ, drums, and guitars provided a perfect subtle complement to the rich voices. When a large woman in a gorgeous blue robe stepped forward to lead "Swing Low Sweet Chariot" tears welled up in M.E.'s eyes. That was the song her mother had requested for her funeral. This act closed with the wonderful rousing funeral song: "Walk im up de stairs" from *Purlie Victorious*. M.E. felt that such bright music, and white vestments, were the real Christian way to bury a friend or relative.

At the second intermission she stayed in her seat and rose just to greet friends who called to her. She debated the facilities but decided she could hold out. Then she felt two strong hands on her shoulders and tilted her head back to see Henry. "You've been hiding," he chided her.

"I'm just exhausted, Henry, and I didn't want to stumble and spill a drink or something."

"Or fall onto a bassoon?"

She smiled, desperately wanting to crush him to her in a passionate kiss. But, like a Charleston lady, she just smiled and held his hand.

"You aren't too tired for dinner, are you?" asked Henry plaintively.

"Are you going to the reception?" asked M.E.

"Nope, I got my cousins from Georgetown to agree to squire my kids home after the reception so I'm free as a bird, but without any wings."

"Would you like a ride to my place? I've got some great nibbles."

Beaming, Henry replied: "You're a great nibbler you are. But only if you promise I can explore every square centimeter of dermal delights."

M.E. blushed and looked around furtively. "Henry! I was going to make it but now you've made me rush off to the facilities. Let go my hand. Bad boy. I'm parked on the uppermost level of the garage—do you want to meet there?"

"I can't wait, and I'm glad these pants are a little baggy."

"Oh, hush up—quit unrabelin yo' mout."

The third act was an abbreviated concert version of Porgy and Bess including most of the major songs rendered by local artists from the gospel choirs. Summertime wavered a little. Bess was beautiful. Serena had the best female voice, rich and lyrical. Crown had a deep velvet bass that resonated throughout the hall. The ending was stirring as always. The crippled Porgy gets out of jail and returns to Catfish Row, a block below Broad Street which ends in the old Custom House. Porgy greets his friends and looks for Bess who has gone off with Sportin' Life. He sings: "Weh Bess?" The answer is "Noo Yawk." His reply is: "W'ich way Noo Yawk?" After admonishing him that he best stay with his friends he is told it is: "Way up nawt' pas' de Custum House!"

He calls: "Bring my goat!" and starts the aria that always brought tears to M.E.'s eyes: "I'm on my way." She smiled because to old Charlestonians like her parents, who insisted on living "South of Broad," there wasn't much of interest "Way up Nort, pass de Custom Hous." It was a vast unknown universe, not suitable for the gentle folks of downtown Charleston who lived in the past and loved it.

The audience broke into thunderous applause, everyone on their feet, for this was Charleston's opera and everyone loved it and knew every word. DuBose and Dorothy Heyward were Charlestonians and their play, that Gershwin set to music, had been published in 1927 when Charleston was in desperate financial straits. It was said Charlestonians were too poor to paint and too proud to whitewash. After the terrible scourge of Friday's so-called opera, at last they were back to their culture, their people ("we people") both as characters and singers, and familiar and predictable ground. M.E. had never seen so many flowers handed and tossed to the performers nor such a long and demanding ovation. She guessed that the remaining performance of this event would be sold at scalpers' prices, a first for Spoleto.

It was almost midnight when she reached her car. The long line of exiting cars, despite prepaying the parking charge doubled this year to $6, made her realize it would be a long wait to the exit. She settled into the comfortable seat, now molded to her figure, and turned on The Breeze. Within five minutes Henry arrived, a little breathless, and announced he had run up the stairs after seeing off his contingent. She opened the door and he sat, turned, and embraced him warmly in a very long kiss. "Take me to your lair, young lady," exclaimed Henry, "before I ravish you publicly and we are expelled from decent society."

"Ravish away," replied M.E., quickly starting the Jag with its usual purr. "From the history of our town there was a lot of public ravishing right from the start, as well as public drinking, public gambling, horse-racing, and such. As I recall the only thing that didn't get a lot of attention was church-going."

"But my dear," smiled Henry. "No one is supposed to see or remember or talk about the Charleston Gentry when they behave outrageously. It just isn't done. You can do anything, as long as you pronounce it correctly, but never talk about it."

M.E. laughed, turned down The Breeze, and began telling Henry exactly what she planned to do when they had closed her front door behind them. "Well, I hope I can take off my coat and hold it in front of me to get from the car to your door."

"I hope not."

Tuesday, 11:50 pm

Bubba made his way across backstage and found Teddy just buttoning up. She smiled and said: "You're a little early, but tonight has been easy. These singers, although not really professionals, have been very orderly and helpful. They are so polite. It must be true about you southerners being ladies and gentlemen. Give me just one minute and I'll be ready."

As they exited through the side door to his police car, Teddy said she's not very hungry and why don't they go to her place for snacks?

"Won't your father-in-law walk in on us," asked Bubba tentatively.

Teddy startled unexpectedly. "Don't worry, I've got the only key to my suite in the apartment. Besides, tonight the bastard is at the Plaza."

"The Plaza?" asked Bubba. "As in New York?"

"You got it," replied Teddy. "Last night after the tragedy he was on the phone for hours. His investors are very antsy about the deaths. He said they wanted to know if anyone would be left alive to open in New

York. And he's very frightened of one big investor named Personnoni who apparently is very demanding. You can't believe how much it costs to mount one Broadway show, much less two, with one of them an opera. You have to kowtow to a lot of rich folks to make it possible. Jean-Louis expects his opera of Charleston decadence to have the same impact as Bernstein's story of New York gangs. By the way, don't mention Bernstein or Gershwin to him unless you want an hour diatribe."

"So when did he leave?"

"He got up about 4 am and caught the Delta 6:10 am commuter to LaGuardia. Said he would be back in a couple of days 'he hoped'."

"Are you going to be part of all this development of both shows in New York?" asked Bubba, beginning to think about what was going to happen when Spoleto ended. Did he want her to stay or was this another of his snatch-and-run romances?

"Absolutely not! I hope to never see him again, at least never alive— I'd applaud at his crucifixion. Besides, I think the old goat has gone crazy. He spends all his time imagining schemes against him and plotting revenge on everyone around. His personal life is insane. He hit on Kasandrá and was furious when she rejected him. He threw out Capone. I think he may be sleeping with Areana. No one at the festival wants to be alone with him."

"I'm so sorry, Teddy," said Bubba, turning right from George onto East Bay. "I had heard he was a little crusty but I didn't know he was that hard on you."

They chatted about her work in the theater and Bubba's background in criminology and his rapid promotions on the police force. He indicated he might practice law as an alternative, but was learning a lot from his current job which was mostly investigating complex and high-profile crimes. "I'm proud of our new white-collar crime taskforce, and we've already prosecuted a number of lawyers, real estate brokers, and doctors for various scams. Last week we caught two child pornographers on the Isle of Palms and the week before we rolled up an internet credit-card scam being run out of Kiawah."

They parked on South Battery and took the elevator up the edge of her piazza. Teddy said: "I'm amazed this building wasn't damaged in the Civil War with all those cannon out there."

"It was," replied Bubba. "First, down here, you better call it the War of Northern Aggression. We don't think it was very civil. At the beginning of the war the Yankees couldn't get any cannon close enough to shell

Charleston. Then an inventor named Parrot put rifling grooves in a cannon and they got one close enough to shell houses below Calhoun Street. Of course everyone who lived down here just moved further up the peninsula."

"But look at all those big cannon just outside. They must have been shooting at something."

"Well, not during the war. They were just put there as a museum long after the war was over. But I do believe that a Confederate mortar just outside this house blew up, but I don't know how much damage it did. I think it was after that they added this piazza."

"War used to be so civilized with rules and proper behavior. Now the terrorists destroy anyone and anything. It seems like the thing to do. If someone makes you mad, just blow them up."

"Life certainly was easier before 9/11. You know when Charleston shelled Fort Sumter that April morning, everyone came out on their piazzas and watched. The only casualty was after the Yankees surrendered the fort and a soldier was killed in the salute to their flag as they withdrew with it."

"Well, be careful of the construction stuff on this piazza so you don't become a casualty just talking about it," Teddy said as she led the way by moonlight to the entry door. They both stopped and looked over the harbor. The lights on Mount Pleasant on the left and James Island on the right seemed to twinkle just like the stars. Fort Sumter was dimly visible. Nearer at hand was the dark Castle Pinckney. A huge container ship, nearly 1000 feet long, slipped down the channel to the harbor entrance, silent and dark and seemingly top heavy. It was not nearly as ominous as the stealthy nuclear submarines that used to ply these waters, but Bubba still wondered why they didn't capsize in bad weather. He remembered being told that containers often fell off and just floated away. Not like the old days when everything that came by ship was carried out by hand and walked down the long wharves that surrounded the town.

Bubba slipped his arm around Teddy's shoulders and said: "Don't you love my crazy old town. There is a continuity here that just feels right. Doesn't it excite you to know that some of your relatives sailed up that same river three hundred years ago?"

"Well, not my own kin but of course my husband's mother's family did flee France to grow sugar cane in Barbados before one young squire, bored with plantation life, turned pirate. Most of the Bonnet family remained loyal to the King and Pope, lived in Paris, and made copper pots until they got into the theater."

Bubba gently massaged Teddy's back with his left hand as she rubbed her right ear on his right hand. She turned and slowly ran her arms around his chest and looked up as he, on cue, kissed her eyes, and nose, and mouth—deeply. His large hands spread out over her back while he noted the absence of bra straps. The kiss was growing more excited until she broke away and said: "Why don't we go inside and get comfortable."

"I'm pretty comfortable right here, ma'am, but I like your idea."

On the eighteenth century Sheraton sofa in the big living room they were soon entwined. As excitement et al. rose, the sofa seemed to grow smaller, and Bubba reached under Teddy's legs, picked her up in his arms, kissed her deeply, and said: "Let's find a spot that is less full of angles, edges, and hard bumpy things. Your bumps don't seem as likely to bruise me."

Teddy giggled and directed him to her bedroom and he paused only to lock the door before laying her gently on the bed. She responded by staring intently at him with those hypnotic eyes as she slowly unbuttoned her dress and enjoyed the obvious reaction as she opened it fully to reveal only a garter belt and black net stockings.

"My goodness," he said. "You're perfect."

"Not really, but we need to talk. Get comfortable but before we go much further I need to tell you some things that aren't nice about myself. Bubba, I'm really scared about this and I need your help. I like you a lot but this is difficult for me."

Bubba, now shirtless, sat on her left side and tried to keep his hands off as he, with a solicitous but urgent tone, said: "Teddy, we don't need to do anything. I'm a very boring straight guy with no kinks, and my greatest pleasure is in giving pleasure as well."

"I know," said Teddy, turning her head a little away. "It's me, not you."

"Well, I would expect to use protection if that's what you mean."

"No, Bubba, and I don't have any diseases. It has to do more with my screwed up life. I would say love life, but there hasn't been any love in it for years. I'm not sure I can satisfy you and I feel all awkward and unsure about this."

Bubba, his experience reassuring him, decided it was not time for a long conversation, and she was just too inviting, and so he started licking all the prominent places as he heard her sharp intake of breath. Soon she was unbuckling his pants as he kissed slowly downward.

An hour later they lay, exhausted and very satisfied, across the bed. "Teddy," said Bubba softly while running his right index finger around her right nipple, "I nominate you for an academy award in lovemaking. Wow, you really are perfect."

Teddy, with a shiver, pulled him closer to her and said: "Thank you. It's been a very long time and I didn't know I could respond like that. You are quite a master, sir."

"Why on earth would you doubt yourself," he crooned. "You are just super."

"Well, when I share my secrets, you may hate me and regret our tête-á-tête."

Bubba smiled, "I am not sure tête-á-tête gets the anatomy just right, but whatever you call it, it spells de-light."

"Now listen, Bernard," Teddy said pressing one hand on his chest and arising on her right elbow while looking deeply into his eyes. "You know how liberated theater people are. Many of my friends have been into some real weird stuff. I've stayed away from the drugs. I learned so many bad things about drugs in five years at The Philadelphia College of Science that I am very careful in that regard. I've never been into control or pain or Satan or animals or the other far out stuff. I haven't really had that many partners, and my HIV was negative just last month when I gave blood, but I have slept with both men and women. I hope that doesn't shock you."

"No," replied Bubba, his eyes widening a little. "I think I'd have a problem with another guy, but two women together I must admit I find exciting. Obviously you enjoy men, or you are one heck of a great actress."

"Don't be silly. Nothing tonight was acting. But it has been a terrible time for me since Steve died and I've avoided men like the plague ever since I was raped. That changed my life and embittered me like you wouldn't believe. I couldn't even be alone in a room with a man for a year and it took three years of therapy to work out some of my hostility. I just couldn't believe a relative could do that."

Bubba, now incensed, sat up despite her pressure and said: "Just tell me who the bastard was and I'll go arrest him right now. I'm amazed how much child abuse there is."

"You promised to listen," Teddy admonished pushing him back down. "It was terrible. But I wasn't a child. It was just after Steve's funeral. He acted as though he wanted to comfort me, but his kisses changed from

Platonic to sensual and soon he was holding me down and violating me. I was in shock. I tried to fight back, but he beat me with his fists until I couldn't resist and then tried to have his way, but he failed. That made him even more angry and he hit me again and again, calling me his son's whore."

"My God, it was Jean-Louis?"

After a long pause, she whispered: "Yes. He hits on everyone. I don't think it is even sex—just power and control."

"That bastard. No wonder you hate him. But you know rape usually isn't sexual and many times the rapist can't complete the act. But did you press charges?"

"No. I hate the guy and will never forgive him. But after all these years he would just laugh and beat the rap. Don't worry, he'll get his just dessert. I'm working on that for sure! Someday he'll feel just as helpless and betrayed as I did."

Pushing him flat on the bed and rising up over him Teddy said: "Now do you see how awful it is and how frightened I was of you tonight. I know you despise and hate me, and you can just get up and leave right now and never see me again."

Bubba tenderly said: "Teddy, you're just super. We've all had problems. I'm sorry this has been so bad for you, but I can't tell you how much I appreciate your sharing it with me. It brings us closer, and all I want to do is help. What can I do?"

"Goodness" she said, "thank you my gentle knight in shining amour. You are beginning to restore my faith in myself, and I don't feel so dirty and worthless anymore."

Bubba, rolling over in bed and pushing her backwards, began to kiss various tender spots evoking moans and words of encouragement. After a few minutes Teddy erupted, pushed him back flat, and said: "It's my turn now. I want to run things up and down this flagpole and see if I can get a salute."

"Oh," groaned Bubba, "more like a 21-gun salute."

"Well," purred Teddy, "make that one at a time."

Wednesday, 4:10 am

Bubba awoke, entangled with Teddy, and bursting for a toilet. Afterward he was thirsty for some ice water, and wandered until he found the kitchen. Ice water was easy, there was even champagne in the refrigerator, but he kept bumping into all the gadgets in the kitchen. He wondered if the old man practiced alchemy, and reminded himself to ask Teddy in the morning what the maestro-rapist-father-in-law was cooking up.

Bubba awoke about 6 am with the sunlight streaming into the room. Stumbling about he closed the plantation shutters and returned to bed, initially for sleep, but Teddy stirred when he wrapped himself about her and soon sleep was not on the agenda.

When they both arose about 8:20 am, they soon were smiling and playing with each other in a carefree way. "Thank you," said Teddy. "You've done so much to make me feel more at home with myself."

"My luscious wonderful lady," replied Bubba, kissing her nose and licking down her chin to her chest, "don't you ever thank me for what you gave me—the most thrilling and satisfying night of my life. I know you must have been using all your acting talents some of those times."

"Bite your tongue masterful sir," said Teddy, while licking his left nipple. "Everything was genuine from my side." Soon lips were too busy for meaningful conversation, but the moans of pleasure were convincing.

About 9:15 am they finally arose and showered. While dressing Bubba said: "I'd go fix you some of my famous hash browns and sausage, but I'd be afraid some of that nuclear warfare stuff in the kitchen would get me."

"Don't be silly," replied Teddy playfully. "My father-in-law seems to be a natural foods freak and he wants to live forever. He uses one herb or another every day in various potions. The still is for *eau de vie*, essence of fermented fruit like Poire Guillaume or framboise."

"Well if you do make an atomic bomb in there," added Bubba, "just take it someplace else before you explode it. My poor town has survived pirates, Indians, smallpox, Yellow Fever, redcoats, hurricanes, tornadoes, Yankees, reconstruction, the collapse of cotton, and even the current invasion by rich people from 'off', but I don't think a nuke would fit in with the oaks and magnolias. Although, last night, I did wonder if you had nuked me a few times."

"I've got to get to theater and get to work," said Teddy as she put on a pair of tight-fitting black slacks that fit devotedly and a loose white silk blouse and tied an Hermes scarf in her hair.

"I hope you didn't put on that bra to keep me away," chided Bubba.

"I bet you'd just rip it off," smiled Teddy. "Actually, Bubba, I'm afraid of the maestro. He's been acting so crazy and has been so violent. I just want to keep away from him and vice versa."

"Would you like me to lean on him a little" offered Bubba.

"Oh, Bubba. That sounds great, and in truth I think your presence, just for a short time, might help. I hope he doesn't come back for a few days. His assistant conductor has been doing the rehearsals. He wants to work with the new soprano and finish rescoring some of the arias for her. Maybe she'll give in to his advances, then we'll never see him."

"Why don't you come stay with me?" asked Bubba. "You know my place isn't much, but the Ashley House overlooks Charleston, the medical university, and the Ashley River. You saw that I connected up a two-bedroom apartment with a one-bedroom and so there's plenty of space, two large living rooms, and balconies out in two directions. The breeze is great. The building is nice and secure and there's plenty of parking. It is mostly filled with medical folks from the university next door and some retirees."

"I really don't want to impose," said Teddy. "Let me think about it. I do need to move somewhere. I'll check in at the theater and see if Spoleto management has found me a new home."

"Well, just call me if you want to move in," said Bubba. "I've got an extra key and a red carpet for you."

fifteen

Hollow-Ground Mystery

ednesday, 9:30 am

M.E. was embarrassed to be a little late for work. Dr. Bill McCord and Dr. Dirk Gadsden were both eager to see her. She called in Bill first and he was grinning ear to ear. "I think you were right and I was wrong about those two possible puncture wounds on the actor's foot. Come look at this. Lieutenant Rhett and his crew found this at the theater."

M.E. examined the plastic evidence bag with a tiny metal object in it. Not very impressive she thought.

"Actually, another actor got this stuck in his sandal during the performance. He threw it in the trash and the police recovered it. I've studied it under the scanning microscope and I think it is a 20-gauge thin-walled hypodermic needle, cut off. The outer diameter is pretty uniform at 0.95 millimeters, about 1/27th of an inch. It is 9.3 mm long, about one-third of an inch, and one end is tapered and hollow ground just like the 20-gauge needles we use. The back end is crimped shut. Take a look through the microscope. I've put one of the usual 20-gauge needles on the microscope platform for comparison."

"Well, that can't be too unusual," replied M.E. looking through the microscope. On the left was a regular hypodermic needle with a plastic hub. On the right was this recovered tube, about the same diameter, with a hollowground point that looked like the needle but a crimped shut hub. "Remember the victim was diabetic."

"Yes, but this is much too big a needle for insulin. The insulin pens he used, with the cartridges of Lilly insulins, had 30-gauge thin needles, much smaller and almost invisible. You can't even feel those tiny needles."

"Well, couldn't he have used this needle to inject heroin or cocaine? Or maybe he needed glucagon for hypoglycemia. Or perhaps it has been lying around for days. The stagehands might have used this needle to inject some prop or as a thumbtack. I use syringes and needles to inject booze into fruit or wine into meat," said M.E.

"Could be, but this needle, the holes in the kid's foot, and the footpiece of the cross may all fit together," said Bill grinning like a Cheshire cat.

"OK. Enlighten me."

"I've a theory, but it sounds crazy," said Bill, tentatively.

"OK, let 'er rip."

He handed M.E. a triangular block of wood, about 8 inches on each side, and announced it was the footpiece of the cross. "Lieutenant Rhett said the stage crew had complained that the victim had demanded lots of adjustments, up and down. You can see all the holes in the back that fastened it to the cross. And there are lots of splinters. But look at the holes on the front slope where his feet would have been."

M.E. took the magnifying glass and scanned the surface. At 6X the surface was uneven and there were several holes. "I see several holes. So what?"

"There are several holes with smooth sides that I think are from nails." Bill pointed out one of them with his pencil. "But look at these two holes," pointing out two others. "They have grooves on the inside and look like they would have been drilled."

"Couldn't that have been part of building this?"

"Perhaps, but the holes are just 12.3 mm apart, exactly the distance between the two wounds we found on the actor's foot. Finally, if you suppose the foot were placed like this (demonstrating with his hand) on the footpiece, the holes would line up perfectly with the wounds. QED," he added with a big smile.

"Terrific," complimented M.E. "That is good work. But how do two tiny needle wounds in his foot contribute to his death? Did someone stop his heart with some poison? Did he get excess insulin that way?"

"Bear with me," asked Bill eagerly. "The inner diameter of the needle is 0.8 mm so the void volume of a needle this length would be about four thousandths of a cubic centimeter. That would contain up to 4 mg of material. By the way, I've measured the depth of the hole and the needle would protrude just 4 mm or about one-quarter of an inch. It would hardly be seen on this roughened surface with some splinters. You might even cover it with some makeup and there is on the edge of each hole some wood-colored material that scrapes off. If you stepped on it, you could drive the needle into your skin. It could deliver a milligram or so of something. That much insulin would be trivial, but there must be more potent poisons. And don't forget we only have one sharp object but there are two holes. That might mean twice the dose."

"Bill, don't misunderstand me. What you've done is super. I can't wait for you to present it to Pathology Grand Rounds. But something is miss-ing. What's the poison? There're only a few poisons that would kill within minutes and even fewer that would have a lethal dose of a milligrams. I guess it could be a potent muscle relaxant like curare that would paralyze him. I'd bet on saxitoxin."

"Isn't that the red tide stuff? When the seawater gets hot the micro-scopic plankton, dinoflagellates, bloom. When shellfish eat them the poi-son is concentrated and you get poisoned from eating the oysters or what-ever. Isn't that the basis of the "R" month story?"

"Very good. Even the CIA uses it. When Gary Powers flew the U2 over Russia, he carried a silver dollar that concealed a needle that had saxitoxin in or on it. Fortunately, he didn't use it."

"And tetrodotoxin, the puffer-fish poison, is almost the same as sax-itoxin and just as potent," added Bill. "Both block the sodium channels that allow nerve impulses to activate muscles, so both cause paralysis, though I've never heard of either being used medically."

"What else can you think of?" asked M.E.

"Cobras and kraits cause paralysis. We occasionally get an exotic snake lover who gets too close. And there are lots of poisonous scorpions and other bugs. The Gila Monster makes something that lowers blood sugar, but I'm not sure it causes hypoglycemia. Then there's botulism, but of course that's a food poisoning."

"Usually. But remember wound botulism. By injecting the poison it may take only one-thousandth the amount needed if taken by mouth. That's why the homeland security people are so concerned. You might be able to spread it through an aerosol via the lungs." M.E. thought for a few moments. What possibilities. She turned to Bill and added: "Our library has a lot of books on poisonous animals and plants. Why don't you see what you can find that looks like it might fit."

"I'll also check with our marine molecular biology group. They might know of stuff that hasn't reached the books yet."

"Bill, you just set me thinking about potency. Do you think a gene itself could be a poison? If you had a gene that led to production of a protein poison, like curare or botulinum toxin, you could just inject a few molecules of the gene and let the body make the poison. Or if someone were allergic to a protein you could force their body to make it and cause anaphylaxis. Or you could inject some oncogenes known to cause cancer, for example. Since they are normal body genes, how could you ever detect them? Or you could knock out the function of a key protective gene using a short antisense strand of RNA that is complimentary to its RNA. Think of the possibilities. Wow, we'd never be able to detect genetic poisons and the dose would be infinitesimal. It could even be given as an aerosol or spiked in a cigarette."

"Well, there is at least one more down-to-earth today-type real poison," said Bill, with a mysterious air. "And I think you might hear more about it later today."

"Which one is that?" asked M.E.

"Aconitine," said Bill proudly.

"Monkshood?" asked M.E., deflating her resident somewhat. "Dr. Peter Gazes used to use that to demonstrate cardiac arrhythmias in the laboratory. Boy do I remember that demonstration in medical school! He cut out a rabbit's heart and hung it up a Langendorff perfusion apparatus that kept it beating. Then he just touched it with a tiny amount of aconitine and it went into tachycardia and then fibrillation. It sounds like it's just a poison, but didn't I read that aconitine is used medically in some countries? Or maybe monkshood itself is in some herbal remedies?"

"You are a genius," said Bill somewhat sheepishly. "Yes, the Chinese in particular still use aconitine in liniments where it is said to relieve pain and cause tingling. But cases I found of death when the liniments were ingested or when people ate grasses that contained the Aconitium plants. I looked up the lethal dose in animals and 50% die with doses of about 0.3 milligrams per kilogram. Your actor weighed in at 53.2 kg. So in him only 15 or 20 mg could be a lethal dose of aconitine. But that's too much for our needle."

M.E. laughed. "I've got a quiz for you. Do you know the story of the

English physician who was hanged for not keeping up with the literature?"

"That's an inordinate penalty, even for our stuffy British colleagues," Bill replied.

"In the nineteenth century an English physician went to a lecture about aconitine that said there was no assay for it. He went home and poisoned his wife with it. Unbeknownst to him, an assay had been developed, it detected his poison, and he was convicted and hanged. *Voilá*— keep up with the literature!"

"I guess monkshood is just another poison mushroom," added Bill. "Remember that Amanita liver rot we saw a few years ago? The grandfather from Romania had always eaten wild mushrooms and in this batch he fed some deadly ones to his whole family. A couple died, several had liver transplants, and the rest were quite sick. The joke at the time was that there were bold mushroom hunters and old mushroom hunters but no...."

"Well," said M.E., "back to the needle. What's your plan of action?"

Bill thought for a few seconds and replied: "Three lines of investigation. First, gently rinse out the void volume of this needle and do toxicology, especially looking for the few potent rapid-acting poisons. I'll research this carefully before we start analyzing. Second, I'll contact the National Toxicology Center, the Rocky Mountain Poison Center, our Marine Biology colleagues, and the literature to be sure we have a comprehensive list of possible potent poisons. Third, when we get to look at the tissue sections of that area of the foot, we'll look for any evidence of foreign chemicals along the track. If we are lucky, very lucky, we might be able to detect a chemical in the tissue using our most sensitive assays. Or, we might be able to get an antibody that could be labeled either for *ex vivo* fluorescence of the tissue section or for an *in vitro* chemical assay for the poison."

"Good!" replied M.E. with vigor. "The only problem is we need to know what we are looking for before we use an antibody. Mass spectrometry is more general, because it will determine the molecular weight of many different chemicals. In fact the guys who figured out how to use it to analyze proteins and DNA just got the Nobel Prize."

"Do you think we have enough to use it?"

"I doubt it. It would be better to use specific antibodies if we can get them and if we can guess what the poison might be. Let's get the consults you suggested and review the literature and try to make a prioritized list of what we think the poison might be. I'm afraid the best guess still is splinters and all this is a red herring, but I must admit that your needle is very unusual. The thing that really fits is that the actor had juvenile diabetes and had almost completely numb feet. He for sure would not have felt the punctures. Remember what Bob Hope said about Ginger Rogers?"

"No, what?"

"She swallowed a pin when she was eight and didn't feel a prick until she was sixteen."

Bill laughed. He had worked hard and he thought he had impressed his boss. That was tough. M.E. might be the best looking doctor on the faculty, but she was probably also the smartest and the hardest working. He wondered if Dr. Simons would succumb to the recruiters from Hopkins, Harvard, and UCSF-Stanford. He grinned as he thought of how she'd shake up the chauvinistic egotists at Haaarvard. Then he turned to making the calls, burning up the on-line search capabilities, and getting the analytical lab to be as excited as he was, even if it were now a needle-in-a-haystack search.

M.E. walked upstairs to the analytical laboratory, bouncing with the thought of what Bill had found. He was a super resident. This would certainly make the actor's case more interesting, even if poisoning didn't pan out. Finding Dirk in his laboratory she said: "I'm sorry I'm late. I got your urgent messages."

"Aconitine," said Dirk.

"Yes, Bill McCord and I were just talking about it. Do you think that might be the stuff in that needle?"

"What needle?"

M.E. wondered what he meant. The needle was the key finding. "I thought you had talked with Bill about his finding on that actor. Isn't that why you bet we'd find aconitine in it?"

"We found it," said Dirk.

"In the needle?"

"What needle?"

"The needle Bill thinks stuck the actor," replied M.E., feeling like she was in a Three Stooges or Abbott and Costello routine.

"I don't know about that. No, aconitine is the mysterious peak in the soprano's blood assay."

"The soprano!" said M.E. startled.

"Remember I told you I was working on one peak that was present in a significant concentration but was difficult to identify?" said Dirk patiently. "We didn't have a reference peak as it is not a drug, at least not one used in the U.S. presently. I finally got a reference sample from the F.D.A.'s toxicology lab FedEx'd in this morning. After running those standards through the high precision mass spectrometer we proved that what we've got is aconitine. I found a good assay See, here it is."

M.E. picked up the reprint and found it to be: H Ohta, Y Seto, and N Tsunoda; Journal of Chromatography (Biomedical Applications) volume 691, pages 351 to 356 in 1997.

"That assay cleaned up the sample enough to get a clear reading from the mass spec. Interestingly, I can't find much of the other alkaloids, like mesaconitine, hypaconitine, and jesaconitine, that are usually in the plants like monkshood from which aconitine is extracted. The relative concentrations vary from variety to variety, from part to part, from season to season, and even with the amount of sunlight and water. There is only a tiny amount of each and I think their absence might be significant."

"I think I know what you mean," replied M.E. thoughtfully, "but tell me."

"It suggests that a purified poison was given rather than the whole mushrooms. You might make a mistake and eat a poisoned mushroom, but you wouldn't go purifying its contents to take it."

"Good. But this is so confusing," said M.E. puzzled. "Bill and I were just talking about the possibility of it being a poison that might have killed the actor. Why would the soprano have aconitine in her blood?"

"Well, I've researched that. The Chinese are using it in liniments to relieve pain and it causes paresthesias. I found one paper," handing M.E. the reprint.

She saw it was from a major Chinese journal: B Peng, HY Yang and SD Liu; Chinese Journal of Pharmaceutical Analysis, volume 15, pages 13 to 16, in November 1995.

"They report on the contents of meaconitine and hypaconitine in two traditional Chinese herbal medicines called Chuan Wu and Fu Pian. So those medicines at least would be a mixture of alkaloids, not just pure aconitine as we found in the diva."

"Great work," smiled M.E. "This is going to be important to research thoroughly. I can feel a featured paper for you to present at our national meeting. It will help you become a Fellow of the American College of Pathology. And a scholarly review of the aconitine poisons would be a great publication. But the real question is did it kill her or is it just an interesting finding?"

"I think it might have killed her," added Dirk. "I've found several papers on the effects of aconitine on the same potassium channel that is screwed up by either Seldane or quinine. Any of the three alone can cause QT prolongation and torsades de pointes or sudden death. I can't find anything published on the combination of all three, but I'll bet that it is highly lethal. Bill and I want to try that out on frog ventricles or perhaps isolated perfused rabbit hearts."

"Call Dr. Pete Gazes," M.E. replied eagerly. "Pete knows everything about the heart and pretty much everything else."

"He is great to work with. I'll phone him right away. Maybe we can publish together if he can help with some animal studies?"

"Sounds good, but let's nail down the soprano first," said M.E.

"I think she was already nailed once," smiled Dirk. "Should I go get another bassoon?"

M.E. smiled but in mock indignation added: "We'll never have an end to those jokes. We might as well start a contest."

Dirk, somewhat sheepishly, added quietly: "We already did. It's a dollar an entry and Sarah the histology technician is handling the pool. We vote next week and it's winner take all."

"Dirk, the key thing is what this means about the possibility of either an accident, as you know how much junk she was taking, or foul play. Can you quantify the amount so we have some idea of the dose? Was there any aconitine in the various liquids and liniments etc. we recovered?"

"Nope. I double checked."

"I'll ask the police to search again and see if we missed something, perhaps something just thrown away. I'll also ask them to let us test anything that might have been used to take aconitine—beverages, food, containers, and so forth."

"We didn't find any in that chalice used on stage and none in the champagne bottle," added Dirk. "With all the weird medicines she was taking, I'd bet on an accident. Without knowing the consequence she could have mixed several of her drugs and maybe added some herbal junk containing the aconitine. Of course without the help of chemistry she could have just gotten woozy and tripped over the microphone."

sixteen

Firebird Flambée

Wednesday, 7:30 pm

Augustus Hanahan was pleased. The Gaillard was not only sold-out for the Stars of the Bolshoi Ballet, they had added 112 portable chairs in the aisles and many SRO tickets. The fire marshals were unhappy, the box office staff had worked most of the night, but the disasters and replacement of the opera with this ballet had actually increased the total revenues as new patrons wanted to see the infamous opera and ballet devotees were delighted with a chance to see the Bolshoi troupe. Even the SRO ticket buyers had been forced to purchase the $100 companion ticket to the reception after the performances, for mostly donated food and inexpensive libations. Spoleto was going to be OK financially, thanks to his skillful leadership.

Hanahan prayed that this evening's hastily-put-together performance of the Stravinski ballets would not have a problem. The rehearsal this afternoon with the full orchestra had been a disaster. Areana screamed at some of the dancers in Russian and, mostly in English, at Jean-Louis' assistant conductor, a young graduate student from Dartmouth. Erik Ochsner. He had mastered the scores for the three acts, as they were from the standard repertory, but the orchestra was uneasy. The events of Friday still haunted them. Henri Vlad, in a Thomas neck collar, had rented a bassoon from New York and returned to his chair. The musicians just couldn't focus.

Rehearsals had been rough. Areana was unforgiving and very vocal. Everyone suffered her derisive comments and imperious commands. She didn't wear a red sweater or throw a chair, but Hanahan thought of Bobby Knight's famous quote that what mattered wasn't the will to win but the will to prepare to win.

The dancers were complaining about everything. Areana had demanded the best accommodations for her entire group and Hanahan had finally been able to obtain the entire fourth floor of the Frances Marion Hotel for the troupe. The hotel, reopened only a few years ago, was at the corner of Calhoun and King Streets, overlooking the parade ground of the Old Citadel. The artists could walk down King for shopping or late night snacks. The dining room of the hotel, part of the Elliott Group, was excellent and the troupe was given carte blanche. Fortunately the hotel manager was a member of the Spoleto Logistics Board and had agreed to make space by walking some reservations to other hotels or bed-and-breakfast locations at no charge to the inconvenienced travelers. Even so Areana was screaming for suites and champagne. She had demanded, and Hanahan had arranged, for the Medical University Sports Medicine orthopedists to examine each dancer who desired it and to treat them during their stay. The 3T MRI at the Medical University was humming, or rather banging, and Hanahan hated to consider the costs. To placate Areana he had even arranged for an orthopedist to sit backstage during the performance and for an ambulance to be parked near the backstage loading dock. Hanahan knew Areana was just taking advantage of the situation and hated to think of her demands next season. He had fleeting thoughts of Areana flying off the stage and onto Mr. Vlad's bassoon. She certainly had angered everyone enough that someone might throw her in Vlad's direction. He wondered if Vlad could sharpen his instrument. Oh well. Two performances, lots of tickets sold, and Areana would be history.

Chief Dan Ravenel was relieved. There had been no threats against the ballet. They still weren't sure if the threat before the play connected with the actor's demise, but it was nice to have no threats at all. Although there were many lowcountry rednecks who still thought of Russia as the evil empire, he guessed that Russians in tutus and ballet slippers didn't seem that threatening. The Chief wondered if the Bambi-hunting, re-

vival-attending, pickup-truck-with-rifle contingent might be more derisive of the putative sexual orientation of ballet artistes than of their na-
tionality. He recalled the bumper sticker he had seen last year right next to
the Confederate Battle Flag: Cure AIDS—kill a queer. Redneck intoler-
ance at its best. The ballet wouldn't be high on their list of performances
to attend, not at these prices. He smiled at the thought of some of his
fellow deer-hunters on-stage in tights.

The Chief hoped that his decision to remove the metal detectors from
the entrance to Gaillard was appropriate. With the ballet sold out, it would
have caused delay and confusion to repeat the weapons collections of Sunday. Sunday had been a scene the Chief would never forget. The audience
arrived in everything from tuxedos to jeans. Little old ladies had had to
give up the cannons in their evening bags. One banker he had observed
had a shoulder holster, a small Glock automatic tucked in his belt at the
back, an ankle holster with a small derringer, and a switch-blade knife
that must have been 9 inches long. The Chief's officers, who didn't agree
with his no-questions-asked policy, observed that there were almost as
many weapons as seats—brought to a religious play at an arts festival! The
check room, built for hats and coats, looked like the arsenal of a Ranger
battalion. No wonder they had to disarm so many Charlestonians stopped
routinely for traffic violations or in the traps for drunk driving. He knew
he would hear from his officers their familiar complaint that they should
have automatic weapons. He was sympathetic, for he knew how his heart
beat when approaching a motorist stopped for something routine. Every
now and again, all too often actually, the officer was left bleeding on the
road.

Henry Woodward escorted his children and four guests to the Spoleto
Festival Society reception room. He and the other big donors were admitted to the main-floor room for free wine and nibbles. This year, Dr. Woodward observed, the Board had provided elegant canapés, and each tray
was labeled with the restaurant that had donated them. He chose a small
delicious crab cake from the 82 Queen tray and a stuffed shrimp from the
AW Shucks tray. As usual, he drank water, foregoing the fancy bottled
kind for just give me some "Goose Creek delight," the local tap water.

Bubba was handsome in his tuxedo. Teddy Bonnet had agreed to
dinner after the performance, and after she told him she would wear red,
he had sent her a corsage of tiny old Charleston Noisette white roses from
Frampton's. Teddy had warned him that it would take her at least 30
minutes after the performance to get everything locked away, especially

because she had never worked with this ballet troupe and Areana was so demanding. But, she'd bring her dress to the theater and change after the dressing rooms had cleared out. Bubba had made reservations at Carolina's. He enjoyed the cuisine, the location behind the old Custom House was central in the historic district, and it was one of the few fine restaurants that would be open after midnight, even on a weekday during Spoleto.

Erik Ochsner was excited, heart pounding, palms sweaty. He had convinced Jean-Louis to allow him to conduct tonight. The maestro was so embroiled with the press and investors that he hadn't taken the time to study the scores. Besides, this was not one of "his" performances anyway. He had given the baton to Erik and wished him luck, saying he had to go to New York to meet with some new backers. He told Erik that the replacement soprano would be in town shortly and to be sure to rehearse version two of the score, that he had already printed last week, with the highest notes rewritten for a normal soprano voice.

Erik thought this opportunity to conduct performances was only fair as he had done all the work in assembling the orchestra and conducting many of the rehearsals. Some of the professionals had arrived early, but the graduate students that filled in most of the chairs had been able to come only as their semesters ended. Under the best of circumstances they were shoehorned into the orchestra pit and were really comfortable only when on-stage accompanying the Westminster Choir. At least that had gone very well and the San Francisco Ballet had been excellent. The rush rehearsals for three new pieces, added at the last minute, should not have troubled such a skilled cadre of musicians, but the circumstances of the two tragedies were weighing heavily on everyone. Thank goodness Pilate's Choice had not been a musical. Erik mused what dance routine could have added to the crucifixion scene or perhaps when Christ popped out of the tomb they could have done the Surprise Symphony. Or the ragtime theme of The Sting would have gone good with the third act.

After a disastrous dress rehearsal, with that Russian shrew screaming at everyone, Erik prayed that his debut on a Spoleto podium would not draw too much criticism from the reviewers. Usually the festival got only a footnote in the news from major cities, but after the two Spoleto disasters already the TV news crews had the satellite uplink trucks parked all around the Gaillard, reporters were in the audience from major cities in the South as well as New York, and to Erik it looked like a Super Bowl. Even so, he was secretly a little disappointed. The press had interviewed everyone in Charleston, it seemed. Henri Vlad had told the story of his bassoon a hundred times, tearfully, as instructed by his attorney. But no one had interviewed the assistant conductor.

Wednesday, 7:57 pm

Areana was screaming at Teddy Bonnet in Russian. The "producer" had misplaced some of the costumes she was supposed to get cleaned, including Areana's favorite red toe-shoes for tonight's performance. Areana had learned that when this officious bitch interfered, she could get rid of her easiest by ridiculing her in Russian so the dancers laughed. Teddy would turn red and stomp away. Areana ran her troupe. What did this stupid youngster with her big tits know about producing ballet? Areana was especially jealous that Teddy had made friends with some of her dancers by giving them herbs or liniments for their aches. To Areana, pain was the constant companion of dance, and a real artiste learned to live with it. Areana would appear as the star of the third ballet, a shortened version of the Firebird she loved, and rehearsal had made her feet hurt more than usual. Perhaps she would try one of Teddy's concoctions. She wasn't really worried that much about the shoes that were lost, she had several other pairs, but for a special performance she really wanted her favorites which that id-i-ot! had lost.

The playbills for the added performances, hastily printed to describe the ballet along with the usual Spoleto advertising, glowed with Areana's descriptions of the brilliant careers of the dancers. Each had won acclaim on stages from the Bolshoi itself to theaters from St. Petersburg to Kiev, Tashkent, and Ulan Bator. All had toured extensively. It was quite an impressive troupe, at least in the program.

Wednesday, 8:00 pm

The audience eagerly awaited the curtain. The orchestra was still warming up. In the third row near the center were two resplendent Spoleto board members. Drayton Hastie Geer, MD, said to his gorgeous young third wife, Chenille: "Remember two years ago when that group of laborers in jeans and boots stomped all over the stage to rap music," Shotzie, as she liked to be called, didn't know much about ballet, but used all her knowledge to reply: "Honeybunch, I wasn't with you that year, remember," as she reached over and massaged his thigh. She bent close to his ear, tongued it briefly, and whispered: "Let's wear just our hunting boots to-night and play like we're in a blind. Do you want me to get your big gun loaded?" Dr. Geer flushed and forgot the ballet altogether. He looked at his wife's slim legs and short skirt, and remembered she had refused to wear underwear tonight, even to the Gaillard. He moved the program to cover his lap. In the four months since their marriage, and during the year before while he was also sharing his aging passion with his second wife, his office nurse, and an occasional seductive patient, he had reached a level of performance he never dreamed possible. He hoped the Viagra effects, even if it made his vision blue, would continue so he could keep Shotzie satisfied at home, as she made no secret of her needs. At least he had outgrown his tendency to mimic his name.

His cousin, Mary-Ann Drayton settled in her seat, arranged her small leather notebook, and selected her "Mozart" Mont Blanc pen from her leather pen-case. Its petite size just fitted her hand and she liked the medium point and smooth flow of the green ink that distinguished her notes. Ever since the Mont Blanc boutique opened next to the old Riviera Theater she had found it was her crack house, and now she had more pens than fingers.

After graduating first in her class from Ashley Hall, she had been off to Radcliffe and then the Columbia School of Journalism, but things in this town didn't change that fast. Since her return she had been living on the Battery with her parents in the family home, but she was usually on the road doing free-lance articles for increasingly important publications. In the last two days, knowing she lived in the site of the now infamous "Spoletho", she had been signed up for feature or color articles by Elle, Der Stern, and the London Times. She smiled at the thought of her by-lines for this festival, and the openings they would create for future assignments.

She recorded some observations about the audience and some of the notable attendees. She knew most of the Charlestonians she had grown up with, and since her debut she had been in many of their homes. She had studied the works scheduled to be performed. Despite the hype about the troupe, she thought the shortened versions of three classic works to make up a very conservative program. She had reviewed videotapes and all the written descriptions of each planned ballet she could find in the College of Charleston library, the Charleston Municipal Library, the Charleston Library Society, and on the web. She had found some biographical information about several dancers that went beyond the public-ity bios she had been given by the Spoleto office. At least she could add some unique features to her articles.

Wednesday, 8:50 pm

At the first intermission Henry Woodward escorted his children back to the crowded Spoleto Festival Society reception room. The hors d'oeuvres had been changed. Slightly North of Broad had provided barbecued pork wrapped in collard greens and their companion restaurant, Slightly up the Creek, had provided Shem Creek shrimp paté on toasted wonton wrappers. His daughter, 16, was getting finicky about food and watching her weight, despite running cross country for Ashley Hall. His son, 14, ate anything and played running back for the Porter-Gaud Academy. He gave each a half-glass of the California jug wines donated by Piggly Wig-gly. He drank little himself but felt that it was better that his children learned to drink responsibly than to prohibit it. Besides, Charleston had always been libertarian and he had recalled drinking in the Anchor, a bar next to the courthouse, when he was 12. Thinking of the Piggly Wiggly he pictured the house of its owner, the former Mayor Hyde's home on Murray Boulevard. The grocery store titan had added cement pigs to the front steps and decorated them for each season. They had just lost their Easter bonnets and he wondered what regalia they sported for Spoleto. Could you get a pig-sized bassoon?

He greeted John Gibbes who was reaching for another treat with his plump fingers. Gibbes, his mouth full, mumbled: "They are really ath-letes, but I hear they all have anorexia or bulimia."

"Well, I do recall that tragic death in the Boston company," said Woodward thoughtfully, "but remember that undereating seems to pro-long life, not just in rodents but also in those NIH monkeys."

"Ha," said Gibbes while chewing on some paté, "if I had a tail and lived in a cage I might live longer too, but who wants to. Remember Sporting Life's song at the end of the first act of Porgy and Bess: 'Methuselah lived 900 years…but who wants to if no gal will give in to no man what's 900 years.'" Drinking a deep draught of red wine he added, pointing at Woodward's chest: "Just remember that wine every day keeps the doctor away." Woodward politely eased away and back to his guests as the buzzer, which he always thought sounded like a cheap doorbell, warned that the second act was about to begin.

The second act was a delight, but at the second intermission, Woodward was accosted by a reporter from the Atlanta Constitution who had been told that he was responsible for the coroner's office. "Nope," he explained. "The Charleston County Coroner is an elected office and it is N. Ecru Filio. Mr. Filio holds inquests and files legal opinions on certain deaths. Our Department of Pathology has a Forensic Pathology division which includes the Medical Examiner, Dr. Mary Elizabeth Simons. She is appointed, not elected, and serves as the scientific and medical investigator for the Coroner."

"Well, what can you tell my readers?" the reporter asked.

"Dr. Simons is working diligently but these things take time," Woodward replied. "Mr. Filio and Chief Ravenel have reported that the preliminary postmortem examinations have shown Ms Kassandrá to have died of accidental trauma and that the actor playing Jesus Christ appears to have died of suffocation possibly related to hypoglycemia—he was a diabetic you know."

"But surely these are not just accidents," pushed the reporter. "When have two performers died so dramatically within three days of each other on the same stage?"

"It is shocking," said Woodward calmly, "but accidents happen. There is no evidence of foul play. We don't yet understand Monday's death, but we do know that in crucifixions the mode of death was suffocation. When you are suspended from the wrists, the chest sags forward rotating the arms backwards relative to the ribs. That makes it much harder to use the accessory muscles of respiration. And if the chin rests on the sternum, as it was observed to do in this case, it tends to close the windpipe and increase resistance to airflow. It is the position that is critical. The Romans learned to speed things up by breaking the legs of the condemned so they would sag faster."

"Sort of like the soprano's pendulous breasts?" asked the reporter.

"I wouldn't have used that simile," retorted Woodward.

"But why couldn't the actor just stand up on the footpiece?"

"My understanding is that the footpiece was placed fairly low and perhaps didn't offer enough support."

"Ah," beamed the reporter. "The death was caused by improper construction of the props, endangering the actors."

"No," said Woodward sternly. "Everything probably would have been safe but the actor was a juvenile diabetic and relatively weak."

"So, the management was irresponsible in allowing a cripple to endanger himself by starring in such a dangerous show!"

"Look," replied Woodard irritably. "There is no fault here. The actor was experienced and had not had a problem in rehearsals. He wasn't the star. Actually he had a very brief role. It would be unseemly, if not illegal, to deny him a role because of his illness. I was told that he and his family threatened to sue if he were not allowed to perform. I think the young actor was straining for realism during the performance and let himself hang more than had been practiced in rehearsal. As he breathed less than usual he may have gotten sleepy, and more relaxed, and sagged more, until he passed out. In rehearsals he would have tensed his muscles and kept himself more erect. Were you at the performance?"

"No, I just arrived today. My editor didn't plan to cover the festival until yesterday's breaking news. Now everyone is covering 'Spoletho.' Even Vegas is posting odds on the next death. So the actor died because his uncaring family pushed him to perform despite the obvious huge dangers."

Woodward, exasperated, spoke forcefully: "Look, you are inventing things. These are accidents. No one did anything wrong!"

"Well, I doubt the actor's parents expected him to die so gruesomely at Spoletho. Who is going to die next, Professor? Vegas has it at 5 to 3 that someone will die tonight."

"I am sure we've seen the last accident," replied Woodward sternly. "In twenty-five years we've had some sore throats, hoarseness, sprains, and one broken ankle I've been told. Remember, that is with at least 5000 performances of various kinds and probably 25,000 performers. So, enjoy the performances. Write about the history of Spoleto and our marvelous town and the great restaurants and the fun you can have. But stop focusing on the tragic accidents."

"Doc, you just don't seem to know what sells papers."

The buzzer sounded, and Woodward, relieved, excused himself to shepherd his clan back to the first row. Sensationalist idiots, he thought. It is bad enough when the reporters are too lazy to learn science and report that cancer is cured when the first mouse lives. No wonder our news is of suspect reliability.

The audience was gradually reseated. Erik strode to the podium under the highlight of two spotlights in the ceiling and accepted his applause. His baton raised, each musician focuses on him as he signaled the beginning of the stirring, and challenging, music of The Firebird.

Areana, tense backstage, took several deep breaths. In the last few years her legs had lost some of their strength, despite her constant exercises. At least she was well rested. Teddy had found her toe-shoes, at the last minute. Areana decided to try some new liniment, even though it was dark brown and smelled bad, and covered her feet and ankles with it. She loved this costume. The red tights with the sparkles highlighted her gorgeous legs. The red costume with the golden bird headdress was spectacular and showed off her still-slim figure. She would use all her artistry with dramatic movements tonight to compensate for a loss of her most athletic leaps. As the liniment began to make her feet tingle she wondered if it would work between her legs. She thought lasciviously of recent conquests, especially of Jean-Louis who sprang to life like a young buck when she had acrobatically taught him a dozen new positions. Of his many promises those nights, he hadn't kept even one and then he'd thrown her out for a second-rate trumpet player whom he said had great lips. But she was already plotting her revenge.

The audience was transfixed. The reporters were furiously writing reviews that would call the performance brilliant—three vignettes of the best Russian works by a company of stars. The financial guarantors of this tour would be very happy when they read the reviews tomorrow. Areana was brilliant. She seemed every bit a little bird, lithe, expressive, moving always with every subtle tone of the music. The large orchestra filled the Gaillard with grand sounds, playing almost flawlessly to the ears of all but the most musically-trained reporters. Only the most crass would suggest that all the bassoon lacked was a soprano voice.

As the finale approached, Areana's performance became even more dramatic. She seemed to be quivering all over. Her arms and legs fluttered, just like a bird. What masterful muscle control. Then, as the climax began to build for her death, she fell to the stage rigidly and her arms and legs beat rhythmically in time with the score, the red feathers on her costume quivering dramatically. As the music swelled to a close, she continued shaking and the curtain swept closed. The audience arose in a burst of applause. Many turned to their companions and thanked heavens that this beautiful classic performance had replaced that beastly opera. John Gibbes turned to his long-suffering wife and pronounced: "That is more like it. None of that 'modern dance' crap. Just classic ballet with gorgeous music. You'll never get me to another of those stupid rap music things with the horrid lyrics and three so-called musicians beating on guitars." His wife just smiled, knowingly, and replied: "Yes dear." She knew he would insist on going to any performance with nearly-naked women who jiggled. Too bad he wouldn't get as excited when they were home naked in bed.

Wednesday, 10:25 pm

Buck Cathcart, the orthopedist standing by in the wings, was the first to react. As the curtain closed and Areana remained supine with her arms jerking rhythmically, he realized she was having a seizure and raced to her side. Her teeth were clenched, she was blue, both eyes were deviated to the right, and he noted that her right arm and leg were having more vigorous clonic contractions than the other side. He slipped his pocketknife out and wedged it between her back teeth, fearing that he had loosened at least one tooth. Her tongue was dark blue. Her carotid pulse was booming at about 170 beats per minute, but he also felt some premature beats and one run of about 10 or 12 very fast beats. He bent to try mouth-to-mouth but could not move much air into her rigid chest and was almost overcome by the garlic odor. By then his colleague from Sports Medicine, Kirk McLeod, was at his side with the emergency kit they had brought. Kirk announced: "We have lots of pain killers and muscle relaxants and oral benzodiazepines, but I only put in one syringe of Valium and no Dilantin or other anticonvulsants."

"Give the Valium," ordered Buck between attempts at mouth-to-mouth, "and make sure it is IV." Kirk couldn't get to her neck so he reached under her costume and pulled down her tights. He opened the foil package of disinfectant and swabbed her groin, felt for the femoral arterial pulse and jabbed the long needle all the way in just at the tips of his fingers. As he pulled back the plunger, blood rushed into the syringe, and he injected the full amount and withdrew the needle. "Where is that paramedic crew?" Buck barked. "Tell them to bring their medicine kit."

Soon the paramedics arrived with large black metal bags. They popped open the triangular tops and inside were many syringes, tourniquets, and IV infusion supplies. Buck ordered the paramedics to start an IV and hand him some more IV Valium. The chief paramedic, a middle-aged bearded white man with a beer gut announced: "We're in charge hare, 'doctor,' until we get 'our' patient to 'your' hospital. You'all skedoodle."

Buck stood to his full six foot five inch height and all 240 muscular pounds of him shook as he bellowed, pounding on the paramedic's chest with an extended index finger: "You pull any of that craapp with me, boy, and I'll pound your arse into a pile of pain. Now hand me that IV and get out of my way or I'll rip off your balls and shove them up your nose."

The paramedic, paralyzed, meekly handed the intravenous catheter to Dr. Cathcart. Turning to his female compatriot he announced: "Go get the police. He can't do that. Did you hear him? I'm not giving him anything else from our supplies. And I'll sue him for assault."

Kirk had gotten the catheter into the femoral vein and as blood began to drip out he turned to the paramedic's cases and started extracting a bag of IV fluid and the tubing. The chief paramedic stepped forward and said: "You can't steal our supplies. I'll see you in jail." Kirk calmly assembled the IV, gave the paramedic a look that could melt steel, and said firmly: "Get ready to transport and call the MUSC Trauma Center. Now! Go get that gurney!"

Buck tried to achieve ventilation with the Ambu bag and mask from the paramedics supplies. He hooked the valve to the green plastic tube leading to the small green oxygen cylinder set to "flush." Then he asked Kirk for a small laryngoscope and an endotracheal tube. Kirk grabbed the paramedic's bag and found a 6.5 mm clear plastic endotracheal tube with the proper white plastic connector on it and, rooting around, a #3 MacIntosh curved laryngoscope blade. He clipped the blade's C-shaped connector over the pin on the battery handle, snapped it open to a 90-degree angle, and handed it to Buck. Then he inserted a stiff copper guide wire into the endotracheal tube. Buck tried to pull back the dancer's head and asked Kirk for help when he couldn't move it. Her breathing was becoming noisier and strained. "Her neck muscles are in spasm. Her jaw is locked shut and I don't think I can get down to her cords without breaking out some teeth. Let's do a tracheostomy as that stridor is getting worse."

Buck heard a soft voice offering help and looked up to see a tall slender gray-haired man bending forward. Recognizing the distinguished anesthesiologist, Jack Gatgounis, MD PhD, Buck breathed a sigh of relief and handed Gatgounis the scope and tube. Buck always asked for Gatgounis on his most difficult patients as he was reputed to be the best gas-passer at the medical school. He quickly briefed Gatgounis on the situation.

Gatgounis, kneeling on the left of Areana's head, cradled her neck with his left hand, and seeing that the nasal septum deviated to the right, gently slipped the lubricated tube into her left nostril and aimed it straight back. It took a little pressure to make the bend at the back of the throat and turn toward the larynx. He put his right ear to the end of the tube as he advanced it gently while moving her head up and down. He frowned several times, pulled the tube back and forth as he listened for breath sounds, and then smiled as he pressed harder and the tube slipped through the larynx. He grabbed the Ambu bag, fitted the valve to the endotracheal tube connector, and a squeezed some air down the tube while watching the chest. He inflated the balloon to seal the trachea and prevent air leak. "Buck," he asked, "listen to her chest." Buck ripped open the front of the beautiful red costume and pressed his ear first to the right and then to the left of her small breasts as Dr. Jack compressed the bag. Buck announced: "The tube is in her chest and the breath sounds are equal."

"Get me some tape," asked Dr. Jack, and Kirk rooted through the paramedics' bags and emerged with a roll of one-inch white adhesive tape. "Thanks," replied Dr. Jack, taping around the tube twice and then circling her head. "That should keep it in place, but we need to be careful transporting her. Her pulse is very erratic but strong and I can get some air into her. Her tongue is a little less blue. But she is still seizing. Alert the Trauma Center that we've got a status epilepticus and may need hypothermia and muscle relaxants as well as anticonvulsants when we arrive. We can always stop her seizures with general anesthesia." Buck was concerned that they had already given her two syringes of Valium, 10 mg each, and it hadn't diminished her seizures.

Buck turned to the paramedics and told them to put her on the stretcher. Dr. Jack bellowed out: "Does anyone know this dancer? Has she been sick? Does she take any medicines? She certainly uses a lot of garlic—like a Korean." Kirk, Buck, and the female paramedic lifted the dancer onto the Gurney as Dr. Jack stabilized her head and continued furiously compressing the Ambu bag.

In a ballet as coordinated as the one on stage, the three doctors and the female paramedic surrounded the Gurney, lifted it to its full height, and rushed it to the door to the loading dock. There they collapsed the Gurney again, lifted it into the ambulance, and with Dr. Jack at the head and Kirk crowded beside the dancer, the female attendant leaped into the driver's seat, turned on the flashers and siren, and bolted away.

Left behind, Buck started looking for someone who knew Areana's medical history. One of the dancers came forward and told Buck in halting English: "Areana had the seizure sickness. She takes pills for it I think. But I never saw her have a seizure before, even during the most difficult rehearsals and performances. She drives herself even harder than she drives all of us."

Buck accompanied the dancer to Areana's dressing room, and found several pill bottles. He pulled out his cellular phone, called the MUSC Trauma Center, and got Kirk whom he told about the history of epilepsy. "I've got one bottle of Dilantin with about 30 pills left and a label that says take two 100-mg capsules twice a day. It was dated four weeks ago so if this is her only bottle she has probably been taking less than half the prescribed dose. One other bottle is for Tegretol-XR, the extended release form. These are 400 mg, to take one twice a day, and they were prescribed on the same day as the Dilantin and about 50 are missing from the bottle. I don't see anything else here, but I'll make sure the police search her hotel room."

Wednesday, 10:55 pm

Chief Ravenel had assumed command behind the curtain. The ballet was over and he told his officers to ensure that the audience went down-stairs to the reception and to reassure anyone with questions. He told them to say nothing specific to the reporters. He radioed for Lt. Rhett to come to the scene and meanwhile assigned three officers to interrogate all the performers and backstage staff about the dancer, her health, and what might have happened.

When Lt. Rhett arrived, the Chief called him over, explained what happened, and said: "Bubba, there is something fishy here. I don't know what it is, but three accidents in five days is impossible. We're gonna have to call in all our troops, pay the overtime, and really jump on this. Have you found out anything suspicious about the singer and Christ?"

"I just left M.E. this afternoon, Chief, and things looked pretty clean. The actor was a diabetic on insulin and she found a number of injection sites in the thighs, abdomen, and shoulders as you'd expect. The only funny thing was she found two injection sites in the sole of his right foot that seemed strange to her. She showed me the photographs and there were two little holes just like a snake bite. She told me they were working on those."

"Did the actor have any tracks from drugs?" asked the Chief. "We've seen them inject junk in the toe webs, under the penis, over the collar bone. I don't think I've ever heard of injecting drugs into the soles of the foot, though."

"Nope," replied Bubba. "Nothing that looked like drugs. We checked all the insulin bottles and syringes in his dressing room and apartment. They'll analyze them, but they look OK to me. Besides, the actor was barefoot on stage and the footpiece on the cross was roughened with a rasp to give more traction. I think it could be he just got a couple of splinters and maybe he had diabetic coma. But M.E. said she'd analyze the tissue blocks containing the puncture sites."

"How about the singer? Anything new?"

"M.E. said they were considering the possibility of heart irregularity making the singer wobble off the stage. She said they had found a third agent that could add to the others and they were working it up. You know, Chief, the soprano to me looked like a top—all that weight balanced on tiny feet and high heels. I think she just got dazed by the effort and the lights, unfortunately tripped on that stage mike, and just happened to fall on the wrong instrument. She could have bounced off the timpani or slid down the double basses. She could have chosen a flute or a saxophone. But nnooooo, she had to fall on the only sharp stick in the whole darn band. Mr. Vlad told me that had he been playing it she wouldn't have been impaled, but it was sitting rigid in a support while he had switched to contrabassoon."

"Well, what do you think about tonight?" asked the Chief. "Do you think one of our duck hunters brought down the Fire Bird or maybe she got into some bad birdseed?"

Just as Bubba was about to answer, the Chief noticed Buck hurrying over with a dancer in tow. The Chief seemed relieved to hear that Areana had a history of seizures and that they had found two bottles of anticonvulsants in her dressing room. Bubba thought of the other evidence to collect, before it got messed up, and told the Chief he'd like to take a Russian-speaking dancer and go to Areana's hotel suite. "I've heard these dancers often use speed and other amphetamines to stay slim and perhaps to get up for a performance. Doctor, won't cocaine also cause seizures?"

"Yep," replied Buck, "but the key thing now is to find out what drugs she has been taking. If she is on Dilantin and we give her more of it, the overdose can also cause seizures. No one here knows of her having any other illness like West Nile encephalitis or head injuries."

Wednesday, 11:15 pm

In the Trauma Center they were having difficulty with Areana. Kirk briefed the Emergency Room attending and gave a nurse the tubes of blood he had drawn and asked her to send them stat for anticonvulsant concentrations, drug screen, and all the routine tests including the muscle enzymes like CK and aldolase. Despite large doses of intravenous Valium her seizures continued and her rectal temperature, first measured at 39.7C, was rising. They packed her in ice, massaged her limbs vigorously, gave her Pavulon to paralyze her, and finally were able to get her oxygen saturation up to 82% on 100% oxygen in the respirator.

Kirk listened to her lungs and announced: "I'm afraid she has aspirated stomach contents or has pulmonary edema from the seizures. We'll have to watch out for heat stroke with prolonged seizures. Her stomach is almost empty, but we've sent off what we got to the lab for a tox screen. Even if she can't move, her brain might be seizing and using up oxygen. We could use a better EEG than we can get here, and I called neurology to help evaluate her. Maybe they will admit her to the Neuro ICU."

Bubba and the dancer searched Areana's suite and found no more prescription drug bottles, but some over-the-counter ipecac, Tylenol, Advil, aspirin, and many herbal medicines, some with no label, and salves, lotions, liniments, and other creams from many cities around the world. Some bottles had labels in what looked like Chinese or Japanese or Korean and others in an Arabic script. "Looks like a drug store," said Bubba, "or rather a health food store. Goodness knows what these are. I'll take them to the hospital and see if the pharmacists or some of the foreign physicians can translate. I hope she didn't take any of that gas the Russians used on the Chechen rebels and their hostages in that Moscow theater."

Bubba gathered up the bottles in an evidence bag and properly signed it. He knew it might just be an accidental seizure, but the Chief would expect him to do an exemplary job and the publicity would be terrible. Three actors in a week. At that rate no one would perform at Gaillard again.

Bubba had asked the dancer to search for any medical records or personal papers. She reported that she found a Russian passport, some receipts, but nothing that looked medical or personal. "How are we going to find her relatives?" asked Bubba.

The dancer answered: "We were required to fill out a long form about our family and emergency contacts and health insurance and things when we came to this country. Someone in the company must have them. I'll ask our manager."

"Wait a second," said Bubba. He pulled out his police radio, contacted his team at the scene, and told them what he wanted. He handed the radio to the dancer: "Just talk in here like a phone and my colleagues will find whomever you wish and let you talk with them. Since you speak the language, perhaps you can work with my friends to try to talk with relatives or doctors in Russia to find out more of her medical history."

"Well, I'll try," replied the dancer demurely. "But I only speak Russian and a little Ukrainian. Unlike your country with one language, my country has dozens."

Bubba winked: "You've never heard our Gullah. And when folks from Noooo Joisey come down here we think they are talking Russian."

Wednesday, 11:55 pm

Areana had been moved to the Neuro ICU and they had given her large doses of intravenous phenobarbital to stop the electrical seizures in her brain. She was paralyzed and on a ventilator. Her core temperature had peaked at 43.9 centigrade, almost 111 Fahrenheit, but fell rapidly to normal in the ice bath and she was now wrapped in hypothermia blankets. She had no signs of life—her pupils were fixed and dilated, nothing moved, and nothing responded to stimuli—even pain.

The laboratory called and reported that her blood test results included Dilantin at a concentration of only 6 milligrams per liter, about one-third of therapeutic, and Tegretol at a concentration of 4 milligrams per liter, just the lower edge of what is expected with antiepileptic therapy. But, the laboratory medicine technician complained: "There is some peak that comes off the high-performance liquid chromatograph right near the Tegretol peak and makes it hard to read exactly."

The neurology resident said with a smirk: "I bet some camel jockey treating her forgot that Dilantin and Tegretol interact and you have to be careful using them together. They both are metabolized by the CYP3A4 enzyme and together they speed up each other's metabolism and have less effect."

The cardiology fellow on call suggested they control her intermittent ventricular tachycardia with bretyllium. He feared that lidocaine might worsen her seizures and quinidine, just one isomer of quinine, would inhibit the 3A4 enzyme that metabolized both anticonvulsants and further complicate things.

Over the next hour Areana's core temperature became stabilized and Charlie Strange MD and his ICU staff prevented the usual overshoot to hypothermia. Her cardiac arrhythmia was a problem but she did not have a true cardiac arrest. Her blood pressure was a little low and they had cautiously given her fluids, not wishing her brain to swell. Her EEG was flat and her BIS score was zero and she had no neurological responses— no signs of brain activity at all, but she was sedated. The ventilator robot had been adjusted to keep her blood carbon dioxide tension at 30 mm Hg, about three-fourths of normal, to help prevent brain swelling.

Joe Kurent, Professor of Neurology, walked into the Neuro ICU to take charge of the firebird. After a quick appraisal of the patient he got a more detailed description of the incident from Kirk who asked him: "How do we tell if she is dead, or brain dead? Our machines can keep her like this forever."

"Good question. We can examine the blood flow to critical areas of her brain with dynamic MRI or PET, but she is too sick right now to move her to the lab. Why don't we just control her seizures and arrhythmias for a day or so and see if she wakes up as we reduce her drug burden. If not, then we can do the special tests."

Just then Bubba arrived and was briefed as he showed Dr. Kurent the grab-bag of drugs. "Oh oh," said Kurent gravely. "There might be all kinds of things to complicate matters in there. Can you get those drugs analyzed or find out what they are?"

Bubba reassured him: "I've already got a dancer who speaks Russian working with one of my men to call everyone who can help. At least it is getting to be daylight over the pond."

"That information might be key," replied Kurent. "We need to know of any complicating drugs or herbs. Our lab already said there was some strange peak on HPLC."

"What does a peak mean?" asked Bubba.

"I'm sorry, Bubba. You know how we use jargon" replied Kurent. "The idea is to separate different chemicals in a sample and to measure how much of each is there. It is like a coin sorter at a bank that puts dimes in one roll and quarters in another. We take a gemish and put it through a long tube that separates the chemicals. It might let the small chemicals through first and the larger ones later. So out of the end of the tube comes a parade of molecules, each neatly separated. Then we use a detector to measure how much of each chemical is there. The signal from the detector is charted on paper that scrolls out of the machine so we see a series of little mountains. Each mountain peaks at a specific time, and we might know that Dilantin for example peaks at 8.3 minutes so we assume that any signal around that time is probably Dilantin. In this case they found two drugs for seizures, Tegretol and Dilantin, on the tracing, but there was an unknown signal or peak as well. Now they have to figure out what that is."

"We use the same kind of system to sniff for explosives, but it detects gases. How do they identify the unknown peak?" asked Bubba.

"The easiest way is to send the sample over to the Medical Examiner's laboratory as they have fancy instruments to measure the precise molecular weight of the chemical. As each atom weighs in at a specific weight, if you know the total weight of the whole molecule you can calculate which atoms have gone together to make it."

"Is that what M.E. called her 'mass spectrometer?'"

"Exactly. See—now you're an analytical toxicologist."

"Dr. Kurent, do you think she'll be all right?"

"Lieutenant, I have no idea. Everything looks stable now except for her runs of ventricular tachycardia. We won't know if she has had brain damage for a few days. She could be perfectly normal, but some of these severe seizure patients never wake up. And she is about as severe as I've seen."

Just as Bubba reached the door, a tall lanky nurse stopped him. Her name tag, amply supported he noted, read Betsy Gilbreth MSN. "Officer," she said tentatively. "I don't want to interfere."

Bubba smiled and said softly: "We need all the help we can get, Ms Gilbreth. What can I do for you."

"Well, I wanted you to know there is something strange," replied the nurse. "When we stripped off her clothes we found some sticky black stuff in her ballet slippers."

"What do you mean?"

The nurse led Bubba over to a paper sack of clothes and pulled out the toe shoes. She put on a glove and ran one finger around in the slippers and showed Bubba a dark colored sticky liniment-like substance. "I washed a lot of this off her feet and ankles as well."

"Did you save any of the stuff on her legs?" asked Bubba.

"I'm sorry, officer, I didn't think of it, but the four-by-four sponges I used are right there in the trash."

"What do you think this stuff is?"

"Well," said the nurse holding out her gloved finger. "It has a peculiar odor. Partly it smells like garlic—real strong. But it also smells like pipe tobacco. I know because my father smoked constantly and his whole house used to stink like this."

"Thank you so very much," Bubba said with a big smile for this lovely creature as he reached out with one large hand to gently hold her shoulder. "Have you got a plastic bag I can use to carry some of this to the laboratory? I've run out of my evidence bags."

Gilbreth smiled up at Bubba, went to the supply cabinet, and handed him two plastic bags they used to wrap biological hazards in. He put the shoes and the sponges from the trash in the same bag, put a twist on the neck, and asked Ms Gilbreth to sign her name on the outside which she did.

"You know my friends kid me that I just carry those bags so I can take home left over food from the restaurant. That may be true, but I've been using them up at a prodigious rate this week, and I haven't taken home any food yet."

Nurse Gilbreth chuckled politely.

"I may need to get a statement from you later," he said, thinking more of a candlelight dinner than an interrogation room. She beamed in reply.

Bubba asked at the nurse's station how to call the medical examiner's office. He phoned, but only a recording answered giving him an emergency number. He called it, identified himself, and aroused the resident on call, Dr. McCord. Explaining the situation he agreed to meet McCord at the laboratory in 30 minutes. He asked the nurse how to get to the Pathology Building. Going down the elevator, through the long corridor to wing B, across the bridge, and finally up the elevator again, he found the entrance marked "Medical Examiner of Charleston Analytical Toxicology Laboratories." The door was locked, and no one replied to his knocking. He waited, thinking of Ms Gilbreth, Teddy, and how bad Spoleto was going to look in the papers with a third injury. At least, he thought, this one isn't fatal…yet.

Paris Match

June 26, 1910

Igor Fyodorovich Stravinsky premiered his new ballet, The Firebird, at the Opéra last night. Commissioned by Sergei Diaghilev for his Ballets Russes, it begins the summer season. The music is challenging and fresh and the choreography superb. The sets are a little primitive but the costuming exquisite. We have come to expect unusual time signatures from Mr. Stravinsky and again he has explored the asymmetrical patterns of compound metres with unusual prolongation and elision. Mr. Diaghilev said that he had commissioned the work after hearing the symphonic poem, Fireworks, that Mr. Stravinsky had written after the death of the daughter of his teacher, Rimsky-Korsakov. The lithe Ludmilla Gnalilev danced the title role in an acrobatic display of precision and beauty. She was in perfect synchrony with the music throughout, in a stunning red costume and headdress. She must have been exhausted at the climax when she swooped to the stage fluttering convulsively. Mr. Stravinsky and his family will remain in Paris through July and then continue to London where he will conduct his works until September when they will return to St. Petersburg. He said that he was working on a new ballet, with Mr. Diaghilev, tentatively to be called Petrushka.

seventeen

Cherchez le Cigar

*T*hursday, 1:15 am

Bubba waited outside the entrance to the laboratory for Dr. McCord, the resident on call, but the first to arrive was a male technician, sleepy and in jeans and a T-shirt that read: *Stuff happens.*

When he saw Bubba he straightened up and asked: "What have you got for us that needs *stat* analysis, sir? Dr. McCord called me and asked me to come right away."

Bubba explained to the technician what had happened to the ballerina and the peculiar smelly goo they had found on her feet. Just then Bill McCord arrived. Taking a whiff of the black liniment he recoiled. "Wow, it certainly reeks of garlic and tobacco—was she afraid of vampires? Is this some Rumanian tradition?" Turning the plastic bag with the goo around in his hand McCord sniffed again. "The odor is so strong I can't be sure what is there, but we can run it through our chromatographs and that will tell us for sure. Do you want to stick around and see how we do it?"

"Sure," replied Bubba, sensitive to the fact he had just awakened these folks and would look pretty selfish if he walked off to go to sleep.

Dr. McCord showed him a row of boxes with many dials and knobs and shiny metal tubes going in and out. Some of them had little circular trays of vials sitting next to them. "We put a sample from each bottle or blood or whatever in these trays and the robots will inject just a little of each specimen into the right machine. See that box with the arm coming out and a long needle at the end? That is the robot and the computers tell it just which vial to get the sample from and which machine to inject with a precise volume. Saves us a lot of work and makes the results far more reproducible."

"But why do you have so many?" asked Bubba. "I thought the whole idea was that one test could identify hundreds or thousands of chemicals."

"You are exactly right," replied McCord, "except that each of these chromatographs is set up to measure a certain group of drugs. Each uses a different solvent, a different packing material in the column that are those thin metal tubes going in and out of the machine, and perhaps a different detector. We used to use lots of gas chromatographs that separated gases, but nowadays we mostly use liquid chromatographs that separate chemicals dissolved in a solvent. But with different conditions we can separate and then identify hundreds or thousands of compounds and certainly all the common drugs and poisons."

"Why do they call them chromatographs? Where is the color?"

"I think at the beginning they were used to study dyes so that a complex dye could be separated into its components and you could see and measure how much red, green, etc. was in the mixture. If you put a dark purple dye in at the beginning of the thin column, and then pushed it through the tube with a solvent, after a few minutes you might see a brilliant red and then later a brilliant blue, etc. as the components came out, each at their own time. I think the FBI uses that today on paint chips to see which kind of car it got chipped off of."

"So do you look for the color of the chemical as it comes out?"

"Pretty much. The detectors measure how much light the chemical absorbs. As you know if it absorbs all the blue it will look yellow. So that is one way to identify it. The other is that the time it takes for the chemical to come out of the tube is key. We pack the little column with materials that will separate the chemicals letting some go through quickly and slowing down others. Depending on the solvents, temperature, pressure, packing, etc. a given chemical will take a reproducible time to appear at the end of the column."

"So do you look up the time and that matches the chemical?"

"Sort of. The conditions change things so we run standards through the column. If aspirin comes out at 8.32 minutes then we believe that a chemical appearing at 8.32 minutes is probably aspirin but one at 7.95 minutes is not."

"Where does the mass spectrometer fit in?" Bubba asked as he watched Dr. McCord pipette a little of the goo into a small vial, add some solvent to dissolve it, shake it vigorously until it was all dissolved, and put it in hole number one on the round tray.

"Most of our chromatography detectors measure light absorption, but it could be that several chemicals will appear at about the same time and absorb the same light. To be specific about the chemical we measure its molecular weight. If we have a precise measurement, we can tell just how many atoms of various kinds make up the chemical and that is a precise identification."

A few minutes later Bubba watched with McCord as the robot sucked a little of the liquid out of vial one, injected it into one of the chromatographs, and the computer screen showed nothing yet at the detector. Over the next two minutes the computer showed a few tiny blips and just made the tracing a little uneven. Then at 2.34 minutes the tracing rose like a mountain to a peak and then fell off again. The computer screen printed out the time of the peak and then its identify: dimethylsulfoxide."

"DMSO, of course!" exclaimed McCord, "that's why the garlic smell. That stuff really stinks."

"Would that cause seizures?"

"I've not heard of that but I'll look it up. It is a horse liniment but it is such a good solvent that we use it around the lab to dissolve anything. If you dissolve a drug in it and paint it on the skin, the DMSO makes the drug penetrate through the skin and enter the blood very quickly."

"Sounds like a good way to administer drugs" suggested Bubba.

"It works, but something was wrong in human use as the FDA has never approved it. I do know some rheumatologists who compound liniments containing it just like they do for the racehorses. But it would give you a very garlicy breath."

"Oops," McCord was startled. "Look at that huge peak coming out now." The computer screen showed that at 12.17 minutes they have a very high concentration of—nicotine.

"Wow," said McCord. "That's a lot of nicotine. Why would you put that in a liniment? I think tobacco farmers get poisoned just from the tobacco rubbing their skin as they work with it."

"But if you smoke it isn't nicotine pretty safe?" asked Bubba.

"Not at all," replied McCord thoughtfully. "Nicotine is quite a poison. It works on something like 17 different receptors—chemicals in the brain and nerves that react to it. A few cigarettes are bad enough, but at really high concentrations I know it can cause seizures and muscle weakness and heart arrhythmias and probably a lot of other bad effects."

Bubba wondered about the nicotine on the ballerina's feet while McCord called Dr. Kurent in the ICU and told him of the DMSO and nicotine. He emphasized that they didn't know how much was in the blood, but he'd try to get the blood levels ASAP.

Bubba asked: "Did Dr. Kurent have any idea about the significance of these chemicals?"

"He told me he didn't think the DMSO would be a problem, but that the nicotine could cause seizures and the heart arrhythmias depending on the concentration in blood. We need the blood sample from the general chemistry laboratory and then we can measure those levels."

Thirty minutes later McCord confirmed to Bubba that her blood contained very high levels of nicotine, ten times higher than in a heavy smoker. McCord added: "It is strange that there is no cotinine, the metabolite of nicotine. In a smoker we see as much or more cotinine than nicotine. I think that means that she got a huge sudden overdose of nicotine, probably through her skin, and was not a smoker or a chronic user."

Bubba had been quiet, contemplative, but now he spoke up: "I hate to keep you up when you've been so helpful, but I'm afraid we now have an urgent police question. Where did this stuff come from? Is it in any of those jars and tubes I brought in the evidence bag? How did she happen to get it tonight? Did she give it to herself or did someone else rub that goo on her? I assume you think she would have been sick if she had done this same thing with a liniment any other night?"

"Lieutenant, I'd like to do some more research," replied Dr. McCord a little cautiously, "but I think you're right. This most likely was an unusual exposure, probably accidental. If she had never used it before, she might not have known it was toxic. Or maybe she usually used a tiny dab to do her and tonight smeared on a lot more. We can't tell if she had ever been exposed to this stuff before. If she rubbed the area it would increase absorption. Or maybe this was the first time she added DMSO. There's a limit to what the lab and I can tell you, sir."

"I know and I don't mean to ask too much, but this is really strange. We've wrecked three stars on the same stage in less than a week. Something bad is going on, and we don't have the faintest idea what is happening. We just need all the help you can give us. I sure hope the Russian wakes up. I really need to talk with her."

Thursday, 5:25 am

M.E. walked into the lab bright-eyed as though she had had a whole night's sleep. "Thanks for calling me, guys," she said happily to McCord and Dirk Gadsden who had just arrived. "This is getting too complicated. A third disaster. Maybe seizures. But you find DMSO and nicotine on her FEET? And the actor has holes in his FEET? If the soprano had just jumped feet-first she probably would have done OK. What the dickens is going on?"

Well," said McCord, "it looks like the dancer got an acute poisoning with nicotine, as well as some DMSO, probably through her feet. Her blood plasma concentration is 1.1 milligrams per liter, about ten times what you would see in a smoker. And the metabolite levels are very low, so she hasn't had the nicotine on board for very long. Looks like acute poisoning to me."

"Where did it all come from, Bill?" asked M.E.

"The goo on her legs tests out at 33% nicotine and 18% DMSO. You can get 40% pure nicotine sulfate in the insecticide Black Flag 40, except the dancer has almost pure nicotine base not the sulfate salt. I scraped off as much of the goo as I could easily get from the shoes and 4x4 sponges, under the videocamera of course, and got a total of 3.6 grams. If injected intravenously in mice, the lethal dose would be about 0.3 milligrams per kilogram or the equivalent of about 15 milligrams in this patient. She must have had at least 1,000 milligrams on her skin."

"Impressive," said M.E. "You've had a good night. Is this another good paper? If Spoleto keeps going at this rate we'll have killed off all the stars but have a year's worth of research papers. What do you think is next? Maybe someone will be hanged from a hot-air balloon at the finale or a cellist will get vigorous and impale someone with an errant bow."

"Actually," laughed Bill, "this one isn't that unusual, except for the DMSO. Nicotine poisoning is pretty common in the tobacco-growing areas like the PeeDee and where nicotine insecticides are used. Dirk and I want to run down the DMSO effect in the lab. It's very possible that she would have been OK with nicotine alone but the DMSO is what caused the excess absorption and toxicity. Maybe we could use shaved rabbits. We can measure nicotine absorption with and without DMSO and get some idea of how long it takes to get blood levels this high."

"I'll bet there is a lot of literature on that," replied M.E. "especially with the nicotine patches used for smoking cessation. Why don't you see if you can find a standard someone else has used. You know, Spoleto is going to double our usual workload. Thank goodness all we've had otherwise has been the usual routine stabbings, GSWs, and MVAs this week. Have you had time to work more on your needle-thing from the actor, Bill?"

"Dirk and I are just beginning. Very carefully using micro techniques we tried to dissolve something off the inner walls of the needle. We think we've got a protein of very high molecular weight, perhaps over 300,000. I think the only way to identify it is with an antibody, but we need to guess what is the right antibody to start with as we don't have much. We've been working on the literature and there are a number of candidates. Some of the potent poisons are not well characterized chemically, but for something that causes paralysis quickly and quietly from a small dose, like in the actor, we can really think of only one common thing."

"Botulism," said M.E.

"Exactly," replied Bill excitedly. "It would fit. If injected, as in wound botulism, the amount of poison you need is $1/1000^{th}$ of that if taken by mouth. It would act in minutes and just quietly block muscle activity, preventing acetylcholine release from nerve endings that innervate muscle, causing paralysis. Usually with botulism you get dilated pupils, dry mouth, sagging eyelids, slurred speech, staggering gait, double vision, and underventilation. I remember two elderly farmers who got it from pickled poke salad and they couldn't move for a month, but did OK in the ICU on ventilators."

"But the problem is that your needle only had a tiny volume within it, and probably most of that would be wasted and not get injected. What is the minimum lethal dose?" asked M.E.

"Ha," laughed Dirk. "Lay it on her Bill."

Bill smiled and said: "One milligram of purified botulinus toxin can kill about 30 million mice by injection and the human dose is estimated to be the amount needed to kill seven mice."

"So one four-millionth of a milligram is lethal by injection," said the amazed M.E. "That is only 0.25 picograms. I've never heard of anything that potent, except a gene. Of course the needle might not have pure poison in it but only a weak solution of it."

"Now you know why no one has found it by chemical assay of the blood and bodily fluids," said Dirk. "Immunoassay can find it in food or in gut contents. Frankly the best test is to protect mice with antibodies and then inject them with the test substance. The CDC uses separate antitoxins to the type A, B, and E toxins and if you protect one mouse with each and inject them all, the one that lives tells you the strain of botulism from the antibody you protected it with."

"Are those three strains the only ones to worry about?" asks M.E.

"Not entirely," says Bill. "There have been cases of D and F, but they are very rare in spontaneous intoxications. If a terrorist grew up some Clostridium botulinum that made a weird type, like G or H, we'd never be able to detect it in the victim."

"My goodness, what a terror weapon. If Al-Qaida got one of those unusual strains for which we have no antibody, in one jar they could make enough toxin to kill millions. Now I'm more concerned about terrorism. But because of the tiny amounts we are only going to be able to do one or two tests. You better guess right on what we are dealing with or we'll never know."

Dirk agrees: "If the CDC sends us the three antibodies as they promised, we could inoculate three mice and stick them with the needle. Or we could extract a little of the contents of the needle and inject the mice with that. If two mice die and one lives, we've identified the poison. I'm hoping the CDC will give us some toxin of each of the three major types as well as purified antibody. That way we can test the antibodies with known toxins before we test the needle itself."

"Is there any way we could avoid killing mice?"

"If we can label the antibodies with a fluorescent label we could see which antibody sticks to the needle. That would be specific if one sticks and the others don't."

"Which strain would you bet on?" asked M.E.

Bill and Dirk started talking at once. Dirk continued: "A tends to occur in the Western US, B in the East, and E in Alaska. E is rare enough I'd suggest we work up both A and B and start with one on the needle and the other on the tissue samples from around the puncture wounds."

Bill said: "I agree with the strategy, but I'm not sure how to pick which to use as this is certainly not a natural case so the geographic incidence might not be of much help."

"Let's not just focus on your needle, Bill, as exciting as it is," M.E.

said thoughtfully. "I think that's a great idea, but it may not pan out. Remember he was a diabetic injecting himself. Have you checked all his insulin supplies and syringes and needles and pens and stuff? Even the lancets he used to sample his blood sugar might be dipped in this stuff— have we found the discarded lancets he might have used?"

"We've finished checking all the insulin, syringes, pens, and used needles, M.E.," added Dirk, "and nothing funny is there. Now I admit we might not be able to find a tiny amount of botulinus toxin, and I wasn't even thinking of that when I did the assays. I'll go back and check again for a high-molecular-weight protein. And the lancets are a good idea and I'll check them. I don't think botulism would grow in insulin, but of course someone could spike his drugs. But, why would anyone want to kill this young actor? Do we know if he had angered anyone?"

"Who knows? We just don't know enough about what is going on. For the moment, suspect everyone and everything. I'll alert Chief Ravenel and the coroner that we have some surprising developments," said M.E., "but as great as your discoveries are it still looks like an accident in a soprano who happened to fall in the wrong direction, hypoglycemia in a diabetic who took his insulin but didn't eat and was hung up in a strange posture, and seizures in a known epileptic who either didn't take her drugs or perhaps had their effects diminished by something stimulating their metabolism."

Thursday, 9:25 am

"Thank youall for coming," said Chief Ravenel. His guests crowded his small office, filled with crime mementos. Mayor Maybank and Augustus Hanahan took the two regular chairs and Bubba and M.E. dragged in two straight chairs from the adjoining office.

"M.E., you asked for this meeting, so why don't you lead off."

"I'm sorry to call us together, gentlemen, but we have some interest- ing findings."

"Interesting I don't need any more of," snorted Hanahan.

"I'm sorry," said M.E. "Let me add that each of these three events could be accidental. The singer probably was tired after her performance. She was old and possibly unsteady. The lights are blinding and hot, she was sweating, and probably got dehydrated. This was the first time she sang this role before a live audience. She could have stumbled over the microphone and by accident hit the bassoon. We've been looking for any other factors that might contribute. We haven't cut her brain yet, but there is no evidence so far of Parkinsonism or old stroke or a muscle disease to weaken her or make her unsteady. But her drugs are a problem. She had a low level of alcohol. By itself it shouldn't have made her unstable, but she also had a so-called 'non-sedating' antihistamine, at high dosage, and together with alcohol it might have made her a little woozy or unstable. Then there is the possibility of cardiac arrhythmia. She had both quinine and Seldane, the antihistamine, in her blood. Each by itself can cause life-threatening arrhythmias but together it is even worse. As far as we can tell she just picked up medicines from all over the world and dosed herself by the handful."

"Now for the complication. We also found a poison called aconitine in her blood. It also causes heart arrhythmias and would probably add to the problems of the other two drugs I mentioned. The confusing part is that aconitine is used in some medical preparations, really herbal remedies, in China for example. She seems to have been taking a pile of alternative medicines. We haven't found a source of aconitine yet, but it could be that she just accidentally happened to combine three things that, in combination, could have made her have a cardiac arrhythmia that made her fall into the pit. We'll never know about the arrhythmia, as there is no way to tell."

"What do you think we should do?" asked the Chief.

"I've asked Bubba to collect everything that she might have eaten or drunk from to see if we can find any aconitine. Otherwise, if we can't find the source, I think it will end up as being some medicinal preparation that got thrown away."

M.E. continued: "The second case is also confusing. What we know is that the actor was a brittle juvenile diabetic taking insulin several times a day. He had had hospital admissions for hypoglycemia and for ketoacidosis, but not recently. On the day of the play we can't find any evidence he ate after breakfast. His parents have told Bubba that they were with him intermittently and urged him to eat but he told them he was OK. They didn't see him check his blood sugar, but they did tell Bubba they saw him inject himself with an insulin pen just before the curtain. We don't have any way of knowing that dose. At autopsy he had nothing in his stomach and, best we can tell, he had not eaten for perhaps six hours or more. This all sounds like he had hypoglycemia. If when he was hanging on the cross his blood sugar went down, he could have gotten weak and with the hypoglycemia he would have sagged on the cross, his head we know had fallen down, he probably couldn't keep his airway open, and his respiratory muscles couldn't work well in that position. He could have just underventilated himself into a deeper coma and died of suffocation. At autopsy he for sure had suffocation."

"Well, did he have hypoglycemia?" asked Bubba.

"We have a problem. We can't tell," said M.E.

"What! What's wrong with your lab?" said Hanahan angrily.

"No, the problem's with Mayor Maybank's paramedics."

"What do you mean," said the Mayor defensively.

"Dr. Henry Woodward was at patientside directing the resuscitation. He was pushed aside by your paramedics, Mayor. He asked them to draw a blood sample but they refused and just injected glucose. Even if the blood sugar were low, that injection of sugar would have raised it and when he reached the hospital the blood sugar was about normal. Dr. Woodward believes that the paramedics might have compromised the care as well as the diagnosis in this case and he is furious. I'm surprised he hasn't talked with you yet."

"We have an appointment in two hours," replied the Mayor with a frown, "but I didn't know the subject. Thanks for alerting me. I'll check with my medical services director."

"Well, it looks like straight-forward if unprovable hypoglycemia. But we have a hooker here too. Actually more like a sticker."

"What do you mean M.E.," asked the Chief.

"There are two tiny puncture wounds on the actor's right foot. They line up with two holes possibly drilled into the footpiece of the cross. Bubba's colleagues were very clever in finding a tiny needle that just fits into either of the holes. This may be just a coincidence, and we don't know how long the needle was lying around on the stage, but it COULD have stuck in the actor and it COULD have injected something."

"But M.E.," asked the Mayor, "wouldn't the amount injected be tiny if there is just a needle and no syringe."

"Very good, your honor," replied M.E., "but there are some very potent poisons out there. Remember the Indians in Peru just coat their blowdarts with curare to paralyze their prey. Curare or one of its modern derivatives could cause silent paralysis and kill the actor. We are also working on the possibility of botulinus toxin, the thing that causes botulism and is in the popular cosmetic Botox. The needle Bubba found could deliver many lethal doses."

"Wow," said the Mayor, "I hope Al-Qaida doesn't find out."

"Darn," said Hanahan, "it does sound like terrorism. Does anyone think we have an international enemy doing this to Spoleto? Has anyone seen any towel-heads around town?"

Ignoring the racist comment, the Chief asked M.E.: "Are you saying this is a homicide?"

"Absolutely not," replied M.E. "I must have misspoken. We haven't found any poison. We are looking. It is just a possibility."

"Well at least the dancer is just a case of epilepsy isn't she?" asked the Mayor.

"Yes and no," replied M.E. Everyone groaned. "She was an epileptic. She was taking antiepileptic drugs—two. The amounts of those drugs were less than optimal. Yes it could be just that simple. But, like the soprano, she was taking a pot full of other drugs, prescription, over-the-counter, herbal, extemporaneous, and so forth. One of the things found in her blood was nicotine."

"So, did she smoke?" asked Hanahan, thinking of his cigars.

"There was much more nicotine than that, I'm afraid," added M.E. soberly. "And, we found it on her feet."

"Come now," said the Mayor chortling. "April Fool's Day is past. Did she hold cigars between her toes or wear tobacco-leaf slippers?"

"I'm serious," added M.E. "Dead serious. She had slathered a liniment on her ankles and feet that contained a solvent, DMSO, and lots of nicotine, possibly from an insecticide. Nicotine is absorbed easily right through the skin by itself and we think the DMSO solvent would increase absorption. Nicotine causes seizures. By itself, this might not have caused the severe seizures the dancer had, but added to the other factors, it could have been the major cause."

"Did you find the source?" asked the Chief. "Did she have some tobacco liniment in her stuff?"

"No," replied M.E. "I've asked Bubba to look again, but we haven't found the source. But, off the record, both she and the soprano seemed to have many extemporaneous mixtures. I don't know of any herbal medicine shops in Charleston that do that kind of thing, but around the world, where those ladies traveled, there are plenty of herbal shops that make all kinds of stuff. You know they grind up beetles and snakes and plants of all kinds. They could have bought anything. And, these temperamental world-class artistes are prone to alternative medicine—acupuncture, reflexology, chiropractice, iridology, and so forth. Even if we've found aconitine and nicotine, that doesn't prove anything so far except poor personal hygiene or bad herbal medicine taking, and remember we haven't found anything yet on this strange needle."

"What next?" asked the Chief.

"I hope we don't say anything in public," intoned Hanahan. "This stuff is crazy enough. The press is having a field day. Have you heard the Spoletho label?"

"It is much too early to go public," said the Chief. "Bubba, don't you think we need to do some snooping in private and not let on that there is even a suspicious of foul play?"

"Exactly," replied Bubba. "Let's not have one word about any suspicion even of the aconitine and nicotine. Chief, if I can add some additional detectives I'll start discrete inquiries. After all, the accidents are enough of an excuse to be thorough."

"Bubba, pick whom you want, just be sure they can keep their mouths shut," replied the Chief. "And I want at least twice-a-day updates."

"We need to search for the source of nicotine and aconitine and DMSO," added Bubba. "I'm not sure if Cross Seeds or some of the other hardware/farming stores stock that stuff. Chief, do you want me to pursue the international terrorism possibility? I've got some friends at CIA."

"Bubba, you always have good ideas," said the Chief, " I haven't been aware of any terrorist connection with Spoleto itself, but of course with all the containers coming in and out of our port there are concerns about problems there. Why don't you ask if they are aware of anything they haven't shared with us? Wouldn't be the first time they kept things to themselves. Let's also expand the investigation to include all possibilities. Right now I don't know which way to jump."

"Mr. Hanahan," asked Bubba, "I'd like your help in reviewing all the folks who've been key in organizing and running this season and what motives and access they might have had. The problem is we don't know if there is any funny business with one, two, or all three of these events. I'd like to do a classical strategy table across all three victims and determine how they are connected and who has motive, means, and opportunity, but most of us don't know the Spoleto artistes and staff."

"Of course, Bernard," replied Hanahan, "I'd be delighted to help. Meanwhile, can you provide some extra security at Gaillard and our other sites. I sure don't want a fourth corpse to make your job easier."

The Chief quickly said: "I've already called in all our staff and asked the Air Force and nearby cities to lend us some plainsclothes and detectives for the next two weeks. It will be expensive, but better than another disaster. I've got two Lieutenants organizing them now, and we'll be discreet but cover all your sites with both uniform and plainsclothes officers. Beside the big auditorium at Gaillard and the Dock Street Theatre where that awful play has moved to, are there any other controversial performances we should focus on."

"Goodness no, Chief," said Hanahan. "None of this was supposed to cause a problem. That Guérard bastard really screwed us with his premiers, but that is old news now. Everything else on the program is pretty benign, unless some Mozart-hater takes revenge on the chamber music series. I would appreciate some special attention at the Dock Street. I don't think they have that many exits and it is all made out of that gorgeous black cypress, that would burn like a match."

"We'll pay special attention there. I think your other sites like Sotille, the Garden Theater, and many of the churches are more modern construction and also have smaller audiences."

"And thank goodness many of the performances are out-of-doors," added Hanahan. "I'd just as soon you not reinstitute the metal detectors at Gaillard. You won't believe the calls I got from upstanding church-going friends who complained about the indignity of giving up their weapons. My goodness, you'd think we were taking away their greatgrandpappy's sword with the Yankee blood on it or something. Maybe we need to set up a metal detector at the door to St. Michael's since we have them on the other three sides of the Four Corners of Law."

The Chief suggested: "I don't want to anger the Lord. We are supposed to be the Holy City, but I bet he is less than happy with that play, and we have many more performances of it to endure. If he is upset, I just hope he aims his lightning at Guérard and leaves the rest of Spoleto alone. Thank goodness we have the Gullah and Gospel Gala coming up. That should soothe him."

"Speaking of soothing, Chief," said M.E., "I do hope you'll pay attention to my boss, Dr. Woodward. I know he is angry about the paramedics, but I heard from the orthopedists who cared for the dancer that they had problems with them too. Unlike Dr. Woodward, they aren't from Charleston, don't know about our traditions of gentility, and like orthopedists everywhere they are jocks. So they just threatened to tear the paramedic apart and that seems to have resolved it."

"I've already seen the complaint," added the Chief. "Assault, battery, interference with duties, theft of equipment, endangering a patient, and on and on."

"Chief, lets huddle on this one," asked the Mayor. "I don't want to have a war here."

"Mr. Hanahan, sir," asked Bubba, "could you spare me a few moments now to work on that strategy table?"

"Of course," replied Hanahan, "I'd be honored."

The Chief closed the meeting and Lieutenant Rhett took Mr. Hanahan to his office nearby.

eighteen

Means, Motive and Opportunity

*T*hursday, 11:17 am

"Would you mind if I turn on the videorecorder?" asked Bubba. "That way my team can appreciate your wisdom and I don't have to take as many notes."

"Shoot," replied Hanahan.

Bubba used a whiteboard that saved every mark in the computer. He drew a grid with three horizontal rows, labeled them "singer", "actor", and "dancer" and added four vertical columns labeled "connection," "motive," "means," and "opportunity."

Bubba began: "What is confusing here, at least to me, is that Spoleto seems to be the only connection between these three victims. We have a citizen of the world, aging retired soprano who had homes in four cities, a young actor unknown in theater who lived in Chicago with his parents, and a middle-aged Russian dancer who lived in Moscow and toured extensively. The first and third seem to have used a gaboonful of medicines of all kinds, but the young boy is said to have been very strict with his diet and meds and used only insulins that seemed to be perfectly OK. Do you know of any particular connection between these three?"

"Only Spoleto," replied Hanahan thoughtfully. "I don't think Kasandrá had worked with Areana before, and they certainly were not friends from what I've heard. I'm pretty sure they didn't know each other before this year. We've known for almost one year that Guérard's opera and play would be highlighted this year. It was just after last year's festival that Mayor Maybank and I went to Paris to visit with the maestro and invite his return. I think he approached Kasandrá and Areana not long after, because at his insistence we tried to fit Areana's ballet into the schedule but they could only do two shows and we needed five to fit well. The maestro was not happy with that, because he really wanted Areana here the entire 18 days, I guess because of his opera, but we settled on her being here for rehearsals and the first week of performances. I don't think the play was cast until about three months ago and I don't know of any connection between that cast and the other performers."

"How did the various artists get along?"

"They didn't have that much contact. The maestro sequestered the actors for his damned play in Summerville at the Woodlands Inn and I don't think they were even let out to roam Summerville much less Charleston until after the opening night. So I don't think they had any contact with the others. As you know, Areana choreographed the opera and had been here at rehearsals for a week before the opera opened, but her troupe didn't arrive from Atlanta until Sunday."

"What about that threat? Any ideas?"

"Well it was before the play. Although few of us knew the subject, that could have leaked out. Certainly the fundamentalists were outraged. And the reference to "God" and "sucking the breath out" is sort of what happened to the actor. But as for who—I don't have any ideas. We don't usually get threats at Spoleto."

Bubba methodically went through the Spoleto permanent staff and the part-time help added for the festival, but nothing seemed unusual and all continued to report to work. The stagehands, however, brought a surprise.

"What do you mean they disappeared?" asked Bubba.

"We usually use locals from the colleges and theaters to help backstage, but two brothers from the large Detroit Cobo Hall had some connections with the maestro and he insisted we hire them, at union wages, as they were experienced backstage and he insisted on having "leadership" as he called it backstage for "his" productions. We made them sort of foremen, one at Gaillard and one at Dock Street. I'm told they were doing a reasonable job and seemed experienced until yesterday, when they disappeared."

"Disappeared?"

"Well, they didn't show up. Our human resources guru got concerned and checked out their rooms at the College and they were cleaned out. And they left without paychecks. Just another of Guérard's screwups I guess, and I bet they call up and demand their full wages."

"Can I get their names and contacts?"

"Sure. We have addresses in Detroit as well as a recommendation from Cobo Hall there. Their last name was Beigi and one was Ismail and I don't recall the other. They were of medium height, slender, bearded, and swarthy. They spoke with accents of some kind, but used good English."

"Sounds like they were Middle Eastern. Do you have any idea of their national origin?"

"None at all."

"I'll have one of my associates work with your human resources staff if that is OK. I think it urgent we find them."

The rest of the interview focused on Jean-Louis and his diatribes, his absence, and his real focus on New York and raising money. Hanahan expressed relief that he would soon be gone and could "peddle his trash in the biggest garbage dump up north, with or without fingers. Maybe they'll just leave his middle finger in a permanent New York salute."

Bubba thanked Hanahan. "If you don't mind I will call on you again and I'd like to bounce off you all the findings we come up with."

"Thanks, that would be much appreciated. Just work fast."

Bubba called the Chief and asked for three more investigators. Two were at headquarters and joined him at the white board diagram immediately. Detective Second Solomon Legare was a tall lanky blonde sailor of note. He had graduated from the Citadel and had earned a solid reputation in the bunko and vice squads. Bubba assigned him to the missing stagehands and sent him off to the Spoleto Human Resources offices. Detective First Sylvia Dennis was the rising star of his special crimes squad. She had worked undercover and broken a number of high-profile crime enterprises, but she also looked like a high fashion model. Bubba assigned her to the maestro and told her she might have to fly to New York as it was urgent that they establish contact with him and he wasn't answering any of his known phone numbers. He knew she could handle herself well in that environment. The third addition, Detective Third Edward Good, was the brainy one. With a masters in criminology and mastery of computers, he led the informatics crimes squad that had a room full of electronics that looked like Star Wars. He was in Mount Pleasant working a credit card scam, but he was pleased when Bubba phoned to ask him to head up the search for the weapons and he enjoyed working with M.E. He told Bubba he'd go directly to the Medical Examiner's office and then check in.

Bubba set morning and afternoon times to report, made the videotape of his interview with Hanahan available, and assigned evening duties to his colleagues at the Gaillard Auditorium and Dock Street Theatre for surveillance. He asked his chief technician, Marian Read, to see if she could set up two of the microsurveillance cameras at the Gaillard to cover the entire backstage area and one or two at Dock Street.

"Bubba, if you want it covered," replied Marian with a grin, "we could wire every seat. The Feds paid for those new micros and they are neat. Good wireless transmitters and remote controls. And they are so small you'd never notice them. But why don't you get the recordings from Friday and Monday?"

"What?" asked Bubba. "What recordings?"

"Didn't you know that the maestro had those two performances videorecorded with 16-channel audio? They brought in a professional crew from New York, but they asked me to help Friday so I moonlighted setting up the audioboard. They had network-quality digital camcorders and recorded the audio digitally."

"Where were the cameras and all?" asked Bubba. "I didn't notice any."

"You wouldn't have seen much," said Marian. "They used two cameras high up on the skywalks above the floor and they were black just like all the lights and other gear up there. A third camera was mixed in with the lights in the center of the balcony, but it looked just like another spotlight. The audio pickups were all those suspended microphones hanging from the ceiling plus the body mikes and the stage mikes. They'll mix the audio later, but there was some rush to do a quick edit of the video for use in New York within a day. Usually a careful edit like that takes weeks—especially to blend the sound into the five or nine channels used in theaters."

"How can we get the video, even raw, of those performances?" asked Bubba.

"Let me call the guys who hired me and see if they are willing, as police business, to make us a dub off the masters—it would fit on one

DVD, if we get the right format. We might have to pay them a few hundred dollars and get a statement that we won't copy it and will return it when we are through. These pros are most sensitive about pirated material, even brief segments."

"Well, do everything you can to get us a copy so we can study every move."

"OK, boss. And don't worry about our surveillance. With those tiny camera/transmitters painted black, no one will see them and they work in very dim light. I'll just set up some of the usual digital recorders in a van outside the theater—the transmission shouldn't be a problem."

nineteen

Dining au Naturel

*T*hursday, 1 pm

Bubba picked up Teddy at the Gaillard for lunch. "How's the performance going for tonight?"

"Great. The San Francisco Ballet is very professional and self-contained. They don't need much from me or my staff. Let's forget work and have a great lunch."

"We could go to something nearby if you think you'll get paged back." noted Bubba.

"I think we're OK. Let's go somewhere different."

"How about SNOB? It is open for lunch and has great seafood."

"SNOB. What kind of a name is that?"

"It means Slightly North of Broad," explained Bubba. "Charlestonians want to live 'South of Broad' and turn up their noses at other addresses. When I was a kid there were three good restaurants in town and one, the Colony House, got turned into a private club and so they started a new restaurant, called it SNOB, and now have three other great places. We could also go to their SUTC—Slightly Up the Creek on Shem Creek where the fishing boats dock."

"Sold. I'm dying for some she-crab soup and crab cakes. Does that sound like too much crab? I had that soup last week and it was terrific. Isn't it a local delicacy?"

"When my grandfather was mayor and lived in the John Rutledge House, his butler, William Deas, invented she-crab soup. Later Deas was the chef at Everett's, a fast food place right near the Ashley River Bridge."

"Sure. Rhett's butler! You made that up. Was your grandmother named Scarlett?"

"No, it's a fact."

"So, do you want to be mayor someday?"

"I'm not sure. I've thought of practicing law or starting a business. Charleston has a tradition of good leadership and that might be fun someday."

As they enjoyed lunch they shared memories of other interesting meals. Teddy enjoyed ethnic foods and loved the variety in New York. She said she'd found sushi, Indian, Vietnamese, Chinese, and Thai in Charleston, but mostly the menus looked just like each other. She asked Bubba what had been his most exotic meal.

"Well, ma'am, it's pretty embarrassing."

"Embarrassing food? Tell me!"

"When the fancy new country club opened on Kiawah Island, I was invited out for a dinner. I certainly couldn't have gone there on my own as I think their initiation fee was at least $50,000. So, I go as the guest of three lawyers from Broad Street and, since I don't play golf, they went first to the steam room. So there I am following three fat middle-aged naked guys waddling into the steam where we sit around with a lot of other naked guys. OK. I'm used to locker rooms and it just seemed a strange way to prepare to eat—I mean I'm all for cleanliness, but.... So when we are limp from the steam they lead me out to dinner. But instead of going to get dressed, they hang a quick right through a door into the dining room! There we are, buck naked, in a formal room in which half of the diners are in suits and half are naked! I couldn't believe it. No ladies, at least I didn't notice any, but then I was too embarrassed to look for friends, acquaintances, and relatives. Then I had to sit, bare-arsed, on a chair and tried to cover myself with a tiny little napkin that kept falling off. I've never been so uncomfortable eating a hot steak—I kept fearing it or a steak knife would fall into my unprotected lap."

Bubba noted that Teddy was laughing so hard tears were running down her cheeks.

"Even the most informal lady's club in the Big Apple can't top that one. What's that famous impressionist painting of the picnic with the naked lady and the men in suits? I've always wondered about that. Can you take me to this fine diningroom sometime?"

"Sure. Just as soon as I make my first million, learn golf, buy a large asbestos napkin, and you've recovered from your gender reorientation surgery."

Bubba learned that Teddy was now living in the Victorian bed-and-breakfast at Two Meeting Street, right on the Battery and a couple of doors west of her former abode in the apartment shared with the maestro. When he asked about dinner, she suggested he pick her up there at midnight to give her time to close up the Gaillard stage and get dressed.

Thursday, 4 pm

"It is inappropriate for you to even be here!" said Dr. Kurent outside Areana's ICU room to the tall gaunt figure with the nametag that read: "Harvey Est, MD. "We can't tell if she is brain dead, Harv, and it's too early to start talking about donations. Give us a couple of days at least. Take some blood samples for typing if you must. I haven't even been able to contact any relatives yet. Apparently she has some cousins or aunts or something in Russia."

Areana was still having cardiac arrhythmias. She had developed a more stable atrial fibrillation, and her ventricular response rate was controlled by beta blockers. They had backed off on the phenobarbital and the blood concentration was falling, and she was not having any more electrical seizures on the EEG. She had gotten full doses of the protective Guilford neuroimmunophyllin within a few minutes of reaching the hospital, but it didn't always work in brain injury and no studies of it had been done in *status epilepticus*. In fact, she had a virtually flat EEG even now that she had normal temperature, good vital signs except the arrhythmias, and normal electrolytes. Dr. Kurent suspected that the EEG would not show much when the phenobarbital was completely gone. He was beginning to suspect that she would end up as an organ donor, just like those kids that rode motorcycles with no helmet. Whenever he saw them on the street he would yell "organ donor" at them—it was such a waste it made him angry.

Thursday 5:45 pm

Bubba was leading a team meeting so his colleagues could share what they had learned. He had selected himself to be responsible for gathering information from and about Teddy and reported on what he had put together, without sharing that it was over sesame-encrusted grouper at SNOB or that the interrogation would continue after midnight. He learned from Detective Dennis that Guérard rented the Plaza Hotel room in New York for months at a time and the hotel staff hadn't seen him for several days. His assistant conductor at Spoleto, Ochsner, thought he might be in Charleston rehearsing the handsome black actor who had been hired to replace the dead actor playing Christ, but the detective hadn't located either of them yet. Ochsner had reported that he'd been told the actor had been hired a week before and promised the New York opening. Ochsner also had begun rehearsing the opera with the new soprano and she too had been booked in advance and promised the New York role. The re-written music fitted her vocal range perfectly and only a few phrases had had to be redone as she had a strong traditional soprano range.

Bubba learned from Detective Good that the Chief had authorized additional manpower and overtime to check local sources for the weapons: monkshood mushrooms and aconitine, botulinus toxin (possibly), nicotine (possibly in an insecticide), and the solvent DMSO. He'd just started to get his new crew working on regional sources and Bubba suggested he check with the local colleges and medical school.

Nothing new had been learned about the threat. Homeland Security knew of no specific threats from the ultraconservatives or religious fundamentalists involving Spoleto or Guérard, but were helping investigate.

The most troublesome news was from Detective Legare, who told Bubba that the Beigi brothers, Ismail and Faramarz, were a problem. They had not made friends in the backstage crews at Spoleto and had just disappeared. Their rooms at the College of Charleston dormitory were cleaned out. Their previous phone in Detroit was disconnected. No one could find their employment papers with next of kin or other contacts. No relatives or friends had been identified and Cobo Hall said they had worked there for a year but two weeks before had gotten into a fight with some skin-head truckers and when they threatened revenge they had been fired. Legare was searching for them now through all the police agencies, and had learned that they had an old Chevrolet and they had not bought airline or train tickets in their names. They did not have credit cards in those names. Their passports were Iranian but they had overstayed their visas.

Bubba had assigned one of the officers to cover the ballet to be a policewoman whom he knew to have taken two Russian courses at the Citadel day school. A few years ago when the Citadel was mistreating women in the Corps of Cadets, their PR folks forgot to mention that women had attended the Citadel, in day classes, for decades with no problems. Charlestonians were furious when some Yankee bad boy, sent by his parents to get straightened out at the Citadel, set one of the female cadets afire. Southern gentlemen certainly knew you didn't have to cook southern ladies before....

The other officer he assigned to the ballet was a thin young woman whom he knew to have done local dance and figure skating. Both reported that they had made contact with some of the dancers and learned that replacing Areana would not be a problem as several of the dancers knew the part and they often rotated roles. Although Areana considered herself to be the leader of the company, the officers heard nothing but derision for her artistry, personality, and leadership. Several dancers complained that Areana was not even the usual dancer in the Firebird role but that she had insisted on it opening night. They learned that Areana was regarded as a sexual predator, even among the closely-knit and highly promiscuous ballet group. When asked if the dancers meant there was something between Areana and the maestro, one dancer snorted: "she likes them younger, more athletic, and more female, but to further her career she'd fornicate a jackass on King Street while it was drawing a carriage full of tourists." Bubba laughed at that one.

The two officers he had assigned to the opera were both great singers. One was a full-bodied woman who stood out in the main Mt. Zion AME Church Gospel Choir and had performed at the Gaillard Tuesday and was due back. Her partner was a short balding man who sang tenor at the Huguenot Church. They reported that they had interviewed most of the opera cast and had been informed that there was no problem replacing Areana. The choreography was complete and needed no further development. Furthermore, the lead dancer had been hired by the maestro with the understanding that she might choreograph and direct the chorus for later performances including New York. The cast was surprised that the replacement soprano had arrived Monday and was already knowledgeable about the part. The cast felt she was so well prepared that they could have performed yesterday, as scheduled, but the maestro forbade any discussion of that. When they interviewed the new soprano, she indicated that the maestro had given her the score two weeks before and paid her to rehearse and keep these dates open. She had been told that Kasandrá was older and feeling fatigued and that at any moment she might have to step into the role with the possibility of continuing to New York as the star. The maestro had agreed that she could wear body makeup and a body stocking so she would not actually be nude on stage. She had been given a rough videocassette of the performance Friday to study the blocking, but she said she was horrified by the ending. She said she felt that the rehearsal Tuesday had gone so well that she would have been ready for a Wednesday performance, especially with one more rehearsal for the blocking.

Detective Good had assigned three detectives, all from Charleston, to find the possible poisons. He told them to look beyond a local source and find what they could on the world wide web. He wondered if there was a URL called "Poisons R Us." Sergeant Rutledge Moore had called all the local farm supply, seed, and hardware stores and found that one, on Orleans Road west of the Ashley, said it had sold its last old can of Black Flag 40% nicotine sulfate insecticide just a week ago. Rutledge had interviewed the clerk who made the sale and he described an elderly, short, stooped gray-haired man in coveralls who paid cash, so there was no credit card record. He was working with a police artist on a sketch, but didn't remember many details except a moustache.

Corporal Beulah Manigault had found one possible local source of DMSO, but it was widely available on the web. The Angel Oak Animal Hospital, on Johns Island, that cared for many farm animals, had a drug store in their waiting room. The veterinarian was sure they had two jars of DMSO on the shelf because a woman had called and asked for it just a week before. When he looked for the DMSO with Ms Manigault, nothing turned up. He checked and they hadn't sold any, and he had no idea where it had gone. He said he wasn't planning to get any more as the demand was so little—it was a good for sore joints in horses, but it sure stank and wasn't very popular with the farmers who had to apply it.

Bubba learned that Detective Sergeant Shauntay Brown had been searching for aconitine and botulinus toxin. She hadn't expected any sources in the lowcountry, and had found none even in the biology departments of the various colleges and universities. She had found several suppliers of monkshood mushrooms, either spores or the adult forms, in herbal stores on the web, but no one sold purified aconitine.

Besides the CDC in Atlanta, Shauntay had found two suppliers of botulinus toxins for laboratory use. Ophidian, in Madison, Wisconsin, made toxin fragments with recombinant DNA for the Defense Department but said they hadn't sold to anyone else in more than a year and they had never sold the intact whole toxin. BioLab Supply Company, in the Woodlands, Texas, sold natural botulinus toxins A and B, to the CDC and universities. BioLab checked their shipments to zip codes close to 29401 and found only one shipment in the last two years to South Carolina. They had shipped 1 milligram of Botulinus toxin A, inside triple aluminum containers, to Marine Biology Experimental Laboratory at PO Box 1729 at the main Post Office on Broad Street, 29401-1729, ten days ago. The purchase had been paid by a Money Order for $329.54.

"Is that lab connected to the Marine Biology Department of the College of Charleston and the Medical University?" asked Bubba.

"Nope," replied Shauntay. "the director, Dr. Nemo, said he had never heard of Marine Biology Experimental Laboratory and insisted his lab had never worked with botulinus toxin even though others used it as a laboratory marker for the acetylcholine release mechanism."

"With all this concern about terrorism how could someone just order up a million lethal doses of a poison with no controls?" mused Bubba. "Well, get over to the Post Office and see what they say about that PO Box and the shipment."

Bubba had assigned the last two detectives to the Spoleto staff and the permanent staff at Gaillard. The box office manager at the theater just complained about the terrible mess caused by the substitution of the ballet for the opera. The security guard talked about how troublesome the Monday night metal detectors and coat room full of weapons had been. The maintenance crew said they welcomed the help of the police sweeping up the stage and hoped that would continue. The Spoleto office staff, still adjusting to their new quarters in the old mansion on George Street, finally opened up and expressed their bitterness at the maestro. They said he was impossible, demanding tickets and limousines for the "Nooo York backers" and treating them like they were his personal servants. One of them said that at Saturday's Gullah and Gospel Gala they had hoped the maestro would be in the coffin when the choir sang that wonderful "Walk 'im up de stairs."

Bubba reminded his team to put their detailed notes on the Lotus Notes program and to drop hyperlinks into the 3x4 grid he had established. He ended the meeting with the reminder: "see how I put the three

victims horizontally so we can add more right down the screen." Everyone groaned and left either for home and family or for their evening as-
signment at Gaillard and Dock Street.

twenty

Peaceful Ballet

*T*hursday, 7:40 pm

Walking up the Gaillard stairs on the arm of Henry, Dr. Simons was radiant in her pearl gray business suit, teal silk jabot, and the simple gold and pearl earrings and brooch she had inherited from her grandmother. She had run by the Ashley House Salon and had Jim Riley fix her hair beautifully, and she wore the wrist corsage, of a lovely gray orchid Henry had sent from Frampton's. She wore a colorful Hermes scarf as a belt and her Gucci white bag and shoes. She looked just perfect as a Charleston lady of old, head high, posture perfect, and that graceful gait of the patrician in complete charge of the moment, despite her three-inch heels. Henry, in tuxedo with a tartan tie and cummerbund, beamed as he introduced her to his children and his other guests and escorted them to the Spoleto Festival Society room for a glass of good cheer as he put it.

The house was sold out with many folding chairs added in the back. Some of the newspeople had left for home, but there were still more re-porters than usual, sho' nuff. M.E. observed that the on-air reporters were resplendent from the waist up even if they had on jeans below. The print journalists either overdressed or looked like the maintenance crew, but they all had bulky notebooks and a clutch of pens. M.E. whispered to Henry that they must have some aphasia that made it impossible to dictate and wondered if they were incapable of leaving messages on phone recorders.

The ballet was a delight. The audience roared its approval. No one died. At intermission Henry entertained her with his cleaning problems. He had left his penguin suit at Arrow Cleaners after Friday and they promised to try to get out the blood spots. He had ruined his best tux helping resuscitate Christ, and apologized for having to wear an old one tonight. M.E. snuggled closer and whispered that he would look perfect in anything, or out of anything. They continued that conversation at midnight after saying good-bye to his other guests, dropping off his children with his housekeeper, finding a parking place on the battery, and making their way to her little house on Church Street. M.E. noticed that Bubba and Teddy were just leaving from Two Meeting Street. She remembered when the big football hero had dated her several times years ago, but he had Roman hands and Russian fingers, as the saying went, and she had stopped seeing him after two dates while she could still fight him off.

Bubba took Teddy to the jazz club on the roof of the new Market Pavilion Hotel right on the corner of Market and East Bay. The view was spectacular with a full moon glimmering in the swimming pool and off the Cooper River nearby. A huge cruise ship had docked at the foot of Market and its lights blinked on and off. Several girls in bikinis were in the water enjoying the warm evening and the attention of the even warmer guys including two Citadel cadets in their summer uniforms. The snacks were spectacular, from the Grill 225 below. The crab appetizer was all crab and the tuna tower had sashimi tuna on a rice base. As they danced each felt a mounting urgency that soon led them to the exit. While the valet brought Bubba's car, he explained the strange front door of the hotel that could be barricaded water tight in a hurricane. The architect, Will Evans, had insisted on thick aquarium-type windows for the ground floor restaurant so that diners could be undisturbed as a storm surge surrounded the outside of the building, a block from the harbor. Bubba suggested Teddy return for a spectacular meal during the next big hurricane. Teddy replied that she'd read all about it from a dry New York apartment.

At her new abode they entered quietly, not wanting to awaken the bed-and-breakfast guests. But in her small bedroom it was hard to restrain her vocal enthusiasm or his athletic performance. The head of the bed kept beating on the wall, so they took off the mattress and put it on the floor. Bubba noticed that the bathroom had only a few of the feminine potions he had seen in her former residence and none of the kitchen gadgets. When he asked Teddy if those accoutrements had been hers, she just replied: "I've got a big strong man to fill me, and I mean fill me with delight. Why would I need food or drugs?"

twenty-one

Frenzied Theatre and Nosey Police

*F*riday, 3 pm

Backstage at the Dock Street Theatre, the stage director of Pilate's Choice was in a frenzy. Wardsworth's Chamber Music series had just ended, with a vigorous performance by the St. Lawrence Quartet and Todd Palmer. It was late to start setting the stage for the first performance of Guérard's play in this new venue. Only five hours to go and they had to get the sets in place and run through the play with a new actor to be nailed up and all new blocking on this tiny stage. There just wasn't time. No time. The maestro would be here in an hour expecting everything to be perfect. At least the new Jesus hung on the cross like he was supposed to, although the director couldn't keep his eyes off his loincloth.

Friday, 3:30 pm

At Bubba's staff meeting they worked on filling in the grid. Sylvia Dennis told Bubba that the Manhattan detectives knew all about Guérard and feared he had gotten in with a rough crowd. They told her he was deeply in debt to "Digits" Personnoni, the Mafia loan shark famous for carving off fingers and toes in lieu of interest on unpaid debts. If they didn't find the maestro soon they speculated he was in "Noo Joisey Sausage."

Detective Legare reported no luck in locating the Beigi brothers. The Detroit police didn't know of them but the Homeland Security forces reluctantly acknowledged that they were on a watch list, but would say no more. He had interviewed the backstage staff that had worked with them and found they were quiet, spoke little, didn't make friends, and were notable only for praying five times a day even when working. They had not made contact with the local Charleston Moslem community and seemed to have disappeared. Legare had put out a watch notice to all police forces for them and their automobile to "observe, report, but don't approach."

Bubba reported that Marian Read had obtained the DVD of the opera and play opening nights and they had reviewed it in detail. The only likely source for the soprano's poison, if any, was the chalice she drank from. Esau Versey had again insisted that he hadn't touched anything in it. In a closeup the video clearly showed a dent in the rim of the chalice above the faux ruby on a closeup, but the one they had recovered from her dressing room was undented and clean. Bubba remembered the spare chalices in the prop room and told them to get a warrant to search for all props. The video of the play didn't help much. The actor had just slumped, become incontinent, and died. Bubba looked twice but couldn't see anything on the footpiece or any strange foot motions.

He was disappointed to learn from Sgt. Moore that the sketch of the man who presumably purchased the nicotine insecticide was so vague as to be worthless. Even Ident-I-Perp hadn't helped. The clerk couldn't remember any details, but did recall him wearing a hat, coat, and dark glasses in the hot weather.

Bubba noted Edward Good beaming and asked him what was exciting. Good turned to Shauntay who had had success with the postal inspectors. Box 1729 had been rented two weeks before and the renter paid with a money order. The clerk who did the rental hadn't recorded a personal name or address and couldn't remember the renter. Basically they would accept anything addressed to that box number. But, surprise, they did have a record of a heavy hazardous-material package that had been sent to the box but wouldn't fit. Because of the biohazard label, the package had been stored in the postal hazard locker until the box-owner came to claim it. The post office had saved the duplicate notice they had put in the PO box and it recorded a shipment from FMC, Green River, Wyoming, to Lowcountry Electroplating, PO Box 1729. The shipment weighed 128 pounds. They had asked all the clerks on duty if they remembered handing over the parcel, but none did. Checking the records for the day and time it had been delivered, they found that Peter Bounetheau was the only clerk that had been on duty then who hadn't already been interviewed. Peter was off for two more days, but they got his home telephone and address and were working on contacting him.

Meanwhile, Shauntay had contacted FMC and found that it had been bought by a combination of Winnemucca Chemicals and Degussa Corporation and had gone out of business. The Green River, Wyoming, factory had been closed and she was referred to CyanCo Company that supplied industries such as steel hardening, electroplating, organic molecular synthesis, and gold mining. She found a website for CyanCo but it indicated that they mostly shipped tank cars of 6000 gallons or steel bins of 1450 kg of their products to major manufacturing sites. She hadn't yet reached them by telephone.

Bubba was disappointed that Beulah hadn't found a source for the aconitine. She was calling all the herbal stores in the region, but hadn't found monkshood either, at least not that she could identify. With the myriad of herbal remedies and their many names, this might be quite a search.

Bubba learned from Detective Sylvia Dennis that the maestro was not to be found. He hadn't been seen at the Plaza in New York and there were no tickets in the Guérard name on any flights to Charleston in the last three days. Bubba thought it important to peruse the maestro's apartment, but getting a warrant might be tricky. Then he had a thought, smiled, and told Sylvia to wait for a minute. He went to his office, called Teddy, and asked if she had kept a key to her former domicile, shared with Jean-Louis. She said yes and agreed to lend it to him.

Bubba drove over to Gaillard, picked up the key from Teddy, rode the elevator up to the maestro's apartment, and knocked on the door, key in hand.

The door swung open and there was the maestro in dressing gown. Stammering, Bubba asked for Teddy but was told, haughtily, that she had moved out. Bubba said he thought the maestro to be in New York, but Jean-Louis looked around and said: "No, feels like Charleston, looks like

Charleston," and with a deep inhalation, "Ah yes, it even smells like pluff mud."

"But no one has seen you for several days."

"Well, I was in New York on business, but when the flights were full I just caught the Silver Meteor, Train 97, as it left Penn Station last night at 7 pm and arrived here, two hours late, at 10 am. Had a nice breakfast of French Toast and good coffee—you should try the train sometime."

Bubba was chagrined not to have considered the train, so few people used it even after 9/11, but decided to retreat. Thanking the maestro Bubba said he would look for Teddy at the theater.

Bubba reported to the Chief all the facts. The Chief had been studying the grid with all the details, but seemed perplexed. "Bubba, what does your gut tell you? The FBI always teaches us that it is the facts, paperwork, and grunt stuff that solve crimes, but I think it is the intuition of the beat cop, the first on the scene, and detectives as long as they don't get so mired in detail they can't see the forest."

Bubba replied thoughtfully: "Boss, my gut ain't talking. We don't have much of anything. We've no proof of any crime—they could be all accidents. We're working on the means but haven't anything solid yet. We can't connect them except through Spoleto. Everyone had access to the dressing rooms. I thought the maestro was out of town, but now with the train he could have been here for each tragedy. For motives, everyone seems to hate the maestro and both divas— skewered and seizured. But after three such accidents in less than a week I doubt the headliners are lining up to star in the next Gaillard production."

"OK, I understand the facts, but what does your gut tell you?"

"You know, one of my criminology professors always used to say: 'a sane man will not saw off the leg of a chair he is sitting in without having a prop handy.' He meant that faced with a sudden event you should look for who might have predicted it. In this case there are several odd facts. A replacement soprano had been preparing with an alternative music score, although she says she was just preparing for later performances in New York. But she was also asked to be available during these 18 days. The new Christ would not have taken just an understudy role but was told he would open in New York and suddenly made himself available. The ballet troupe seems just fine without their leader, in fact overjoyed. I don't know how to fit these pieces together, and it may be just that in theater you always have backups for contingencies, but it does look like a lot of planning had been done."

"I see where you are headed. If Guérard were guilty of something it would make a lot of the Spoleto board delighted. They'd probably sacrifice another artiste or two just to get him good."

"Well, one other funny thing is that Jean-Louis is into some Mafia loansharks who don't play around. He seems to be desperate to raise money and I'm told publicity, even bad news, would bring in backers. Maybe he was counting on the press to help him get funded."

"Money and sex are always the two best motives."

"Well in regard to sex he seems to be an omnivore. What gets into those New York art folks anyway? Another interesting tidbit is that he videotaped both premier performances and did a quick edit to show them around New York. The tape gives us great evidence of a crime if there were a crime. Do you think he was the only one to know those would be singular events, never repeated?"

"Good point. Any more on our three victims?" asks the Chief.

"They haven't found any source for the aconitine in the singer and are still looking. Its funny that it seems to be a pharmaceutically pure preparation, not just the mushrooms themselves. They suspect botulinus toxin might be a possibility in the actor, but they can't prove it in the laboratory. M.E. did say they were getting reagents from the CDC in Atlanta and I arranged for Delta to expedite it just like they do organ donations. The dancer is officially alive, but her doctor isn't very hopeful. We may have found the source of the liniment that was on her feet. A jar with the same mixture of nicotine, Black Flag 40% insecticide, and the solvent DMSO was in her collection of oddments, but it only had her fingerprints on it. Also we found a source of DMSO over on the Stono and some may have been shoplifted and the last can of the specific insecticide, Black Flag 40% brand, was sold to an old man by that hardware store out on Orleans Road. We are trying to identify the buyer but don't have a very good description and it was several weeks ago."

"Be sure your crew is careful in the interviews to keep this quiet. Don't let them have idle chatter outside the house here. Nothing like a rumor, especially a grisly one, in this town, and we don't know yet if there was anything fishy about any of these three. You might want to be the one contacting the maestro. Be very careful. He is old but he is very sharp, very bitter, very mean, and has resources to cause us a lot of trouble. This may be a troublesome Spoleto, but I don't want us to be blamed for making it the last one."

twenty-two

Terror in the Hole?

*F*riday, 6:35 pm

In the microscopy laboratory, M.E., Bill McCord, and Dirk Gadsden gathered at the fancy two-headed microscope. M.E. and Bill began looking at the brightly-colored H&E sections of the tissue blocks cut from the foot of the actor. M.E. said: "I agree that the wound looks like a puncture from a needle and there isn't enough cellular response to make it old."

Switching to the second block with the other wound, they concluded that both wounds looked similar and like fresh punctures.

Bill eagerly said: "Now let me show you the antibodies with the fluorescence labels."

M.E. switched the light source to the laser they used for fluorescence microscopy.

Bill slipped another slide on the stage and tried to find the puncture wound in the tissue. Now the tissue was very dark with tiny green speckles in some of the cells. Under this light source everything was black except where the antibody with its fluorescent tag had attached to its target. Soon he brought the wound into the center of the field. "Note there are only a few dots of fluorescence around this wound."

"Which antibody did you use?" asked M.E.

Dirk, standing next to Bill, said: "This is the more distal wound, closer to the toe. We agreed to use the 'B' antibody on it and the A on the other one first."

"Do you have an A antibody test on this wound?" asked M.E.

"Not yet," replied Bill. "Remember we are afraid of running out of sample. But just wait a second," as he replaced the slide with another, holding it so he could read the label. "Just give me a second. We tested the other wound first with the 'A' antibody."

As M.E. watched through the microscope, Bill adjusted the slide on the stage and used the micrometer to move it under the lens. At first most was dark and then, approaching from her left, she saw the hole from the needle brilliantly lit up with fluorescence. "Wow," she exclaimed. "I hope you have pictures of this and the other one. Obviously the wound is filled with whatever the 'A' antibody binds to."

"It is all documented on videotape and on still digital images. This nails it," said Dirk.

"Let's be careful," urged M.E. "You are sure the two antibodies are specific for the A and B toxins."

Bill and Dirk answered "yes" in unison. Bill added: "we also checked them out in vitro against the purified toxin the CDC furnished us. Neither antibody reacts with the 'E' toxin. CDC also sent us a little of the rare fish botulism toxin 'C' and they don't react at all to it. Both antibodies only react with their specific antigens, either on the A or B toxin."

"What did the CDC say about a chemical identification?" asked M.E.

Dirk replied: "They said forget it. No one has proven the structure of the whole botulism toxin, which is supposed to have a molecular weight of as much as one million! They said each strain has two chains held together by one disulfide bond. The heavy chain is the site that initially binds to the nerve ending but when the light chain gets inside the cell it cleaves some essential protein, like SNAP-25 or VAMP, that is needed for acetylcholine release. At that point the nerve doesn't function, the muscle is paralyzed, and church is out. People are pretty uptight these days about something this lethal. They reminded me that one laboratory worker had died from inhaling vapor contaminated with a little toxin and a patient had died after just touching a spoon of canned beans to his lips and immediately spitting it out. They only sent a small sample and said to treat it like an atom bomb with all the precautions. We haven't taken it out of the laminar flow hood, and I've done all the manipulations of the main store myself."

"Is there any possibility this is just Botox? I hear the New York crowd is having parties and just injecting themselves to look young. It gets rid of all those wrinkles we work so hard to acquire."

Bill replied: "That's a good point. Actually there are two Botox drugs on the market, one from strain A and the other from strain B. But the doses are tiny. In the Botox vial you get 5 nanograms or 5 billionth of a gram and that may be enough for 50 injections."

Dirk continued: "But we knew you'd ask so I went up to ophthalmology and got several doses. We injected a mouse with a whole syringe of the stuff and he died. Then we did a frozen section of the mouse muscle and stained it with our antibodies."

"OK, let me see."

Putting a slide of the mouse muscle on the microscope Dirk hunted for the needle track he left from the injection. M.E. saw that there were only a few grains of fluorescence lighting up the track. "And this is the straight Botox stuff? It must have only 1% or less of the toxin in the actor's puncture wound."

"Yep."

"Well, I guess that rules out an accident. I've never heard of Botox in the foot anyway. Do you get foot wrinkles when you get old?"

Dirk laughed: "I think you get wrinkles everywhere when you get old, but don't come near me with any botulinum toxin even if I look like one of those wrinkly dogs."

"Do you think the actor's poison could be from a Defense Department source? Do we need to worry about the CIA or some other black op?" asked M.E.

"I'm sure we are prepared to use it in biological warfare," replied Bill. "Just imagine if it is as lethal on inhalation as you might guess. Just one test-tube of botulinum toxin could kill an entire army, and you could immunize your own troops in advance. But I bet our guys wouldn't use any of the standard strains—the enemy might have immunized 'their' troops. It would be easy to isolate the gene from the Clostridium that makes the toxin and Fort Dietrich could engineer a special strain that only our side would be immunized against. You could find the gene segment that coded for the active site and then transfect yeast or E. coli or perhaps Clostridia to make pounds of it in a fermentor. You could make antibodies in sheep or goats, and now they also use chickens and harvest the antibodies from the eggs."

"OK, but how are you going to immunize the troops except for giving them large amounts of passive immunity from injecting antibodies?" asked M.E. "If you injected the toxin to raise antibodies in the troops, they'd all be dead. Remember the joke in the chemistry textbook that describes this toxin—they describe its color, the crystal shape, I think it was the first biological protein crystallized, but say 'odor unknown.' Darn right, unknown, the person who first smells it will have to describe it fast on the way to the morgue."

"I see your point," replied Bill, "but I think they could engineer a part of the protein that is not so toxic but is antigenic. With a molecule that big there would be lots of epitopes that were immunogenic but not toxic. Also they could use a DNA vaccine and inject a gene into muscle cells or inhale it or use nose drops that would make the body's cells make the antigenic but nontoxic molecule. Actually, some of the people getting multiple Botox injections form antibodies that decrease the effect a little."

"Sounds like a lot of work to improve on what is probably the most toxic molecule on earth," answers M.E. "I guess if we can afford $650 toilet seats our tax money must also be figuring out how to kill everyone on the planet without using plutonium."

"No," replied Dirk seriously. "The idea is to kill only the 'other' people."

"Oh," smiled M.E. "The 'we' people will get the vaccine and the people from 'off' will die of the poisoning? I know how to tell the 'we' people when we are talking about Charleston and Gullah. Sometimes the little kids on the street who want to sell you a dance for a quarter or two will approach one of us and then, hearing our accent, they'll jump back and say: 'great gawd, she one of 'we' people'. But when you get to the political world, how do we tell if the Bosnian Muslims or the Serbs or the Croats are 'we' or 'off'?' Sometimes I'm glad to work with the corpses and not the killing itself."

"But M.E.," retorted Bill. "When you see those corpses roll in from the Saturday Night Knife and Gun Club, especially when the welfare checks go out on Friday, downtown Charleston looks a lot like Kabul."

"I see what you mean," replies M.E. sadly. "And here we are with two and a half corpses from an arts festival and we don't know whether the boogie men killed them or not. I sure hope none of them are spies or have the KGB after them."

"There is no more KGB," responded Dirk.

"Guys," said M.E. sadly, "if you examine the five thousand years of our history you find that in every era in every culture on every spot on this planet there is a KGB, just with different initials. Dirk, Bill, I really enjoy working with you guys," adds M.E. sentimentally. "Down here when you work with corpses and pieces of patients you can get very callous. But I know you two, like me, went into medicine for the human element and helping people and by God I will fight those bureaucrats until my last day if they interfere with good patient care."

"Bravo, boss," said Bill. "I hope if I get sick I get to see your shining face before I get put in a body bag."

"So much for philosophy," added M.E., "have you tested the needle thing yet with your antibodies."

"Nope, waiting for you to OK it," replied Dirk. "Now that we've got the tissue positive my suggestion is to try to remove just a tiny bit of the stuff in the needle and test it with both B and A antibody, expecting the A antibody to be positive like the tissue. If the 'B' antibody is negative it will be a good control. Does that suit you?"

"Sounds good to me," adds M.E. "Let me know the result. I'll tell the Chief we have a positive on botulinus toxin and that makes it murder for sure. I can't imagine this being an accident. Now we have to look more carefully for a source of the aconitine and rethink that nicotine. Maybe they were accidents with weird herbal mixtures and maybe they were purposeful. Maybe we have a rogue scientist with a garden of poisonous herbs. We better read up on exotic snake venoms, funnel web spiders, and Ebola. Wasn't Jack the Ripper supposed to be a surgeon? Maybe one of our local doctors is mad with Spoleto, perhaps he got poor seats, or more likely someone is angry with Mr. Guérard. From what I hear there would be a line waiting to kill Guérard. Maybe they thought killing his children, his productions, would wound him even more?"

twenty-three

Needles and Spikes
and
Everything Nice

*S*aturday, 7:45 am

Bubba kissed Teddy good morning, ran home to shower and change, and arrived early at his office. Half his team was already there, working on the phones and computers. As he came in one of his detectives jumped up and rushed over: "I think I've got it."

"What have you got," Bubba replied.

"Monkshood," trumpeted Rutledge Moore with Beulah Manigault right behind.

"What about it?" asked Bubba.

Rutledge deferred to Beulah who elaborated: "We found a store on the Grand Strand called: 'Needles and Spikes' that specializes in tattoos and piercings. Lawdy, you'd never believe where they attach some of that piercing stuff. Anyhoo, they also do herbs and they sold two ounces of Chinese monkshood mushrooms just about two weeks ago. They said they got it by mistake in a shipment of many Chinese herbs and realized it was dangerous before they sold it off with the ephedra, rhino horn, and other oddments."

"Well, who bought it?"

"The 'Needle and Spike' guy said a teacher from Trident Tech bought it for her botany class. She had asked for Amanita, the death angle mushrooms, but seemed happy to find monkshood instead."

"Did they get a name?" asked Bubba.

"Nope, she paid cash. But the spaced-out clerk remembered her. Boy was he a work of art. Tattooed everywhere I could see, with bolts and wires sticking out all over. Looked like he'd just recovered from a week-long binge and had been run through an assembly line. Anyhoo, he said the teach had dirty-blond short hair, lots of makeup, pale complexion, frumpy clothes. He remembered her as being so different from their usual clientele. He especially said she had 'school teacher shoes' and no piercings or tattoos!"

"Could he do a sketch? We could send JayJay Brown. He's a genius artist."

"No, he didn't remember many details other than what I've said. He thought she might be 5'4" and perhaps 120 pounds. He did remember those 'grandmother shoes.'"

"Did you find her at Trident Tech?" asked Bubba.

"No way," replied Rutledge. "The two professors who teach botany are both men, one old and one young, and no women are involved. They said they have lots of examples of mushrooms, including poisonous Amanita, but get their specimens from biology supply houses. They knew about monkshood but had never handled any."

"Where are we on our postal clerk Peter Bounetheau, Shauntay?" asked Bubba.

"He wasn't home all night and a neighbor said he was on a fishing trip with his son. The neighbor said he usually fished around the Edisto and I got his registration number from the Coast Guard and they are looking for his boaat."

Saturday, 9:05 am

Bubba reported all the most recent news to his Chief.

"Darn," echoed the Chief. "I was hoping these deaths were all accidents. Think of the publicity. So it looks like the divided diva might have been poisoned after all with some mushroom stuff, the kid with the diabetes got food poisoning through his feet, and the dancer got tobacco poisoning through her feet too? Have we got a killer with a foot fetish? Did the diva get it that way too, through her toes?"

"We are looking into the diva's aconitine. We're not sure how she got that and we haven't found a source—just possibly some mushrooms. I am afraid the other two look like murder."

"OK, de-tec-tive," said the Chief. "Who dun it?"

"I can't connect the three victims except through Spoleto," opined Bubba. "It could be someone on the local Spoleto staff, but why? Some old grudge or new grudge? It might be someone among the traveling artistes. Everyone seemed to hate the diva and the dancer, but no one seemed to care much about the kid. I'm not sure it's personal, although I guess murder is always pretty personal."

"How about the maestro?" asked Chief Ravenel. "He is cranky, vindictive, angry, egotistical, and nuts. Sounds like a good candidate for anything. He certainly hates the local Spoleto crowd. Maybe he didn't want anyone else in the limelight. Or was he promoting publicity for his New York shows by bumping off his stars? You said if he didn't raise some money some Mafia don was going to cut off his fingers and toes. That could motivate you. Or maybe his paranoia just got out of control like in other serial killers."

"We've got some physical evidence," said Bubba. "We have potential sources for the aconitine mushrooms, DMSO, nicotine, and botulism toxin and we have that funny needle thing. We could search for evidence that connects with these. What do you think?"

"Who do you want to search?"

"Well, I'd start with the maestro," suggested Bubba. "He's got a bunch of strange cooking stuff including a still and he certainly has been around lots of plots and murder mysteries, travels all over the world, and apparently is a gourmet chef."

"Boy," said the Chief. "When you pull that plug you will really ignite a storm. Can you imagine. He might walk out with his artistes and cripple the rest of Spoleto. Is there any way we could connect him without a search warrant?"

"The nicotine insecticide was purchased by an old man, but the description could fit anyone his age," suggested Bubba. "The DMSO just disappeared, but the store thinks a woman asked about it. The mushrooms, if they are connected at all, were purchased by a middle-aged school teacher woman. Doesn't ring a clear bell for the maestro does it."

"Have you shown the store clerk who sold the nicotine a picture of the maestro?" asked Ravenel.

"Not yet, but we will."

"If that doesn't work," added the Chief, "I'd get search warrants for the maestro but include that relative of his who produces the shows, a couple of the local Spoleto bigwigs, and the management staff of the Gaillard Auditorium. That way it doesn't seem vindictive."

"How are we going to get a judge to include the locals?" asked Bubba. "That is a giant step."

"Just try. It may protect us from the wrath of Guérard at least."

Saturday, 10:30 am

"Boss, we've hit paydirt," exclaimed Bill and Dirk, speaking more and more in unison as they got more excited.

"OK, what have you got?" asked M.E.

"The aconitine," answered Dirk. "We found a trace residue in one of the chalices—not the one in the dressing room but one in the locked property cupboard. They look almost identical, but this one has a dent above the fake ruby, just like the one on the video of the performance when the diva quaffed her *cocktail de fenestration.*"

"That's strange," mused M.E. "Why would someone put an unused chalice in the dressing room sink. Did he think we'd not look at the duplicates? Or maybe not know about them? Good work. Call Bubba and give him the news."

Saturday, 11:30 am

"Judge Trott, we appreciate your seeing us," said a supplicant Chief Ravenel. "Let us explain why we need some delicate search warrants."

After a detailed explanation the Judge intoned: "OK on Guérard and Bonnet and I guess OK on the Gaillard senior staff, but no way on the Spoleto executives. Are you nuts or just wanting to be ostracized for the next century?"

"Thanks, Judge Trott," intoned the Chief. "We'll start with what you've allowed and go from there if that doesn't work. I'm not too optimistic."

Saturday, 12:15 pm

No answer to Bubba's ring on the maestro's doorbell. He led the crime scene team up the elevator and to the suite door off the piazza, warning them about the construction gear. Still no answer to the knocker and so they picked the lock, announced their presence, and noted that no alarm sounded. Bubba directed one pair to the kitchen and the others to search the rest of the suite and confiscate anything that might yield evidence.

The kitchen pair bagged the still, blenders, and the more usual kitchen equipment in evidence bags and stacked them in the truck. The cupboards yielded a bottle of isopropyl alcohol, cottonballs, two 10-ml syringes, and five sterile 20-gauge needles in plastic enclosures. They searched every tiny crevice, tapped for hidden compartments, and found hidden Viagra, two dildos, a black vibrator, and a X-rated videotape titled "Betty Does the Battery." But they found no evidence of the poisons.

Within 30 minutes they had made a clean sweep, left a note on the floor inside the front door with an inventory of what they had confiscated, and carefully relocked the door.

At the Bed and Breakfast at the foot of Meeting Street, a large Victorian mansion with a beautiful piazza overlooking The Battery, they asked the owner for access to Ms. Bonnet's rooms and provided the search warrant. Bubba was hoping he hadn't left anything identifiable or that she had written anything naming him. But they found only a few cosmetics to impound, no kitchen equipment, no medical equipment, but a few herbal medicines all with proper commercial labels. They left a note with an inventory of what they had confiscated and then relocked the entrance.

They inspected the home of James Condes, the manager of the Gaillard Auditorium for the last seven years, and he helped them. They just confiscated a few kitchen utensils. At the home of Sarah Townsend, the chief of maintenance and cleaning, they found some insulin syringes and needles, insulin, and a myriad of other drugs including many herbs and over-the-counter. Ms. Townsend was quite cooperative and expressed her disbelief at the events of the last week. Edgar Coulomb, the head of electrical and heating-ventilation-air conditioning engineering, was upset by the intrusion. He had lots of tools, grinders, mixers, and containers of all sizes and shapes. As they were confiscated he grumbled over and over that he had nothing to do with those "prissy arsed" artistes on the stage. "If it gets hot or cold or breezy or bright or dim, all they do is bitch and want the HVAC up or down, up or down. No one ever considers how much work it is to keep that huge barn comfortable and to suit all the lighting requirements of one show after another. Those lights burn a lot of amps and that means heat and we have a huge electrical supply panel."

As the team was leaving Mr. Coulomb volunteered: "If you were really concerned about someone getting hurt, you should worry about the audience and how easy it would be to get to them."

"What do you mean?" asked Bubba.

"Well the accidents so far have all been on center stage, in full view, with little possibility of concealment, but also no chance of hurting more than one target. If you really wanted publicity, you'd blow up the building, poison the water, or blow viruses into the air supply. You know the whole auditorium has only two HVAC systems that refresh the entire volume every 6 minutes. Standing in front of them is like bracing in a hurricane."

Bubba thoughtfully asked a sergeant if when he had searched the auditorium with the dogs he had specially inspected the HVAC system.

"No," replied the sergeant. We stayed in the public areas and backstage. I didn't even see any big airhandling ducts. Where are they?"

Mr. Coulomb explained that the major supply ducts were high in the ceiling of the auditorium, with a few smaller ducts to enclosed spaces such as the exhibition hall and lobby. The major returns are at the back of the backstage areas. "They are all exposed but painted black to blend with the walls and ceiling. The design was to avoid expensive interior walls and just have a big open space."

Bubba asked: "Mr. Coulomb, are you working the Gullah and Gospel Gala tonight?"

"Yep. During Spoleto we work constantly—no time off. I'll be there about 7 pm unless my colleague has a problem earlier."

"When you arrive, please call me on this number," said Bubba. "I'll be there and I'd like your help to look over the HVAC before the show."

"See you there. And take care of my tools. I want them back in one piece and back neat like I had them."

Saturday, 12:53 pm

Shauntay Brown had been investigating the heavy shipment to PO Box 1729. She couldn't get an answer to her telephone calls to the CyanCo Company. It seemed to be closed for the weekend. Searching the web

Shauntay found references to it providing supplies to miners and metal-workers all over Western North America. Their major products seemed to be for gold mines, and Shauntay called several gold mines until she found one engineer working on a weekend who knew the company. He said that they usually bought 6000 gallon tank cars of "30% solution", but he knew they also sold dry powder in 1000 kilogram "big bags." He added: "It's a lot easier to control in the tank cars as they are sealed three times and everyone knows how dangerous the liquid is. But I wouldn't want to handle the dry powder. One whiff and poof, you're history."

"What do you mean," asked Shauntay.

"Well, the sodium salt is wicked stuff. You should see the space suits we use and all the precautions. You can't really mine gold without it, but we send someone to the hospital every four to six months for a stupid mistake. And we are always afraid of a major disaster."

"So what exactly is this stuff?"

"Sodium cyanide. They sell powdered pure stuff or the 30% solution we use. I guess a tank car like we get could kill about 50 million people."

"Wow!" Shauntay was stunned.

"You know that company you asked about, CyanCo, is really good about providing safety programs and devices. I have an emergency number if you want to contact them directly."

Shauntay dialed the number and quickly reached John McDermott, an engineer at CyanCo responsible for client safety. He confirmed that their main product was sodium cyanide in various forms. He said the smallest standard shipment was a 50 kilogram or 110 pound steel drum. He agreed to check their computers for a shipment to Charleston. He said: "I know Poe wrote the Gold Bug while he was stationed on Sullivan's Island, but I didn't know you had any real gold mines around there. Of course, our stuff is also used in plating and other industries."

Saturday, 3:12 pm

Peter Bounetheau was startled from a doze and almost dropped his fishing rod as the powerful Coast Guard Cutter bore down on him and swung around his bow. "Mr. Bounetheau," the Petty Officer in charge called through a megaphone. "We need to see you right now. It's about the Post Office."

"Sure. What's the emergency? Did we lose your tax return?"

Boarding Bounetheau's boat the Petty Officer handed him a radio and told him it was connected with Lieutenant Bernard Rhett of the Charleston Police Department. Bubba identified himself and explained to Peter the importance of the package delivered to box 1729 and what he knew of its weight and origin.

At first, Peter had trouble remembering this particular delivery. "It was a week ago. Just one of a million packages we handle."

Bubba reminded him about the hazardous materials and that it came from the hazard locker and was heavy.

"OK, OK, I'm beginning to remember," added Peter. "She certainly couldn't even push this huge box around. I'm not supposed to cart things like that, but she reminded me of my sixth grade teacher, Mrs. Tenney, and so I got a hand truck and took the box down the stairs and put it in the trunk of her car. I remember the trunk lid wouldn't close and I helped her rope it shut."

"What did she look like?" asked Bubba.

"Oh, typical middle-aged school teacher. Maybe 5'2" or 3", 130 or 140 pounds, wire-rim glasses, dowdy dress down to her ankles, dirty short brown hair. She had on a lot of makeup for a teacher, but I remember she had ugly shoes and no jewelry—not even earrings or rings."

"What was her automobile like, besides the small trunk?"

"Aahhh, I'm not sure. Four doors, blue-gray, a simple model. I think it had one of those Spoleto signs on the doors. You know they get the dealers to lend some demonstrators for the artistes."

Saturday, 5:25 pm

"Thank you for assembling so quickly," announced Mayor Maybank to many of the Spoleto board, and Chief Ravenel. They had hastened to this meeting when told there was a major disaster looming over Spoleto.

The Mayor asked Chief Ravenel to review the recent events.

After reviewing all the data and the CyanCo shipment, the Chief asked the Mayor and Spoleto Chairman Hanahan to cancel all Spoleto performances for that night until they could locate and make safe the presumed cyanide.

"Don't be crazy," blustered Hanahan. "Are you nuts. If we do that we can forget Spoleto. No one will go to anything tomorrow, next week, next year—NEVER. Not after 9/11. We're doomed."

"This is serious," intoned the Chief. I've notified the Federal Home-land Defense folks and they're flying in a team. They'll want us to shut down the whole city—roads, boats, airports, trains, etc. They'll be here later tonight and will take over. I've already got the FBI trying to boss around my people."

After a heated discussion of money, deaths, and reputations, money and reputations won. The police wanted to postpone performances; Spoleto folks and the Mayor wanted to keep problems secret. Mayor Maybank added: "Do your best, Chief, to safeguard each site. Of course begin with Gaillard and postpone that performance if you must. I'm hoping some-one just sent that teacher a passel of books for her classes, maybe from the Cyan County Library. I doubt she's so angry about the lack of teacher's raises next year that she is trying to exterminate South Carolina."

Saturday, 6:10 pm

"Bubba," said Shauntay. "I just got word from the CyanCo engineer that they did indeed ship 110 pounds of sodium cyanide to Lowcountry Plating at PO Box 1729 just over one week ago. He doesn't have any records of prior business with the company, but they prepaid with a money order. There is no record of any such firm in the state—I checked with the state incorporation people, who were not happy to work on a weekend. I checked the yellow pages and the web. I also called two metal wholesalers in the state who have never heard of them."

"How do we connect the school teacher, and perhaps the old man, to Spoleto?" asked Bubba. "Are they one of the performing troops? Are they on the permanent staff or just pickup helpers? I know they have a huge list of ushers, drivers, and other part time help."

Saturday, 6:30 pm

Chief Ravenel had called a meeting of his staff in the large police assembly room. "Thank you all for assembling so quickly," announced Chief Ravenel, in complete charge of the crowded room filled with his officers and detectives. "We have a potential disaster of major propor-tions. So far we have learned that the three Spoleto victims were probably murdered. We have two possible culprits or conspirators—an elderly man and a middle-aged school teacher-type woman. Neither fits the profile of any perps we are considering and may be red herrings. The most serious problem is cyanide—enough to kill everyone in Charleston. Shauntay Brown, Rutledge Moore, and Beulah Manigault, through good detective work, have found that a shipment of about 110 pounds of sodium cyanide was received at our Broad Street Post Office about a week ago from a company called CyanCo that sells tank cars full of cyanide. It was sent to a fictitious company and has disappeared. That's the same Post Office box that received the botulinum toxin, so it's central to our investigation. The person who picked up the cyanide resembled the woman who bought a poisonous fungus in Myrtle Beach. Now we don't know much more at this point, but I asked Dr. Henry Woodward, Chairman of Pathology at our Medical University, to brief us on cyanide and what we should look for. Dr. Woodward."

Dr. Woodward stood and strode to the dais. A tall imposing figure at any time, on this occasion he had the rapt attention of everyone in the room. "Cyanide is a perfect terrorist weapon. It is cheap. It is uncontrolled. You can buy a ton of the stuff. Yet it is one of the most deadly chemicals on earth. The person who first synthesized it died. Workers exposed to it often have life-threatening poisoning or die. We have very few ways of treating cyanide poisoning. During the depression so many people were killing themselves with it that the chief scientist at Eli Lilly and Company, Dr. K. K. Chen, invented the Cyanide Treatment Kit which was given away for decades. Now you can buy it from several sources, but no one stocks more than a few kits. The kit suggests you first have the victim, if they are still breathing, inhale amyl nitrite, commonly known as poppers. Actually, that does little good and we don't use it any more. Then you inject sodium nitrite intravenously. That oxidizes the hemoglobin in the red blood cells that carries oxygen. Oxidized hemoglobin won't carry oxygen, and if you oxidize too much the patient will die of asphyxia. That sometimes happens with nitrite poisoning from well-water. Oxidized hemoglobin will pick up cyanide and form the harmless cyanmethemoglobin. Then to flush out the cyanide we give sodium thiosulfate intravenously, and the kidneys take care of the rest, excreting a harmless thiocyanate."

Chief Hanahan asked: "Can we get lots of those antidotes?"

"Nope. That's just one of the problems. Now it sounds easy, and I've saved four victims when I was in an emergency room, with all the equipment, and lots of help, and plenty of lab expertise to help measure the hemoglobins. Out in the field you'd be firing blind and guessing and I doubt you could treat more than a few patients, even if you had enough kits. The Medical University pharmacy is having a special shipment of treatment kits flown in from the wholesaler later tonight, but we probably won't have them until midnight. My staff is alerting all the local hospitals and EMS units, but they only have a couple of kits apiece."

"What does the cyanide do to you," asked Shauntay.

"It blocks metabolism so even if you have oxygen you can't use it. The tissues, starved for oxygen, die quickly as they have no other source of energy. Remember, this is the stuff that is used in gas chambers. They simply dump some solid potassium cyanide into a bucket of sulfuric acid and in a couple of breaths it is all over. So you can't give oxygen or ventilate the patient as the oxygen can't get to work in the cells."

"How bad is it in crowds?" asked Beulah.

"It can kill everyone. Remember the incident in Bophal, India, in December 1984, when a plant released methyl isocyanate and killed thousands of people in a nearby village? It just formed a silent cloud that spread through the town."

"Just how toxic is 110 pounds?" asked Bubba.

Dr. Woodward thought for a moment: "Well it takes about 100 mg to kill an adult. That is about 1/50th the weight of a nickel. In 110 pounds there are about a half-million lethal doses!" That stunned the audience.

"But how would a terrorist deploy it?" exclaimed Bubba. "In food, in drinking water or the air?"

"Any way will work. Remember the contamination of Tylenol capsules in Chicago two decades ago. Of course that killed just one person at a time. You could put it in Goose Creek and poison our water and probably get thousands of us. Chief, I'd get some officers out to the water supply right away. Probably the easiest way to kill crowds is to convert the powder into hydrogen cyanide gas using an acid, such as sulfuric acid. For a pound of sodium cyanide all the cyanide could be converted to gas by 8.4 ounces of concentrated sulfuric acid. The acid would make the gas bubble up and it could be spread quickly in the air. Anyone close would be dead in seconds. And just one pound of cyanide could kill about 4500 people, almost twice the capacity of Gaillard Auditorium for example. Here we may have more than 100 times this much."

"What kind of trigger would a terrorist use?" asked Rutledge Moore. "I assume he'd like to be far far away."

"Well," mused Dr. Woodward, "any explosive device could shatter a glass jug of acid in a sack of powdered cyanide. Or a device that rotated, like a clock, could spill an open jug of acid onto the powder. I'm sure there are many other ways of doing it. One puff from a pen sprayed into the face could be enough to kill one victim silently and quickly. And at the scene it would probably look like a heart attack."

"So where do we look, Bubba?" asked Shauntay. "We haven't found any 110 pound packages in the homes we have searched. We haven't even found any suspicious powder. Would the dogs sniff it out in the theaters?"

"Dogs wouldn't work" said Woodward. "Not only are they not trained for cyanide, but sniffing it would kill them. You must be really careful around that stuff. We've alerted the area HazMat teams and even the Air Force is sending us a crew. They will be in suits with oxygen supplies. Let them handle anything suspicious—I'd like to see you at roll call tomorrow."

Chief Ravenel started handing out written duty assignments and announced: "I've called in off-duty officers and divided up the jobs to search tonight's venues. Besides Gaillard, Dock Street, Sotille, Robinson, Garden, Grace Church, and some small venues, we have Piccolo performances all over town. Each team will work with a HazMat person in full gear. I hope they can stand the heat. Paramedics will have as many of the treatment kits as we can get. I've sent an officer to the airport to collect the incoming shipment of 187 more treatment kits. Please be careful! We know how deadly this stuff is."

"Chief," asked Shauntay, "why not postpone tonights' performances and be safe?"

"I begged Hanahan to do that but the Spoleto folks are so scared of getting bad PR that they feel any such act would lead to no attendance at any of their events and end the festival, probably forever. They might be right. It's a big risk, but the Mayor is backing Hanahan and his board. We'll see if any of them and their families show up tonight. I know the Gullah and Gospel Gala at the Gaillard is a sellout like the first performance, and I think most of the other major events are pretty full. Actually, that decision may be out of our hands because when the Federal Homeland Defense folks arrive, I bet they shut down the city, the bars, the restaurants, and everything moving. This is really a potential disaster. Until then, lets sweep the sites and try to avoid any catastrophe."

Saturday, 7:00 pm

"Good evening, Mr. Coulomb," Bubba said eagerly shaking the hand of the Gaillard electrical and HVAC engineer. "Thanks for being on time. We have a very important job. We think there may be 100 pounds or more of cyanide poison somewhere in Gaillard with a trigger to set it off. It might be a powder and in one container or it might be in lots of little containers and it could be a liquid. It could have powerful explosives connected with it, so we have to be doubly careful. Your HVAC is the best bet for distributing it. We have two other teams searching the rooms, offices, bathrooms, hallways, etc. Detectives Rutledge Moore and Beulah Manigault, and this HazMat officer, Ms I. N. Hale, and I are here to help you search the HVAC, from top to bottom."

"How bad is this stuff?" asked Coulomb.

"One whiff and you're dead, in seconds, and it may be enough to kill everyone in the city! So, we don't want to set it off or even get too close. If we spot it, HazMat takes over and we evacuate the area."

"Can't we keep the audience out while we search?" asked Coulomb. "Why risk their lives?"

"Don't look at me!" retorted Bubba. "I think it's crazy, but the powers that be insist on everything being quiet unless and until we find something. They are betting the future of Spoleto versus thousands of lives, and we are the key part of that bet so let's get to work. But we'll keep them out of the auditorium until we look at your ducts."

Coulomb led them to the main return ducts backstage in the auditorium that gather all the air. "Air is sucked up by these huge tubular cage fans," he explained, "and then blown past the heat exchangers and out the supply ducts to the auditorium. Each of the major plenums has an access door so you can see the whole duct and that's how we clean them."

After they searched the largest ducts, big enough to stand in, they worked their way to the smaller ducts to and from the exhibition area, lobbies, stairs, restrooms, and the nonpublic areas.

Bubba did a rough calculation: "If the auditorium is 50 feet high, 100 feet long and 150 feet wide that makes 75,000 cubic feet. If 50,000 grams were distributed evenly in that space, and each gram can kill ten people, then there are about six lethal doses in every cubic foot."

"Rutledge, go close the auditorium entrance at the glass doors," Bubba decided. "Tell the ticket takers we are just being extra cautious for their safety and that we'll be open in awhile. Let the concessionaires and anyone already inside stay, and don't hassle the performers and musicians, but let's keep out the other 2800 people for a few minutes."

Saturday, 7:25 pm

Dirk Gadsden, in the forensics laboratory, telephoned M.E. on her cell phone. Connecting, he eagerly asked: "Where are you?"

"I'm in the upper lobby of the Gaillard admiring the prize-winning art and drinking the free champagne they are handing out. They won't let us in yet. Something about a late rehearsal."

"I'll bet you it is that cyanide scare and not a rehearsal. They already performed this concert a couple of days ago. You be careful. That stuff is nasty."

"Well, I'll try not to breath. Why did you call? Just concerned for my health?"

"I think we've got the perp!" Dirk said with obvious excitement.

"What have you got?" asked M.E.

"Most of the confiscated stuff the police collected tested clean except for two items. The still in Mr. Guérard's apartment has a trace of aconitine as well as three related alkaloids on the ground glass surface of the connection between the hot pot and the condenser. He must have cleaned everything else but forgotten that the ground glass holds particles on its uneven surface."

"Is there any chance he was just making mushroom soup?" asked M.E. "I hear he is a gourmet."

"Well, if so it was lethal—heart stopping I'd say."

"OK, what was the second hit?"

"The bearing under the blender blade in one of his blenders had residues of nicotine sulfate," added Dirk. "It is the same stuff we found in the insecticide."

"That explains it," replied M.E. "The liniment we tested contained nicotine base but the insecticide contained the sulfate salt. I wondered about that at the time. The base would be absorbed more rapidly than the salt, and I wondered if someone extracted the base. That would be easy to do—just add a solvent like alcohol and change the acidity. You could then evaporate off the solvent and have the pure base. A blender would be just the place to mix the insecticide with the solvent. Good work."

"Well, one problem is the police can't find the maestro. Bubba told me they went to his apartment and found that the inventory note they had left at the search was gone. The maestro probably realized the police were close and took off. Hopefully, that means he won't be around to use the cyanide or something else. They'll catch him eventually, I'm sure. I thought the maestro would explode when he found out the police had searched him and confiscated his stuff. I guess running is a pretty clear indication. The police have covered the airports, trains, and buses, but can't easily close the port and the roads."

Saturday, 7:45 pm

The Mayor sought out Chief Ravenel in the Spoleto lobby. "Chief Ravenel!"

"Yes your honor," replied the Chief.

"Let my people in! You haven't found anything. You've searched all the air conditioning, right? Nothing. No wacko bomb or powder or spray cans! You've got a lot of constituents who paid a fortune for these seats and they want to hear gospel not stand out in the lobby swilling cheap champagne. Open those doors NOW and I'll apologize. Get me a megaphone."

"Bubba," the Chief called over the secure radio. "The Mayor has ordered me to open the gates, so the audience will be on you in a minute. Is everything clear?"

"Well, we've gone through the HVAC minutely and I'll swear there is nothing big there. A tiny bomb might be concealed, but nothing with pounds of stuff in it. We've searched the auditorium itself, under the seats, up where the stage lights are hung, and even up on the exposed catwalks above the audience—nothing suspicious. Of course this is a huge barn and all painted black up above. We've done a pretty good job with the dressing rooms and other backstage areas, although the musicians and singers weren't too happy to be interrupted. The orchestra pit is clean and the musicians are taking their places as we speak. We are still going through the offices and restrooms, but they are lower priority."

"The stuff we confiscated at the various homes and offices has mostly turned up negative except for two items," added the Chief. "Guess who's the perp?"

"Well, how about an old man named Jean-Louis and his school-teacher conspirator," replied Bubba.

"Very good! Verry good. The problem is who's the dowdy old lady and where are they?"

"What was the evidence that pointed to the maestro, Chief?"

"You remember that big still in his kitchen? It had traces of the poison mushrooms. Dr. Simons said it would be easy to distill out the most deadly aconitine poison from a mushroom soup made with monkshood. That was the stuff the dowdy school teacher bought in Myrtle Beach."

"Anything else? I'd hate to think we just caught a gourmet chef experimenting with a new dish."

"Well one of his blenders had nicotine in it. I guess he could have been grinding up cigars, but M.E. thinks he used it to extract pure nicotine from that Black Flag insecticide that had some salt of nicotine. She said it would be easy and the blender could have mixed up some solvent, like vodka, with the insect goop. Then when the nicotine was in the solvent, you could evaporate off the solvent leaving pure nicotine base."

Bubba said thoughtfully: "That sounds pretty conclusive."

The Chief replied: "I'm still worried about it being more than one person. Do you have any idea who he is close to or sleeping with or in business with? Who could the little old lady be?"

"Chief," replied Bubba, "He sleeps with everybody and is hated by all. I think he is the most disliked person in the Holy City. The Spoleto staff hate him. The major artists all have egos in competition with his. He treats people like servants. This week he has spent a lot of time in New York with his financial backers and we hear that he is in trouble with a Mafia kingpin."

"How about the schoolteacher angle? Do you know of any gray-haired, middle-aged dowdy ladies?"

"Ha! Not his type and none I've seen hanging around him."

"Was anyone seen around his apartment here or with him frequently at receptions and things?"

Bubba paused. "Chief, there is a possibility. The maestro is an old hand in the theater. He works with props and makeup and disguises all the time. He could probably appear as a woman, a derelict, or even a shaggy dog. Remember, he's a showman."

"Good thinking, Bubba," added the Chief. "But I thought you said both the schoolteacher and the old man in the hardware store were supposed to be short. The maestro is pretty tall. If he can shrink himself that much he is a magician, but I guess everything is possible in the theater."

"That's a good point," added Bubba, just as the first notes of 'Climbing up the Rough Side of the Mountain' filled the auditorium. A young gospel singer was really belting it out, with a full orchestra behind her, to the audience's delight. Bubba peeked out from the wings and was startled. "Chief! He's here."

"Who?"

"Guérard. He's sitting in the middle of the first row next to a young blonde. I think that's his new soprano. He's all gussied up in white tie with a big smile."

"Are you sure?"

"Absolutely. Well, that is a relief."

"What do you mean, relief?"

"Well, he won't bubble up cyanide on the audience if he's in the middle of it, will he?"

"Maybe not, but I don't trust that guy. Keep an eye on him. If he starts to slip out I'd get really worried. I'm not sure I like beginning tonight's show with a funeral hymn. Let's make sure it isn't prophetic."

"Chief, there is one thing you should know," added Bubba, softly. "You recall the maestro's daughter-in-law, Teddy Bonnet, the producer of most of the Gaillard shows? She was staying in his apartment at the beginning of Spoleto. She moved out. She's supposed to hate him."

"Isn't that the gorgeous young woman you've been dating, sir?"

"Yes sir."

"She doesn't look like a schoolteacher to me. Does she have gray hair under a wig?"

"No, I can vouch for that."

"I bet you can!"

"But, you know, Chief, she is an actress and she is about five feet four inches tall," Bubba said reluctantly and softly his mind racing.

"Good thinking, Bubba," added the Chief. "But what motive? I've been thinking the maestro hates our guts and would be happy to see the Spoleto festival and Charleston go under. He certainly didn't like sharing the billing with the diva and dancer. I was wondering if the publicity got him more money for a New York opening and maybe got him out of trouble with that Mafia loan shark. And he already seemed to have made preparations for backup artists for each of his premiers. Would his daughter-in-law be in cahoots with him? Are they close?"

"They haven't spoken for ten years, I don't think," added Bubba. "And he raped her, more or less, after his son's funeral."

"Nice guy! Just as we all knew. But would she be helping him?"

"Maybe it's the opposite?" mused Bubba. "Maybe she is using this to get back at him. I think she really hates him. Blames him for the death of her husband as well as her mother-in-law."

"Why was she staying with him then, especially if he raped her?"

"Spoleto put them together, not knowing. She might have been planning to kill him, but this could be even better revenge if he looked jinxed and his shows were ruined for Broadway. Probably the Mafia guy would Cuisinart him and she wouldn't have to raise another finger."

"Where is she now?" asked the Chief.

"She's backstage producing, and I'm heading that way."

"Be careful! Remember Dr. Woodward's description of cyanide and the billions and billions of dead people. I don't want to see you 'Walkin up de Stairs' tonight. I'll send Rutledge and Beulah to help you."

twenty-four

Walk 'im Up de Stairs

*S*aturday, 8:55 pm

The audience is thrilled. The hall is filled, SRO. The Spoleto management, aware of the threat, are conspicuously absent, but in the middle of the front row, sporting the young blonde new soprano on his arm, is Jean-Louis. He is greeting the crowd and acknowledging their accolades as though he were the savior himself.

The Gospel singers, drawn from Lowcountry churches, are magnificent and everyone who is "we" people can sing these songs from memory. But with a full orchestra, under the baton of Erik Ochsner, the hall is really jumping. The second act of the Gullah and Gospel Festival will be the beloved Gullah stories and playlets and then the finale will be excerpts from Porgy and Bess. That New York Times reviewer gave the first performance on Tuesday rave notices and tonight they've packed chairs in every aisle and tickets have been going for a double and triple premium from scalpers, a real first for Spoleto.

Bubba spots Teddy backstage, with her headset and microphone, by the rope board that controls the flys and counterweights and the row of electronic controls of the fireworks each with its blinking pilot lights.

Each fly is roped through pulleys to its counterweight that will pull it up or allow it to be lowered into position at the back of the stage. The thick ropes are wrapped around belaying pins, just like on a sailing ship, with the pins fastened in proper chronological order, each labeled, in a board. At just the right moment the pin is pulled out, the rope is free, and the counterweight "flys" the backdrop into place. Teddy was standing by the board watching a cue card and holding pin six. As Bubba approaches he can see the label on pin six that says: "Walk him up—stairs to heaven."

"Hi, Teddy," greets Bubba with a smile.

"Oh, hi Bubba. I didn't know you'd be at the performance tonight. Such craziness. Your police are all over and we were 20 minutes late with the curtain. I hear there is a terrorist threat."

Bubba paused, looked deep into Teddy's eyes, and slowly said: "We need to talk, Teddy. There are some things we need to go over. Were you or your father-in-law using that still and the blenders in his apartment?"

"Oh…" Teddy said thoughtfully. "I'd like to tell you the maestro did it, and he does distill some *eau de vie*, but he hasn't been around that much these last two weeks. Besides, he expects everyone around him to treat him like a king and be his slave. The old bastard."

"Where's the maestro been, Teddy?"

"He's been in New York raising money. Right now he's in the front row, with his new love, the blonde soprano he signed up to be next on his hit parade. I thought the money would dry up with the problems here, but I hear he did OK with the investors and even old Digits Personnoni will have to wait to get his fingers. But a terrorist attack would make headline news worldwide and would be coupled with him forever. Just like 9/11 makes everyone think Bin Laden, a Spoleto massacre would be linked with Guérard. That would screw his reputation good—just what he deserves, the bastard."

"Is that why, Teddy? Do you hate him that much?"

"You'll never believe how he treated me. I just told you a little. He killed my husband. Steve was so sensitive. When the maestro killed his mother, it devastated him. Then he rejected Steve and criticized everything he did. He took away my only love, my life. And then he did everything he could to destroy my career. I was hoping Personnoni would take a long time with his knife. Now, its up to me."

"The maestro killed Steve's mother?"

"Check the records. She was diabetic and wealthy. He was sleeping around with everyone and she was ready to divorce him. He kept threatening that she'd never live to leave him and the next thing she died of an insulin overdose. I'm sure he gave it."

Just as Rutledge and Beulah started to edge closer, Teddy slipped her hand to belaying pin seven. "No closer. I shouldn't have waited. It's time. I was going to get him after that sacrilegious play, when the audience had left, and blame it on the religious fundamentalists. But the bastard ran out early at the second intermission. And, you came along and were kind to me—the first in many years. Bubba, get out. Right now. Run to that backstage door. Don't breathe. Do it now!"

"Stop, Teddy. I'll help you. Whatever you've done, I'll stand by you. Everyone will understand what you've gone through. But did you do the aconitine and nicotine and botulism?"

"Of course. I told you I graduated from the Philadelphia College of Pharmacy and Science. I know drugs and herbs and poisons. Poisons of all kinds and these were easy."

"But why, Teddy?"

"I just wanted Alexandrá to be sick. With the role written just for her unique voice, I thought if she dropped out it would screw his big new opera. But no. He had a replacement and had already rewritten the score for her. I thought the aconitine would just make her sick—I didn't know about the Seldane and quinine or I would have chosen something else. Even so, she would have been OK if she had collapsed on stage like I thought rather than falling into the pit like a pig being barbecued. Who could imagine a healthy woman dying of a heart arrhythmia surrounded by a thousand physicians—its like dying at a medical convention."

"See, Teddy, it was an accident. We can work around that."

"I thought the play was so outrageously sacrilegious that everyone would applaud it being shot down. I still can't believe they let the kid die. Botulism just paralyzes your muscles. If you just breathe for the victim they will recover on their own. I thought when he got in trouble he'd call out and they would just ventilate him for a couple of days, but it would screw the play. But somehow no one noticed him in trouble until too late. And then the maestro got so excited he ran out at the second intermission to rewrite the play to include the resuscitation. Instead of killing him I gave him an idea—I can't stand it."

"Again, Teddy, it sounds like there are good explanations and that was mostly an accident. Let's work through this."

"Areana was so nasty and vindictive I just wanted her to suffer. She was stretching to dance the firebird and I thought some nicotine might make it harder for her when she started sweating and having palpitations and things. I didn't know she had epilepsy. I had thought of just giving her phenolphthalein and inducing explosive diarrhea—that would have only hurt her ego."

"See, Teddy, it was mostly an accident. You know my feelings for you. I'll help. We'll get through this."

"No, a spectacle is a better way to go," as she starts working pin seven loose.

Following the rope from that pin upward, Bubba spots high in the flys, at the ceiling, barely visible, a large black metal drum with a huge sandbag hanging from one handle supported by the rope. It blended in with the other backdrops and the black ceiling, so you'd never notice it except for that rope.

"Bubba, its time you leave. Right now. One jerk and that container you see inverts and the powder inside tears through the thin paper cover and pours down into the auditorium. It won't take but a minute to fill this whole space. Why don't you just run out right this second—and hold your breath."

As the choir begins the rousing "Walk im up de stairs" from Ossie Davis' Purlie Victorious, Bubba says calmly, reaching his hand toward Teddy: "You don't want to be remembered as a terrorist, Teddy. You are too living and kind and loving. Let me help you. I'll stand by you. Each of the three deaths could be accidents. No one is certain. You've got a good defense. And if nothing happens here, who knows."

Teddy hesitates. Pin seven is loose and a jerk will free it, the rope, the counterweight, and then oblivion. No one in the auditorium would have much chance of making it outside. Jean-Louis would be the centerpiece of a tragedy equal to 9/11. She had hoped the little plastic breathing hood in her pocket would save her, but now she would be delayed getting outside and might as well forget it.

Rutledge has his weapon in his hand, but is unsure of whether to show it and take a shot. She probably can get the pin out. Bubba stands with his hand extended.

Teddy looks deeply into Bubba's eyes and says: "I did hope it would work. Love again. A normal life. Would it have been possible?"

She slips her hand from pin seven back to pin six, quickly wraps the loose rope end around her neck, and pulls out the pin. As the rope flies upward, pulled by the heavy counterweight, the backdrop of the stairs to heaven rises behind the choir and, before it, swinging, her neck obviously broken, S. Ted Bonnet is hung suspended, half way to heaven.

The audience gasps. The conductor is the first to see what has happened and after another bar Ochsner signals an end, and the orchestra sputters into silence. The singers, caught up with the rousing chorus, gradually become silent and look above them. The audience is in shock. Bubba tells Rutledge to lower the victim and walks onstage to cradle the body of the fourth Spoleto victim. Perhaps the last.

Charles Towne Reporter

Sept 27, 1718
Colonel William Rhett has captured the notorious pirate
Stede Bonnet of Barbados. In a furious battle in the Cape Fear
River, the Henry, under Captain John Masters, cut off the flight
of the Royal James which ran aground. The Sea Nymph, under
Captain Fayrer Hall, also grounded along with the pirates. In
the ebb tide the pirate's vessels exposed only their flanks, but
Rhett's decks were exposed. Neither side could bring their
cannons to bear until the tide floated them. Rhett's fleet floated
first and with withering small arms fire forced the pirates to
surrender unconditionally.

October 30, 1718
Lest they die of their wounds, all but four of the pirate crew
were hanged off the Battery. Today, Stede Bonnet came to trial
in the Court of Vice-Admiralty before Chief Justice Trott with
the sentence of hanging assured.

December 10, 1718
Stede Bonnet, the gentleman pirate, was set hanging today
off the Battery near van der Horst's Creek. This closes the season
with a final score of 49 pirates hanged, 9 imprisoned. The
Eagle, captured by the pirates, was found to contain 36 women
indentured servants bound for Virginia and Maryland. Judge
Trott declared them to be chattel and ordered them to be sold.
Several of Blackbeard's crew have become free agents and thus
will be included in next week's draft.

Maurice is a high school teacher, assistant to the Editor of the Women's Page of the local newspaper, lecturer, historian, and preservationist who has prepared audiovisual materials for science and produced multi-thousand person meetings worldwide. She met and married Leigh while they were at the College of Charleston. When he worked one year so she could complete her baccalaureate she agreed to reciprocate, not knowing that he intended to be a student until retirement. After earning his PhD (Pharmacology), MD (Johns Hopkins), and Internal Medicine Residency (Johns Hopkins and NIH) she put him to work.

Leigh built three of the first Intensive Care Units, ran analytical laboratories, became Professor of Medicine, edited ten textbooks and authored 285 scientific papers while lecturing worldwide. He pioneered live medical telecasts to physicians and hospitals and was a prize-winning medical news reporter for NBC-TV and then joined Eli Lilly and Company and retired as Chief Scientific Officer. He is a member of many boards and consults globally to health care, pharmaceutical, and biotech corporations.

Maurice and Leigh, multigenerational Charlestonians, live in a colonial home and enjoy the local people, cuisine, arts, and Gullah culture. This is their first novel, written about their hometown and its major Spring arts festival.

If you enjoyed this tale of murder and intrigue at the Charleston annual arts festival, you will be captivated by the international intrigue, terrorism, murder, and revenge in the Thompson's newest novel:

CN

(cyanide).

It begins where Spoleto ends with the use of cyanide in a terrorist attack but goes on to realistic use of bioweapons and chemical weapons all directed by al Quaeda. The sleuths are the Special Agent in Charge of the NY FBI office, a former seal, and the expert in computers and ciphers from MIT, Danielle Gilbreth. When not engaged romantically they crack the codes and locate the terrorists with the help of the Delta teams. But, a doomsday ship filled with explosives and cyanide and radioactivity is bearing down on New York....

The bench was hard. It was old, hard wood, with scabrous paint. It sat lonely on the Long Island Rail Road platform. He sat lonely upon it. He was scabrous as well and looked old and hard. The bench should have been crowded. People flowed like lemmings down the Penn Station steps. Nearby two elderly women with canes could have used it. A stooped over lady with a shawl and walker surely wanted to sit. But he was surrounded by a halo of six feet of space. Probably that was the diffusion radius of his most malignant odors. He was one of New York's untouchables. Once treated in hospitals they were liberated to protect their right to be the worm in any portion of the Big Apple. He was invisible. No one made eye contact. They avoided him, the bench, and the LIRR sign behind him extolling its virtue as the oldest continuously operating railroad company. Not one in the hump day crowd could have picked him out of a lineup. None could have been sure if he were black or white. Actually he was neither. No one could have described accurately his dirty matted hair and beard that had taken him so long to create. They might have described his odor but not his carefully chosen filthy floor-length coat buttoned to his chin, mismatched shoes, and grimy work gloves that he wore over his latex surgical gloves. He was relieved that he had had to brutalize only one homeless bum to acquire the ensemble. That was more efficient that he could have done at Bloomies or Sax with a thin waist and a fat wallet. He thought of himself not as a homeless wretch but as the avenging sword of Mohammed about to extirpate at least part of the cancer in Sodom and Gomorrah. Like a lion on the Serengeti he awaited his prey--motionless but sensing everything about him. Soon through the crowd that stood like tall grass in his line of vision he first heard their higher-pitched Semitic voices. Then the yarmulkes appeared, bobbing up and down like gazelles heading to the water hole. The intelligence was perfect. He had been told they took the 555 to Lynbrook after the Midtown Hebrew Academy released their Zionists onto the other filth of this city of infidels. Their black and white costumes stood out like dorsal fins as their phalanx knifed through the crowd like an orca through baby seals. His double-gloved hands grasped more firmly the handles of the filthy old grocery bags on either side as the prey gathered, as he had been told, near the rear car. It was one of the reconditioned GE M1 cars. He had studied the construction to calculate the dose. Eighty-five feet long, 10 feet wide, an average of 9 feet high makes for just 7,650 cubic feet inside those two double doors. The large windows were sealed. Yes, they could break them open in an emergency, but he didn't think they could last that long. Not with a whole 244 moles. And each bag weighed only 23 pounds with the fine white powder in thin plastic bags plus the glass gallon containers in the bottoms. If it distributed evenly, each quart of air in the car would deliver 30 milligrams—a lethal dose in half a minute of breathing. And, best of all, when it began to work they would breath even more of the poisoned air into their lungs. The train pulled in and the doors opened disgorging its polyglot. The audio system blared some announcement he couldn't understand. His five languages did not encompass U.S. train platform announcements. Holding back until the car was nearly full, he squeezed in just behind the Zionists. One young boy turned and rather than looking disdainful, smiled and reached out a hand to help him over the threshold. Fool, he thought. If he expects a reward in his heaven he'll find it soon enough. As the doors began to close he held the bags widely apart and swung them together, hearing the glass jars break. He ejected himself backwards through the narrow aperture as the doors clanged shut. In seconds the train was moving. To the remaining few passengers on the platform waiting for the next train to Jamaica in five minutes it seemed as though he had been thrown off the car, stumbling backwards onto the platform, and without his filthy bags. For good measure he shook a fist at the departing cars, stumbled a little, and then made his way to the stairs. His steps became surer and swifter as he mounted the stairs to the marble public restroom on the main level, the headquarters of others who looked and smelled just like him. There, in the handicapped stall, he quickly stripped off his filthy coat, shoes, work gloves, cap and wig, and stuffed them in the elegant Hermes bag he had rolled up in one pocket of his powder-blue pinstripe suit coat. He loosened his Hermes tie, red with the little giraffes playing down it, and the collar of his crisp white shirt. Using paper towels he removed the dirty makeup from his skin. He carefully peeled off the beard and mustache and removed the adhesive from his skin. He combed his short black hair. He slipped the Hermes thin loafers out of his coat pockets and eased his feet covered with the black opaque pantyhose into them. He took the Hermes cologne sample towelettes the clerk had given him and wiped them on his face, hoping none of the stink remained. From his shirt pocket he withdrew the chromic glasses with the neutral lenses that darkened in the light and slightly hid his dark eyes. A conservative Hermes scarf covered any residual makeup on his neck and chin. Finally he withdrew the Gucci black leather gloves from his right pants pocket and drew them on over the latex surgical gloves. Packing his costume tightly into the Hermes bag, he emerged from the stall refreshed in just nine minutes. None of the homeless, drug-addicts, pimps, or out-patients nearby paid any attention nor had any observed the remarkable transformation.

AVAILABLE SPRING 2003

Printed in the United States
1021300004B

9 781930 859548